A PRACTICAL ARRANGEMENT

Hope you enjoy the book

A PRACTICAL ARRANGEMENT

Verity Trevethan

Troubador Publishing Ltd
Unit E2 Airfield Business Park,
Harrison Road, Market Harborough,
Leicestershire. LE16 7UL
Tel: 0116 2792299
Email: books@troubador.co.uk
Web: www.troubador.co.uk

ISBN 978 1805142 089

British Library Cataloguing in Publication Data.
A catalogue record for this book is available from the British Library.

Printed and bound in Great Britain by CMP UK
Typeset in 11pt Minion Pro by Troubador Publishing Ltd, Leicester, UK

Matador is an imprint of Troubador Publishing Ltd

To my family. My hope for their forgiveness should they ever find out that I wrote this book!

part one

AN ORDINARY LIFE

THE FIRST TIME

The fruity acidity of the soft drink he had gently warmed between his hands helped the off-white powder dissolve. The citrus flavour just about blunted the drug's metallic taste, although there was no mistaking that his drink was not just the sugar- and taste-free lemonade his wife insisted on buying. But after nearly half an hour of looking at, if not exactly watching, a sadistic fitness trainer thrashing an obviously overweight man to within an inch of his televised life, he felt no different after drinking his new blend. The armchair still felt uncomfortable and still needed reupholstering. The only remaining unmodified molar on the left of his lower set of teeth still throbbed gently as it had for the past few weeks. Outside, what had been a bleak and colourless winter's day was almost coming to an end, although it was barely five o'clock. And his mood. His black dog. That familiar animal – who typically arrived at the most inconvenient of moments – was still staring at him from the sofa across the room, and the dark angel was still hovering near the door. Two faithful but uninvited and unwelcome companions. When would the 'up' arrive? Perhaps it never would with this compound, and it would all turn out to be just another failed experiment. That this untested drug hadn't killed him yet was, at least, of some consolation to him.

A second dose was contemplated. Perhaps he had been too cautious in extrapolating the dose that worked so well in rats at his company's laboratories to calculate that needed to work on the brain of a middle-aged Englishman running to fat. He considered returning to the attic hideaway where he had stashed a handful of vials of the experimental drug that he had 'borrowed' from the company, to pick out a second dose. But just before he could climb out of his armchair – and just after the fitness trainer man-hugged his newly slimmed, if not entirely slim, protégé – it happened. At first it was a barely noticeable tingling, trickling down his spine like a lover's gentle touch. This soothing sensation was then joined by a gradual release of tension, starting from his neck and shoulders and then moving to his head, bathing it in a vague, fuzzy warmth. This was what Andy had anticipated from the data they had collected in the lab: a gradual easing of anxiety.

This compound was not supposed to provide an acute 'up'; an immediate buzz. But then that particular train did arrive. The euphoric sense of confidence cascaded through him as if powered by one of the more convincing evangelical preachers. It was truly bewildering. Enthralling. A feeling of calm and complete control over what he was and what he could do, bereft of the cynicism he typically experienced on encountering such absurdities of thought. An overwhelming, unsurmountable optimism had replaced his weary, default setting of barely justified pessimism. It was as if someone had corrupted the hard drive that was his brain. The lines of code that had for a long time made him the rational, conservative, responsible man he was had been overwritten in a language so very unfamiliar to him; one resplendent in words of emotion, possibility, hope and freedom. Words and feelings that he had for so long forgotten.

It was this quite remarkable sense of overwhelming confidence and well-being that stayed with Andy over the next few hours as he waited for his family to return home. An ease with all around him and the future that faced him. Not even the thought of a house soon to be filled with noise and children could perturb him. Not even the dread of the forced jollity of a New Year's Eve 'celebration' soon to be spent with his in-laws (and which had led to him taking this concoction in the first place) could force its way into his consciousness. Was this nirvana? Maybe. Huxley's soma? Possibly. The complete, life-affirming medication that was supposed not to exist? So it seemed. But surely not. Life is not like that. At least, not Andy's life.

That night he made love with his wife with an urgency, relentlessness and passion that startled them both. It was an echo of a time before the children had arrived; before the energy-sapping sleepless nights. When money was to be spent rather than watched and worried about. When work was aspirational with unbounded opportunities stretching into the future, rather than a worrisome chore. When time was limitless.

How had it all come down to this?

DRINKING

The dying echoes of the slammed door resonated through the plasterboard walls of the cramped, over-bright hotel room. This was not an expensive hotel. His mood was such that he wished to leave little doubt in the mind of the woman standing in front of the full-length mirror as to why he felt as he did and who was to blame for that. As if in sympathy with his demeanour, the slamming of the substantial fire door encouraged a small lamp on the bedside table to wobble briefly before settling, somewhat precariously, near the edge. It was saved from extinction by the close proximity of the ubiquitous hotel alarm radio and an unread Bible taken from the lowest of a flimsy set of bedside drawers; a book which, only hours before, had been the subject of warm and shared humour between the one-time passionate lovers.

The evening had clearly not been kind to him. Although the cut of his well-tailored white shirt and navy trousers, and obsessively polished black shoes, implied that no little effort had been made in his pre-entertainment preparations, a crooked and unravelling tie and a stained, rolled-up shirt suggested an evening of excess. A damp patch of sweat was starting to break through the back of his shirt. She, as always, had weathered the evening far better. Wearing a simple, knee-length black dress, tasteful and modest jewellery, and black suede court shoes, she was experienced in concealing the effects of time on a not unattractive face and figure. Her youthful experimentations had taught her well the lessons of overconsumption, and these days she knew better than to indulge to excess. She was now carefully removing what little make-up she had applied earlier in the evening.

He took two steps further into the room, slowly moving his right hand over his face and through his thick, curly black hair in a theatrical display of exasperation. "How many times do we have to go through this? Even *you* must see that this is completely unreasonable behaviour. We agreed. We've talked it through. Jesus, we've even talked about counselling. It's not fair on me, it's not fair on the kids." He paused, both for breath and for dramatic effect. "I just don't know what to do." Another pause, and a change in posture. His head was now fixed downwards, his chin tucked into his chest. "Perhaps leaving you *is* the only way you are going to change."

Her eyes focused on an imagined object near her partner's feet. Make-up free, she moved smoothly over to the telephone, coffee maker and TV remote cluttered table, brushing past a cheap, brightly flower-patterned duvet folded crisply at the top. No cost-cutting measure had been considered too trivial by this national hotel chain's management and owners. She then became interested in a framed photo of a Cotswold village scene hanging above the bed. Anything to avoid looking directly at him. Seemingly unmoved by his argument, she picked up a packet of cigarettes, took one out and placed it in the corner of her mouth, and in doing so stained the filter from a small patch of pale pink lipstick which she had seemingly failed to remove. Then, finally turning to face him, she pushed away the thin strands of bottle-blonde hair covering her face and removed the cigarette. "Come *on*! Have you lost your sense of humour completely now? I appreciate that there was precious little of it left by the time we married, but everyone could see that it was just harmless fun, flirting with Don. He's been our friend for years. Everybody could see I was just playing around – except you, of course. Lighten up for once in your life. Chill out. Get a life. Do us all a favour." She was taking a calculated gamble, but this approach had worked before and seemed, at this moment, to be the best way to defuse his obvious anger. She had enjoyed the night and now just wanted to get into bed and go to sleep. "It was nothing. It's what good friends do on a night out. People know what I'm like." The cigarette was replaced, lit, and, in the same movement, she walked around the bed towards the darkened bay window. In doing so, she passed in front of him.

"Don't you turn your fucking back on me."

With that, he stepped forward and brought down his clenched right fist on the back of her neck. The blow was certainly not delivered with his full force and had not really been meant to hurt. It was a result of his pent-up frustration at not being in control. But it caught her off balance and, almost comically, she fell forward, her forehead striking the knee-high white windowsill of the bay window; her hands desperately attempting, but failing, to grip the long curtains.

It quickly became obvious to him, from the way that her head snapped backwards and from the unnatural posture of her body on the bedroom floor, that this was serious. Very serious. Breathing quickly, his first thoughts were entirely selfish. *Just an accident. She fell over my foot. A few drinks. Could happen to anyone.* Moving slowly towards her, he crouched down, trying to see her face but irrationally anxious not to touch any part of her. Her eyes were open but without emotion; her mouth too was open and lifeless. Blood trickled from one ear.

He could feel the perspiration cooling on the back of his neck as he rose to look out through the window to the sparsely lit car park three floors below. Cars queued patiently to leave the hotel grounds. The party was over. A thousand thoughts raced through his head, almost all without an obvious conclusion. *Must phone reception straight away – otherwise it sounds suspicious.* He quickly moved over to the table, picked up the telephone receiver and dialled 100 for the hotel reception. Then he slammed down the receiver almost immediately. *Don't rush, take your time; have to get the story right first time. No second chances with this one.* Pacing nervously around the room, he studiously avoided looking at the motionless body and willed himself to think of the most believable story. It just didn't seem real. He almost felt like an actor in some cheap American murder mystery TV show, waiting patiently for the detective hero to get his man. *But wait! There's something going on outside the door.* He froze almost in mid-stride, afraid to breathe, his heart pounding out of his chest. Friendly, happy-sounding voices. Yes, voices – still distant and incoherent, but getting louder. Perhaps the partygoers who had chosen to stay the night were retiring to their bedrooms. The police? But how would they know what had just happened in the room? Then a bright light of almost biblical proportions washed, suddenly and dramatically, through the room.

Consciousness is a funny old thing, isn't it? What is it? How can you tell if you have it? Does it matter? All I know is that it should be avoided at all costs, although unconsciousness rarely comes cheap at today's prices, whichever road of substance abuse you take.

But let me introduce you to someone who needs no such props to tumble into the depths of the unconscious – for him, middle age and a working life suffice. He's someone I was soon to get to know very well indeed: Andy Jones.

"Wake up." Gently, Graham shook Andy's left shoulder.

"Come on, Andy, drink up. I can see Geoff getting tense, and we wouldn't want a repeat of what happened last month, would we?" added Ian, half in humour, half in fear. "An amorous French kiss. That'll wake the lazy bugger up."

"Jesus," spluttered a newly conscious Andy. Not surprisingly, he had been jolted back to life by his friends' persistence, and found himself sitting bolt upright at a small, round table, facing Ian, Graham and an almost full pint of the very flattest of 'traditional' real ale. His transition to full consciousness was aided by the recognition of the familiar surroundings of the pub. What helped him to determine a more precise bearing was the presence of the dangerously overweight, glass-wiping landlord behind the bar. A balding head, an inappropriate and gratuitous moustache, and an air of exaggerated indifference – he could only be Geoff. Andy was, once again, drinking in The Royal Oak. "How long have I been asleep?"

"How long have we been here?" answered Ian, again mustering his laconic brand of exaggerated sarcasm.

"Sorry about that, fellas. I've had a real pig of a week," lied Andy, rubbing his eyes.

"Happens to the best of us when we reach *that* age. That and a prostate the size of a horse," commented Graham, wondering just how much more tired Andy would be had he seen the number of middle-aged, worried-well patients Graham had had to soothe that week.

Ian fidgeted with his coat in an ill-conceived gesture aimed at bringing the evening's proceedings to an end. It was too late to get another round in, and he had to get back to his own fridge in order to crack open and enjoy his next drink.

"Incredible dream. Full-on colour; close-up action," insisted Andy in an attempt to hide his embarrassment.

"The usual, I suspect? Sex, drugs and rock 'n' roll?" quipped Graham, but with little enthusiasm to hear more detail, as there are few things more boring to hear than monologues of other people's dreams.

"No, no. This was murder – at least, I think so. Very believable and very real. It was as if I was committing the crime myself; at least, I think it was me. Not the first time I've had that sort of dream, I can tell you. Wonder if they mean anything? What do you think, Dr Robins? Or even you, Ian?" The last phrase was delivered with emphasis, almost demanding a response. These recurring dreams, perhaps even nightmares, had been troubling Andy for the past few months, and were of sufficient concern for him to share them openly and canvass reassuring opinions from his new friends, despite him having to confront in the process the taboo of revealing emotions in male company. However, he would never disclose the more disturbing, borderline psychotic episodes encountered in some of his dreams; nor his recurrent headaches. After all, he was a middle-aged Englishman and, worse still, a fully paid-up, anally retentive Yorkshireman.

Hastily, he recounted the details of his most recent dream, dwelling only on the somewhat ghoulish and grotesquely configured body in an attempt to maintain the dwindling interest of his audience. He thought it best not to mention that the victim in his dream had borne a striking resemblance to Graham's wife.

"Well, you're the professional, Graham. Put the man out of his misery. What does it all mean?" interjected Ian with barely concealed impatience.

Graham felt compelled to answer, although he too had quickly become indifferent to Andy's tale. "Don't ask me; I'm only a lowly GP. I just patch people up or send them on to someone who actually knows what they are talking about. But why don't you ask Janey? She's really into all that sort of stuff, and she's bound to have a viewpoint. Got all the books. Sort of does my head in, but there you go."

Andy always felt a guilty unease at the mention of Graham's wife's name, and this occasion was no exception, especially given that he had just murdered her. He had always considered that this particular hang-up – a long-term, embarrassing awkwardness when among attractive, self-assured women like Janey – was most likely due to his single-sex public-school education. Not his fault, of course, though in his case that awkwardness was aided and abetted by his leering attraction to his friend's wife. His teenage years had been blighted by girls being seemingly from a different planet, although an actual alien might have been easier to get to know, as at least the unfamiliarity and incomprehension would have been mutual. "Yeah, sure. Why not?" he replied, without any great conviction and in a voice trailing off into a mumble. Really, he'd known all along that his gamble at being open would not pay off, but at least, contrary to more typical male behaviour and his worst expectations, he had not been mocked. Yet.

"Time, gentlemen, *pleeease*," announced Geoff to no one in particular, whilst fighting back an incoming coughing episode. Three minutes early, as tradition demanded. The not unusual scarcity of custom barely warranted this evening's laboured bell-ringing routine, but nonetheless he felt it to be both necessary and appropriate.

Andy bolted down his only drink of the night with indecent haste, failing guiltily to match the empty glasses of Ian and Graham. Almost inaudibly, he muttered something about not being able to drink as much as he did as a lad to his friends' unlistening backs as they made their way to the bar. The three friends thoughtfully deposited their glasses at the bar and headed for the rear door. Not untypically, no word of acknowledgement, thanks or even recognition was forthcoming from Geoff as they passed through the door and into the dangerously under-illuminated car park. At least they had been spared one of his rants on whichever population had offended him most over the preceding week; a category which ranged from mask wearers to anyone who was not clearly a middle-aged white Englishman.

Andy fumbled for his car keys in the claustrophobic darkness of the moonless countryside night.

"Miserable bastard!" ventured Ian. "Little wonder he has fuck-all custom."

"You're right," added Andy resignedly, not for the first time feeling rather alarmed at the forthright language of the geography department deputy head at Ulstown High School, of whom he expected better. Moreover, Andy's aspirational upbringing led him to believe that this level of obscenity was rather presumptuous of their still relatively new friendship. He made a mental note to redouble his efforts to look for alternative schools for his eldest, although there were still some years to go before Joshua would be leaving primary school. "Can't understand why we still come here. There must be somewhere better than this – I mean, it's not as if it's even local. It takes us twenty minutes to drive here."

"Ulstown is the ultimate drinking gentleman's desert. We've been through this *before*," with the emphasis on a long, drawn-out 'before', was Graham's truthful, although uneagerly anticipated retort. The Royal Oak was the only pub in the locality that sold real ales. Not that any of them had any particular interest in real ale, but each thought that the other two did. Such are Englishmen.

Andy eventually managed to aim the electronic key in the appropriate direction, and, with the central locking mechanism released, all three could retreat from the cooling night air.

"Cold again tonight," observed Ian with a reassuringly English obviousness, although it had been no colder in the previous few weeks and correlated perfectly with the unremarkable weather rather typical of this very fortunate part of the world.

"Frost by morning according to the forecast. May be the last of the winter, I hope. Can't wait to get started on the garden," was Graham's hopelessly optimistic meteorological opinion.

Starting the engine on his first attempt, Andy carefully manoeuvred his new company car through the pub gates, past the grass-bordered road sign posted to Ulstown, and onwards to home. It had all been too easy for the salesman. No need for the hard sell. Commission-eroding discounts could be kept in hand for more demanding customers since, before even entering the showroom, Andy had convinced himself of the good taste and status his pre-chosen car – a nearly top-of-the-range Volkswagen saloon – reflected on its owner. 'Full leather interior and surround sound entertainment system,' shouted the brochure. It remained for the grateful salesman only to sell the colour to the proud new owner, and to make knowledgeable and encouraging noises while Andy considered the merits of air conditioning versus a tinted sunroof. The sunroof option had eventually been selected on the basis that its electronic operation added still further cachet to his choice. Who could possibly justify the fitting of air conditioning in a car driven only over the highways and byways of Great Britain? Climate change could wait.

Graham *was* right, of course. Ulstown was a drinking man's desert, and they had indeed been through this before. Several times. The search for a decent drink was now very much part of a Friday evening's entertainment (nominally exercise night) for the three friends.

The mutual need for regular vigorous exercise was a New Year's resolution agreed by all on a cold December morning outside Andy's house. That occasion had been the first time the neighbours had talked together for any appreciable amount of time, and had become the beginning of their gentle friendship. Their families shared a small cul-de-sac and had moved into their new-build, 'individually designed executive houses' within a month of each other. Although a thinly veiled (but universally accepted) excuse for a night's drinking, Andy, Ian and Graham tried almost their hardest on the exercise course laid out for them at the local recreation centre. Indeed, their initial sessions had been quite competitive, but within a few months this had settled down to mutual false modesties.

First up in their search for an acceptable post-exercise drinking house had been Ulstown Recreation Centre's very own sports bar, which was tried once and only once, being a soulless room sharing all the worst features with airport departure lounges but without the benefit of being able to fly away from it. Inexplicably worn, uncomfortable chairs surrounded plastic tables of insufficient strength and balance to be trusted with any meaningful volume of drink. The noise from a ferocious air-conditioning unit competed with the Eurosport feed from a large monitor which was not quite loud enough to hear but sufficiently loud to prevent easy conversation among the patrons. But the coup de grâce was provided by the bar staff who, in keeping with their obvious inability to run a sports centre, demonstrated only the most tenuous grasp of basic communication skills, barkeeping and attendance. Not an experience worth repeating, all agreed.

Having unanimously rejected the plastic, happy-hour-obsessed pub chains in the town centre frequented by the lager-drinking eighteen-to-thirty community, and thus avoiding the embarrassment of leering at the acres of young women's flesh on view, their second visit had been to the newly built pub designed to cater for the needs of their still-growing housing estate. The traditionally (and thus, in the view of the three men, promisingly) named Green Man sought to justify its moniker by attempting to capture the perceived essence of a typical English country pub. De rigueur horse brasses competed for the customers' attention with reproduction woodwork, generic grey-and-white pictures of bygone days, and a bookcase of never-read (and never-to-be-read) distressed books. All this manufactured antiquity might very well have been tolerated by the friends had it not been for the shocking choice and quality of real ales offered, and the presence of slot machines and loud music, neither of which one would expect to find in a real country pub. Strike two.

Their third attempt in their search for Shangri-La had been the result of some inside information from one of the older receptionists at Graham's surgery. Delsie had insisted that The Royal Oak was well worth the drive out from Ulstown, although she and Lionel had not been there for many years. "But those traditional English country pubs are timeless, aren't they? Lionel always enjoyed the beer there before his… you know… *problem*. You'll have a great time. Just what you're looking for."

It happened to be Graham's turn to drive on their first visit to The Royal Oak. The pleasant surprise of the relative brevity of the twenty-minute car journey (originally advertised by Delsie as being over half an hour – Lionel's driving was almost glacial in speed) was somewhat dissipated by an alarming sideways skid on the rapidly frosting road as Graham belatedly glimpsed the pub's entrance in the gathering gloom. His quick and fulsome apology was insufficient to prevent Ian from once again questioning the need for the childless Graham to drive around in such an unwieldy off-road four-by-four monster. *Janey gets what Janey wants* was, of course, the unspoken answer. Ian and Andy would have looked knowingly at each other had they been able to do so without Graham noticing.

The pub's facade was unremarkable but not unappealing. On the outskirts of the smallest of villages and some fifty yards away from a row of thatched cottages, it certainly had everything in its favour, as English country pubs go. Upon opening the small front door, the new customers were first struck by the obvious lack of patronage for peak time on a Friday evening. Two silent old men standing at opposite ends of a narrow, beer-towel-free bar were separated by the intimidating, expressionless features of the barman. The man to the left turned sharply to confront the intrusion on his evening's entertainment. As he was wearing glasses with lenses of a sufficient curvature to be considered a fire hazard on a sunny day, Graham, from a professional point of view, was very sceptical as to whether he could see as far as the door. In his effort to visualise the strangers, the smaller old man's face cracked open in a forced, toothless smile. There was little doubt regarding the provenance of The Royal Oak. It was clear that very little money had been wasted on its upkeep. Uneven stone floors were bordered by heavily stained, yellowing walls, on which hung photographs of unremarkable, long-forgotten village 'events' often featuring the pub. Non-matching tables were surrounded by a bewildering choice of individual chairs. Thick, uncleaned wooden beams struggled to hold up a nicotine-scarred, worryingly sagging ceiling. The tiny windows were barely transparent. The Royal Oak's final, conclusive authentication as a real, traditional English pub was its complete absence of any offer of food. This was the place for them!

Shuffling nervously towards the bar, the friends were confronted by a minimal choice of real ales, albeit those few were of excellent repute. Their order was given, accepted and delivered with not a word wasted from the barman to his new clients. Momentarily confused by the breadth of choice, they finally opted for the table near the dying embers in the fireplace. Their first drink proved as uneventful as all had hoped, as was to be the case through subsequent nights out, with their only concern being the landlord. All three would have gladly settled for the anonymity of The Royal Oak, were it not for the presence of one Geoffrey Winston Howarth. What could one say of the man? Somewhere between fifty and seventy years old, if one were invited to guess. (He will be fifty-six this year.) An unmarried, unloved giant of a man, prone to wearing ill-fitting clothes seemingly chosen to closely match the hue of the pub's smoke-encrusted ceiling. An unhealthy, pallid complexion born of someone who only ventured outside to admonish poor car-parking etiquette. Like many of his fellow publicans, Geoff was only tolerated by the brewery owners because of the wholly unwarranted deference granted to him by Englishmen of a certain age.

Driving home from their most recent visit to The Royal Oak, conversation about Andy's unconscious adventures soon faded away to window-gazing silence. Andy quickly exploited the unwillingness to talk by turning on his top-of-the-range music system. Unwilling to expose his music collection to potential ridicule – Ian and Graham were big blues and jazz devotees, often to the point of boredom, or so Andy thought – he selected the radio option on the remote control. An irritating country-and-western-style jingle announced hopelessly optimistic claims for the windows and conservatories of a local company before finishing with the company's phone number and a sweeping disclaimer.

"That's enough of that shite," announced Ian, rudely reaching across to switch off the offending sounds.

Andy, of course, was too compliant and afraid to cause offence by pointing out his bad manners, even if his annoyance with Ian's presumption was balanced by it being the right decision.

The radio now off, the darkness of the flat, borderless fields was gradually exchanged for the light afforded by the small clusters of houses which signalled that the outskirts of Ulstown had been reached. They were soon past the High Street and turning towards the new, out-of-town housing development where they all lived. Reversing carefully into his driveway, Andy switched off the engine and the friends once again stepped out into the chilled night air. Bidding their farewells, they strode off keenly towards their respective houses before being urgently reconvened by Ian.

"Yeah, I forgot to say. While you were busy dreaming of murdering middle-aged women, Andy, Graham and I were talking about a summer camping holiday with the families; maybe even Easter if April's not too cold. Just a long weekend, probably somewhere in the West Country, or perhaps on the South Coast. What do you think? Graham's up for it."

A compliant nod from Graham confirmed that he was indeed up for it. Andy could understand Ian's wish for what Andy classified as a rough-and-ready holiday, as the Stevenses had all the kit and often took camping breaks, according to Ian. But urbane, hotel-dwelling Graham, who would not see fifty again, and pretty, pampered thirty-something Janey, who spent more on make-up and clothing than the cost of any camping holiday, on a camping holiday? Surely not. Graham had probably just gone along with Ian, knowing full well that Janey would have no truck with such a venture and so he could use her as his excuse – or so Andy hoped.

"Come on, Andy. The kids will love it. Camping is not like it used to be, you know. All the mod cons these days with this glamping craze. Jacuzzi, central heating," joked Ian.

"Yeah, sounds great," said Andy, fighting desperately to prevent his face reflecting the attack of tensed stomach muscles and sphincter that the thought of being stuck in a tent with hyperactive children had brought on. "Better check with Susan first, though; see if she's already arranged anything," he qualified, with somewhat fervent hope.

"We need to sort out some possible campsites. I'm really busy tomorrow with the kids – can you do some phoning around, Andy?" queried Ian.

"Like yourself, fully booked tomorrow," lied Andy. "Kids swimming, piano lessons and the rest. You know the score. How about you, Graham? What are you up to tomorrow?"

"Rather fancied a lie-in, old boy, then perhaps lunch and a quick round of golf at the club. I think Janey has booked us a table at Whites for seven. I suppose I could tap into the internet to see what's available," offered Graham without any great conviction.

Why the hell would anyone ever think that Graham and Janey would want to go camping? thought Andy.

Graham's outline of a relaxing, self-indulgent weekend sent a wave of envy and memories of long-forgotten personal freedoms crashing over both Ian and Andy.

"OK. Let us know how you get on. I've got a few websites we often use if you need any help," added Ian.

The men once again said their goodnights and disappeared into the executive splendour that could be found in the houses of Malvern Drive.

SUBURBANITES

Come now. Come with me.

Not to Milk Wood, but to watch a frosty, early March dawn break over the semi-rural, semi-urban, new-old town called Ulstown in deepest, darkest south-east England. Follow me up the straight, slight incline of the old High Street; past the dimly lit facades of the various mobile phone shops, opticians, charity shops and gambling dens, and past the town's single grocer whose only competitor has long since been reduced to financial ruin by the out-of-town, two-for-the-price-of-one, trolley-infested, car-parking supermarkets. Then on past the shiny, funeral-black, crow-squabbling church directly opposite the brand-new mosque with its pristine minaret, and into London Road.

Listen. Time passes.

Follow me to the right, under the brightly lit signs to the motorway and London, and past the glistening entrance to the town's frost-painted, duck-infested park. At the roundabout, turn left into Cambrian Way, but take care not to stray onto the unfinished gravel-encrusted footpaths or the temporarily raised and chipped kerbstones. Look to your left, toward the gaudily illuminated 'mini' local shopping arcade, concentrated with businesses deemed essential for the modern lifestyle of the new estate by innovation-deprived town planners. Travel agents, hairdressers, building societies, estate agents, and late-opening, stale-bread, violent-video-game, plastic-toy-purveying 'convenience' stores all competing for customers' attention. Now follow the stark, bright yellow signposts leading to the new housing development and turn into Mendip Road, and then right into Malvern Drive. How very disconcerting it must be for the residents of this new housing development to live in streets named after mountain ranges when all about them is so very flat.

Listen. Time passes.

Please be patient and stay awhile with me amongst the mock-Tudor-fronted houses of Malvern Drive, and watch the dark disappear, the dawn edge nearer, and the frost melt away to dew. A cat needles its way across the top of the splinter-sharp, garden-centre-fresh, creosoted fence of Number 2, leaving evidence of its travels and travails. The marking of territory is important for all the residents of Malvern Drive, man or beast. Squirrels disturb the silent night vigil of desiccated broad-leafed trees as a dog, a rabid car chaser and serial postman harasser, is allowed to bark hysterically from one of the distant, less affluent neighbourhoods.

Listen. Time passes.

Watch with me as the poorly paid, weekend-working souls go about their early-morning tasks. See the redundancy-fearing milkman, the paperboy and the postman pick out their destinations. 'Well-built, attractive, individual homes for the modern executive family,' was the estate agent's promise. Descriptions of tiny gardens, cracked plaster, falling tiles, and car-unfriendly garages were absent from even the smallest print of the glossy-fronted brochure introducing the development.

Come with me now, up to the driveway of Number 4. Past the newly seeded, patchy-grassed lawn; the two shiny, dew-sweating, gratuitously expensive German cars, one for him and one for her, powered only by electricity and the self-righteousness of their owners; and between the white plastic pillars to the brass-knobbed white front door. Let me open the door for you. Inside the house now, up the extravagantly framed portrait-adorned stairs, and into the 'double-windowed master bedroom with en-suite facilities' of what was the show home of the new estate, beautified still further by the appearance-infatuated owners.

Only you can hear the gentle snoring of the recently married Janey Robins, her unmade face surrounded by a fan of long, loosely curled hair. Dark today. Strawberry blonde last week. Beautiful and fragile. Desired but unobtainable.

In the adjacent single bed lies the whirring, clicking, tick-tocking mind of the semi-conscious, insomniac Graham. Cure thyself, Doctor. Should I have referred Mrs Jervis? Can't afford to be wrong again. *Ever cautious, ever worrisome.*

Listen. Time passes.

Let's go back outside. Watch the bleary-eyed early risers leave their houses to go about their business. Where's Number 9 going? Early for him for a Saturday, would be the opinion of most of the respectable local net-curtain twitchers. Must be important – suit and tie. Or has someone died? There, look. Number 11. Full complement. Mother, father, son and daughter. Must be visiting family. You can read it in their faces.

Over here. Let's go into Number 5 at the end of the cul-de-sac. Oh dear. What happened to the cars here? Rust in Malvern Drive? Surely not. Through the door and up the stairs we should go. Duw, Duw, *what a mess. So many toys, so little space. How can houses which share so many features on the outside look so very different when the threshold is crossed? Jake Stevens is awake and content with spinning wheels on a toy car, despite his movement being restricted by a sodden, ground-hugging nappy and a staircase-guarding gate. All the bedroom doors are open – come in and look inside. Only you can see the dreams of bunk-bedded Uma and Jessica Stevens; of colourfully dressed and combed blonde-haired Barbie dolls, and purple plastic unicorns, and make-up and mirrors, and wannabe curling tongs. Side by side in the master bedroom lie Meera and Ian. Meera, restless and fidgety, dreaming of the imminent arrival of her parents and the exhausting childcare duties of the weekend to come. Ian, alcohol-assisted, funeral-still, and asleep without a single care in the world.*

Listen. Time passes.

Finally. Let me take you just over the shared tarmacadam drive to the front door of Andy and Susan Jones. Number 6 Malvern Drive, Ulstown, deepest south-east England. No rust here. A large, modern people carrier – for her, you understand – and a small, meticulously manicured, understated executive car – owned by the company, don't you know. Inside the house, simple but tasteful decoration, just as the owners would like you to think. Now, up the bare-wooded staircase.

"We really must get a carpet for the stairs and landing, Andy."

"Do you appreciate how much that costs? We haven't paid for Christmas yet. Don't forget, we haven't long moved in, and we're already talking about getting the builders in." Conversations past, present and future.

Silence upstairs but for the gentle murmuring of the spoiled Jones children. Their dreams are not so easy to see. I wonder why.

Welcome to the houses and residents of Malvern Drive, Ulstown. Welcome to the new England. And behold the benefits of a Welsh education!

Andy lay awake, staring malevolently at the digital alarm clock as if daring it to announce 7am and thus signal the start of another supposedly relaxing weekend. That this was a Saturday was of little consolation to Andy, since his weekend job was as a not-for-profit taxi driver for overindulged, unoccupied children. He much preferred his salaried role, despite all its problems. Although, these days, he was tired all the time, Saturdays represented his nadir. It was almost as if he was participating in the children's activities instead of just being a prostrate, semi-conscious spectator. Added to the exhausting morning responsibilities was the afternoon weekly food shop at the local supermarket, where his senses were regularly accosted by outrageously misbehaving kids destined for a long life of crime and aisle-blocking conglomerations of trolley-heaving family groups who considered their weekly shopping to be a day out for the whole family. Still, it was better than leaving Susan at large with a credit card and having to manage the fallout from her annoying habit of buying fresh food within an afternoon of its sell-by date. But maybe he could postpone that to Sunday this week. Fingers crossed.

Reaching over to intercept the imminent alarm, Andy swept back the pastel print duvet, planting his feet on the thickly carpeted floor, and sat as upright as he was able to at this time in the morning. A sharp, stabbing pain swept up from his groin and lodged itself in the small of his back, where it became a dull ache. This was the first time he had felt this pain for some weeks now, and he had hoped it had gone forever. Afraid to either tell Susan or consult his GP, he had put up with it for several months, alternating wildly from thoughts of cancer and imminent death to the view that such aches and pains should be expected as one approaches forty. The creeping approach of middle age had, for Andy, heralded a state of chronic hypochondria which stretched far beyond any actual illness he would ever suffer. Long gone were the days when lashings of alcohol and spicy food had been sufficient to ward off ailments. Determined not to let this latest bodily dysfunction consume his day by looking up the symptoms on the internet, he made a mental note to somehow discreetly broach the subject with Graham. Perhaps next Friday, and when Ian was out of earshot. At least those headaches and the brain fog he had been suffering on and off since the New Year were not bothering him this morning.

Andy walked noisily through onto the landing and downstairs to the kitchen, holding and prodding his back in a futile attempt at a convincing diagnosis. The tactic of treading on only the loosest and creakiest floorboards had the desired effect: he could hear Susan and the children stirring in their beds. Shocking workmanship. "Floorboards shouldn't creak in a new house," Andy moaned to himself.

There was sufficient natural light coming into the kitchen for him to make coffee for Susan and tea and microwavable cereal for himself without switching on the light. Susan's first action, as she stumbled bleary-eyed into the kitchen some five minutes later, was, nonetheless, to switch it on. Ignoring, for the moment, this minor irritation, Andy pushed the steaming cup of coffee in her general direction as she slumped at the small, circular, antique pine-effect breakfast table. Having faithfully completed its morning's task, the microwave was opened and its super (albeit unevenly) heated contents of oats and assorted desiccated fruits were rescued by Andy and placed on the table. This was, by some margin, the healthiest meal he consumed in a typical week.

In replacing his almost empty cereal box in a high cupboard, he briefly caught sight of the other breakfast options. "Why do we buy this crap for the kids? Have you read the packet? Chocolate-flavoured, dinosaur-shaped dehydrated cardboard or something like that. No nutritional value at all as far as I can see." He didn't expect – or get – an answer from his barely conscious wife, but he did hope that his harangue would lodge somewhere in Susan's long-term memory, to be accessed when concocting the list for the next visit to the out-of-town 'superstore'. Besides, he had far more important decisions to discuss with her.

"Didn't you arrange for us to go to your mother's caravan this Easter?" He sat down at the table, cradling his mug of tea and determined to finish his breakfast without having to taste it. He looked intently towards his wife.

"After what you said about her last time?! I don't think so. We *were* going, if you remember, but I cancelled after your latest tirade against my family and my mother especially. *She* has a name, you know." Susan thought it best not to reveal that it was actually her mother who had put paid to their planned holiday.

"The Devil has many names, dear," replied Andy, somewhat unhelpfully. He did indeed remember his (now) regrettable post-Christmas tirade, which had been out of character for someone more used to keeping forthright opinions about others to himself. But he had been in a shocking mood, he reasoned, so it was hardly his fault.

"Why are you always arguing about Nanny?" Joshua asked to no one in particular as he took his seat at the breakfast table. "I think she is very jolly and always smiling at me."

The twins had already taken up their seats and were creating a stable for their multicoloured ponies out of the cereal boxes Andy had placed on the table.

"Joshua, son, don't ever confuse good humour with a kidney complaint," was Andy's unhelpful parental advice to his eldest. "It's often difficult to tell the difference between a real smile and a grimace."

"*Andrew!* Was that necessary? Anyway, why are you so interested in what we are doing for Easter all of a sudden? You're not thinking of taking us on a surprise holiday for once in our lives?" breathed Susan, who, in keeping with her tradition, had risen from the table to start clearing away the bowl and mug that Andy had barely finished using.

"That's not fair. It was only last year's holidays that we missed, and you know that was because of the house move," Andy stated forcefully. "And before you ask, the answer is no. There's no way we can afford to go away at Easter – perhaps in the summer. We'll see." Immediately he regretted rejecting a potential excuse for not going camping with the Stevenses. "Bugger," he said under his breath.

"Mummy, Daddy!" interjected Sophie, having parked her freshly combed, pink pony next to the picture of a brontosaurus standing defiant across the front of a cereal box. "I thought you said I could make the breakfasts on Saturdays."

Andy looked at Susan. Susan looked at Sophie and smiled.

"Yeah!" shouted Sophie, before badgering her siblings on what they should now eat for breakfast.

Susan did not have the energy to argue that a short Easter break at her mother's caravan on the Norfolk coast would be unlikely to lead to them becoming destitute. An argument for another time, perhaps, when she had smoothed things over with her mother. "Living next to a different set of Joneses now, you should be aware," she pointed out to the kitchen window, having started to load the dishwasher, "that Janey Robins over the road has spent thousands on hair extensions, and she's even got Graham to agree to breast enlargements. None of which she needs, of course."

"I'm very surprised to hear that she doesn't mind everyone knowing what bits have come off or on. Pretty private stuff, I would have thought," mused Andy. "I didn't know you knew her that well." A topless, post-operation Janey wandered provocatively through his mind, the full-frontal image lasting long enough to temporarily disrupt his train of thought.

"For some reason, she also seems very interested in your job. Making drugs. A bit weird, I thought," added Susan.

"I don't *make* drugs. I carry out research into new medicines," protested Andy, who, over the years, had described his job to many people, few of whom seemed to really understand what he actually did for a living.

"Whatever," answered Susan, although both knew that she was very proud of her husband's achievements.

The thought that the delicious Janey was actually interested in plain, boring old Andy was not a little titillating. "Anyway, I'm sure we can stretch to a breast enlargement for you, love. Much more fun than a bracing weekend looking out across the North Sea. Which one will it be? It'll have to be one at a time, mind – all we can afford at the moment, sorry," he jested in an attempt to lift the general mood and avoid another miserable Saturday.

"Very cheap and just maybe a little bit funny," retorted Susan. "Just like your aftershave. Off and get changed now, girls. Daddy will clear up, won't you, Daddy?"

Joshua had already disappeared into his bedroom, excited by the prospect of slaughtering yet more virtual dinosaurs on a computer game deemed to be non-violent by his parents as no humans were harmed.

“Look, I don’t want to get into another money argument. Not this morning. If you really want to increase our spending then you will just have to go back to work like Meera Stevens across the road,” lied Andy. “How else do you think they could afford that house with only Ian’s teacher’s wage coming in?”

You had to be fair to Susan, though, he mused to himself. She could be a right bitch about money and often was, but she tended to the family and home pretty much without Andy’s help. All this as well as putting her own career as a buyer for a fashion chain on hold to make sure there was someone there for their growing family. An important, non-negotiable contractual obligation, long discussed and agreed before the children arrived. Almost a marital vow, at least in her eyes. Because of his long working hours and commuting time, Andy rarely saw the children in the week (outside of a few frazzled hours in the evening) and never lowered himself to undertake household chores after coming home. Most of the parenting had been done by Susan, and Andy would forever be grateful to his hard-working wife for the well-behaved if somewhat unremarkable children she was guiding safely into adulthood. That both parents wouldn’t have wanted it any other way did not do justice to the sacrifices Susan had made for the family since Joshua had arrived in their tiny, rented house some seven years ago. She had also looked after herself over the years, still almost fitting into the clothes she had worn on their wedding day and rather modest honeymoon during the hot summer when they had both graduated from the same university. Her small, pretty face smiled sweetly out of the many photographs of that memorable day which took pride of place in 6 Malvern Drive. Her considered discipline in eating and exercising sensibly had not been mirrored by her husband, whose increasing girth was now of concern to himself as well as to Susan, and made him a figure of fun for young Joshua.

On the whole, Andy felt that they were both pretty content with their married life. And Susan? She had not been happy with her stagnating career or the mind-numbing daily commute to London from the wrong side of Harlow, so the chance to take a sabbatical as a full-time mother had been timely and welcomed. The stresses of the screaming, vomiting baby years, exacerbated by the very tightest of household budgets, had gradually given way to mild altercations concerning the whereabouts of the TV remote control or the car keys, or the inclination of the toilet lid. Serious arguments raged only when Susan's family was the topic of discussion. With respect to money, Andy conceded, it could easily be argued that Susan deserved more of life's luxuries after the early privations of their married life, even though he felt that she had been rather too eager to sacrifice her career so completely on the altar of motherhood.

Although Andy and Susan had enjoyed but few luxuries in those early years of their marriage, they did share an obvious affection and respect for each other which had endured through to more prosperous, recent times. Theirs had never been a great love, with both happy to conform to the safe and steady model of married life inflicted upon them by their parents. Sex had gradually become more of a routine function than a spontaneous act, and was performed with mutual selfishness but no little enjoyment. Public gestures of affection had been rare even at the start of their relationship and had disappeared almost completely shortly after the twins had arrived. Again, this was not a source of conflict, as it was acceptable to – indeed, preferred by – both parties. Neither felt the compulsion to act otherwise just for the benefit of other people's preconceptions of what 'true love' looked like.

With Andy's career seemingly going so well, they had gradually been able to reach their common dream – that their parents had never been able to realise – of being members of the upper, more wealthy middle-class cabal, and this despite Susan not bringing in a wage. It was only after Andy had left the closeted, northern market town he had been brought up in and arrived at Birmingham University that he'd realised that he was not really a part of the middle classes, as his parents had led him to believe. His was just another family from among the masses; the rather unenviably named lower middle class, a population unable to benefit from either the wealth of the true middle class or the self-righteousness of the working class. Worse still was that this section of society was burdened with aspirations they were expected to fulfil but lacked the requisite financial means. Had Andy and Susan really been able to move up in the world? Maybe. Because – despite the money, the house, the car and the apparent status – there was always one more loft conversion, one more kitchen extension and one more set of patio doors that Susan needed.

Leaving instructions for the children to be ready in half an hour, the freshly breakfasted Andy climbed the stairs for his daily shower, welcoming the opportunity to hatch foolproof excuses to avoid a Stevens-inspired camping holiday, and to arrive at a diagnosis for his on-off headaches. Having failed to achieve either objective, he quickly completed his ablutions, which included a thirty-second session of personal admiration in the pinewood-framed bathroom mirror. Maybe not the best-looking man around, he conceded – even his own mother had said that his face was too crowded – but still, there was something there, despite the thinning hair and the collapsing stomach muscles, the latter of which would surely be rectified by his ongoing exercise regime with Ian and Graham. Putting on his rather plain Saturday clothes – he was too busy to buy nice ones – he rushed downstairs to avoid being late to start on the children's exhausting schedule of Saturday-morning activities.

Within ten minutes the children were rounded up and Andy was hurriedly strapping his youngest into the people carrier he had dreaded buying and had no pride in owning and less still in driving. At least he had convinced Susan to agree to buying a black Ford – as inconspicuous as he could have hoped for in the circumstances. In closing the rear car door, he caught a glimpse of Graham closing his front door. Almost as a reflex action Andy jogged over to Graham, taking care not to slip on any area of frost yet to be visited by the sun.

"Graham, have you got a minute?" he said, now regretting his knee-jerk reaction in approaching Graham in the first place, and glancing back at the people carrier to make sure the children were not doing anything to bring shame on the family. He was talking now to Dr

Graham Robins the respected local GP, and not Graham his exercising and drinking friend.

"Of course, old boy," replied Graham, temporarily abandoning his search for the car keys he was sure he had brought out with him.

"Well, it's a bit awkward, really. Hey, I thought you were due for a lie-in today?"

"I was until Janey woke up with one of her heads. Didn't feel up to the week's food shopping. You know the score. Gone off somewhere to clear her head. So muggins will be doing the shopping today"

"Yes. Funny you should say that about Janey, as I was going to ask for your opinion on this chronic headache I have had since Christmas. Even a sort of annoying brain fog from time to time. A bit tough to explain. Probably nothing really; just a consequence of getting old, I suppose," said Andy rather apologetically.

This was just the sort of encounter that most GPs hate. An out-of-office consultation without the benefit of being back in the surgery hiding behind a desk, nor even the means to really do anything about the complaint other than recommend what the person should really have done from the first: make an appointment to see their bloody GP!

"With your background in medical science, you know well, Andy, that those sorts of symptoms can arise through at least a dozen different causes, most of which are trivial and temporary." Graham always tried to reassure his patients, regardless of how close they were to death. There was little point in adding a depression diagnosis to his workload. "I really need to examine you to get a better idea," he added, with the patience and good grace from which all who knew him benefited.

"OK. I'll make an appointment with Dr Anand sometime this week," lied Andy, who had rapidly gone off the idea of doing anything at all. *How pathetic must I sound?* he worried to himself.

"No, listen. Come and see me at the practice after work. I'll make some time for you as this is obviously concerning you."

"Dr Anand is my doctor, though, Graham. Perhaps it would be better if I saw her?" interjected Andy, desperate to avoid an early and perhaps disturbing verdict on his condition.

"I'll sort it out with my good friend, don't you worry! Expect a call from our receptionist. That's final. Must dash, old boy," said Graham, resuming his quest for the long-lost keys.

"Thanks." Slowly Andy turned and walked pensively back to his car. *Are these headaches really worth wasting anyone's time?* He was at least grateful that he had not mentioned the back spasm that had visited him earlier that morning.

Graham looked out of place because he *was* out of place, even if this was the sort of supermarket where customers were prepared to pay just a little bit more for exactly the same produce that could be bought more cheaply at bargain basement outlets. *One has one's reputation to maintain.* Although he was far from new to supermarket shopping, his unease was ever present throughout his tour of the aisles. A six-foot-four, formally dressed, fifty-something GP doing the weekly food shop alone was, somehow, just not right, at least in Graham's perception. If only he had the patience to work out how to order online. But he didn't. To exaggerate the inappropriateness of it all, Janey just "didn't do lists" and so it was left to him to laboriously decide – by circling, vulture-like, the aisles – which items were needed to sustain the household and any guests who might be indulged during the following week. The only rule of thumb that Graham had to work with was that, if there was a choice, he was to choose the most expensive option. He hated shopping with a passion. The supermarket was too small a place for so many people, each of whom could potentially be a patient of his, intent on stalking him for anything from a friendly chat to an on-the-spot diagnosis. It was one of the more annoying downsides to his comforting bedside manner. And more to the point, why did he always give in to Janey so easily? Every time for anything. As if he didn't know. To do otherwise would be to open a box he just wasn't emotionally equipped to close.

"Well, hello, Dr Robins. How are you? Fancy seeing you here. But I suppose doctors have to eat as well," remarked a middle-aged woman barely taller than the trolley that she was struggling to control.

"Very well, thanks, Mrs Laity. I hope you too are keeping well," replied Graham, taking some pride from the fact that he was able to recognise one patient out of hundreds and remember her as one of the worried well. He then practised the smooth and outwardly polite walk away from a potential conversation which he hoped would be his only such exchange today.

Mrs Laity waved weakly to his rodlike back, happy that such an important man had taken the time to wish her well. It was more than her horrid sister would likely do, she mused.

The well-meaning familiarity of the gentlefolk of Ulstown was to be expected given the longevity of service the Robins 'franchise' had bestowed upon the town. Three generations – grandfather, father and mother, and their only child, Graham – had provided respected healthcare for the steadily growing community. The next generation of Robins doctors was assumed to be guaranteed following the public announcement of the birth of Alice to Dr and Mrs G. W. Robins, and the grand christening that followed. Despite (or maybe because of) the respect this fine family commanded in the community, no little scandal had been occasioned by the separation and subsequent divorce of Dr and Mrs Robins. Graham had taken several years to overcome the anguish caused by his ex-wife's determination to take their daughter effectively out of his life to "start a new life" in Spain. It had been even longer before he'd fully regained his self-respect and his old, easy-going confidence during social occasions. Not that there were many of those. The only lasting reminder of those dark days was the surfeit of grey hair that remained, but somehow it only enhanced his dignified persona.

Carrots. Chantenay or Imperator? How should he know? The most expensive option was deposited in Graham's trolley as per Janey's guidelines, and it was a hint of one of Janey's more expensive perfumes that alerted him to the vague presence of someone to his left. Bent over the chiller cabinet comparing pea-packet malleability, she very much reminded him of what he had always found so attractive in Janey: a natural, beauty with a porcelain complexion and graceful movement, all wrapped up in elegantly understated clothing. 'Class' would be the colloquial conclusion of most, if not, perhaps, Graham himself. With her full concentration upon frozen foods he was able to almost stare at her freely. He wondered if that outward beauty disguised a shallow, rather selfish personality similar to that which Janey seemed to be steadily adopting since their wedding. His beautiful, seemingly untouched English rose had grown thorns. Or maybe they had always been there, and he had just not seen them.

"Sorry. Do I know you?"

"Er, no. At least, I don't think so. I wasn't staring at you; I was just miles away in thought. Sorry. My apologies," blustered Graham, who would have blushed furiously if he had been capable of doing so.

She maintained eye contact for long enough to convey that she simply did not believe his excuse. Graham tipped his head downwards and scuttled his way to the cheese aisle, passing a morbidly obese couple engrossed in the relative merits of the finest sausages and bacon the supermarket could offer. Graham's own deliberation over the selection of something French, aromatic and likely pernicious, versus something English and safe, was interrupted by a sharp, piercing cry followed by a deep, guttural moan from a child somewhere close by. *Why do people insist on dragging their feral children around supermarkets?* Half expecting a call to come from the PA system requesting the assistance of a doctor, Graham made his way towards where he thought the terrifying scream had originated from, and stumbled across Ian and Meera Stevens who were within seconds of embarking on a weekend-defining argument.

"Ian, Meera. How are you both? And the children?" Graham nodded towards the whimpering, red-faced Jake sitting in the supermarket trolley. Uma and Jessica were standing to attention to either side of it. Graham would have preferred to avoid them and would have done so had it not been for the screaming. He still felt a little uneasy in Ian's presence, even after enjoying their post-Christmas weekly visits to the sports centre and subsequent pub nights. His rather uncouth behaviour? The too-often-shared radical views on almost any subject? Graham couldn't put his finger on it but there was something not quite to his liking about Ian. Andy was much more his type. Perhaps Ian would grow on him in time. "Is little Jake all right? I heard a frightful scream."

"Jake? Oh, he's OK. Just had a little disagreement over sweets, didn't we, Jake?" replied Ian, his moustache glistening with stress-induced perspiration and the supermarket lighting reflecting somewhat unkindly off his gently balding scalp. "Don't often see you here," he added in an attempt to divert Graham's attention from his inability to control his young son, who, fortunately, had fallen silent in the presence of the towering GP.

"But hey. Just remembered. You and Janey up for this camping trip Ian said you were discussing last night at the pub?" stammered Meera, adding her own contribution to changing the subject.

"You can definitely put me down for that, Meera, but I

completely forgot to bring it up with Janey," lied Graham. "So, we will have to get back to you on that one. Anyway, I'd better tootle along as Janey's waiting for me to bring back the food. Glad everything is OK. Bye, kids." He strode, with conviction and not a little gratefully, towards the tinned meats and spreads.

"The Robinses going camping? My arse! One more cry from you, Jake, and we will be back home with no sweets. Understand?" threatened Ian once Graham was beyond earshot.

Although Jake provided no indication that he did understand, Ian was happy enough to get the supermarket trolley rolling again in their search for frozen pies. The girls were off foraging for items from the mini list their mother always gave them on supermarket days.

"Well, if they don't come it'll be because they don't want to share any time with a miserable little shit like you," said Meera, to no one in particular.

"Right! That's it. Come on, Jess. Let's go to your tap lesson early. Daddy will take you," shouted Ian to his eldest, who was across the aisle looking for the third item on their mini list.

Jessica flung up her arms, exasperated that her shopping excursion had been cut short before she'd found the ice cream.

Now facing his wife, Ian spoke quietly but firmly. "Look. I've just about had enough today. I'm made to get up early and forced to come around this fucking supermarket. I mean, fucking hell. All this after a never-ending week stuck in that bloody school. And then all I have to look forward to before another week in school crashes on me is a whole weekend having to be nice to your parents. Again. Roll on fucking Monday is all I can say. Come on, Jess, it's only a short walk."

Meera's left hand grabbed her husband's coat, thus preventing an easy escape. Unlike Ian she had made an effort to dress herself well and, as usual, had managed to conceal the parts of her body which had collected most of the post-baby fat. Her long black hair had been tied up and a smattering of make-up applied to her pretty, round face. "Now. You listen to me," she seethed through clenched teeth and with minimal lip movement. She glanced from side to side to rule out the close presence of anyone they might know in preparation for providing her husband with some forthright guidance. "*I* got up first this morning. *I* got the children ready, and *I* am doing the shopping. *I* will look after my parents, and it will be *me* who does the clearing up. You have a real problem with my parents, don't you? Well, despite all their faults, at least they can be bothered to get off their *arses* once in a while and visit our *fucking* kids. So please, be my guest and fuck off to the recreation centre."

The swearing was administered sotto voce, as was Meera's preference in public situations. Her softened tone by no means undermined her venom. Now free of his wife's restraint, and with no adequate comeback to her acidity coming to mind, Ian literally pulled their eldest away from the potential crime scene and did not turn around to hear Meera's parting words.

"Bye, darling. See you back at the house. Don't you hurry back, now."

Ian managed to beat the automatic door but failed

to allow sufficient time for Jessica's safe exit. By the time they left the supermarket car park he had finally managed to calm his bruised daughter. It was a quarter-mile walk to the recreation centre. *What a cow*, he thought. *What an absolute fucking cow. One more step out of line and I'll be right out of Dodge – fuck her and the kids. She brings nothing to the marriage except whingeing. One more time. That's all. One more time.* But he knew full well that this particular argument would be long forgotten by the time they were all back home, and that he would never leave his wife. That was, of course, until the next argument. He just didn't deserve her.

They made it in good time to Jessica's outrageously overpriced and under-taught dance lesson. Through the glazed front door of the recreation centre Ian could see Andy in the reception area, as he often did at this time on a Saturday morning. *Now, Andy's a good mate*, he mused. *Down to earth. Not like Graham, who's always up his own arse. There's something not quite right about him and Janey.* This prejudice had been reinforced by Meera, who could only cope with Janey in the presence of Susan.

"Andy!" called Ian as he backslapped his clearly surprised friend. "How's it hanging, mate? Still up for the camping trip. We bumped into Graham at the supermarket just before I got here and he's gagging for it," he lied blatantly.

"Oh, hi, Ian. Hello, Jessica. Camping. Wonderful. Can't wait," offered an expressionless Andy. "Sorry, Ian, but I'll have to slip off or this bunch will miss their lessons, won't you, kids? Mummy wouldn't want you to miss your lesson, would she? Catch you later." Andy treasured any little, precious peace-and-quiet time he could eke out of his busy Saturday mornings, and he certainly was not going to waste it by talking about a holiday that he was desperate to avoid.

Having expected some sort of conversation, Ian found himself jilted. Still, his rhinoceros-like skin always kept out any slight, whether real or imagined, from friend, wife or work colleague.

Worryingly short of breath, Andy charged up a short flight of stairs towards the changing rooms. *What is this camping fetish about?* he wondered. He was convinced that all this 'glamping' malarkey was really just a ruse to convince the well-heeled that being holed up in a field without en-suite facilities could be enjoyable. *Can these people really be that gullible? Or are they just trying to pretend that they are better off than is actually the case?*

"Come on, you lot. You're going to miss swimming if you don't get a move on. Don't forget, outside the changing rooms straight after your dance lesson," he called after Sophie just before losing sight of her. He knew he could rely on Sophie, who had a maturity beyond both her five years and her twin sister.

After shepherding Joshua and Rachel to their swimming lessons (the classes Little Shrimps One and Two had been etched onto Andy's psyche by his organised wife), he laboured up the spiral staircase to the spectators' balcony. A slightly damp collection of the supplements from last Sunday's newspapers were untangled and read in between glimpses of the splashing, shouting children below and the gratuitously perfect body of the wholly unobtainable young swimming teacher.

Once all the splashing and shouting had stopped and the dripping children had been ordered back to the changing rooms by the perfect body, Andy carefully descended the now dangerously wet stairs to deposit the almost completely unread Sunday supplements into the bin on the ground floor. In delaying for as long as possible his appearance in the changing room in order to avoid the chore of helping the children dress, he glimpsed Janey Robins walking down the main corridor, in conversation with a bottle-tanned leisure centre 'representative' more suited to being with a surfboard on a Cornish beach than in a recreation centre over two hours' drive away from the sea. *What is it with this place and those who live in Malvern Drive?* fretted Andy.

Simply attired in a floral-patterned dress which perfectly outlined her curved body, Janey immediately changed tack in order to intercept Andy on his route to the changing rooms, leaving the representative with a coquettish wave. She had obviously had a good workout with her private masseur, based on the red glow of her face. Janey was always up for a bit of prick-teasing and Andy represented the very easiest of victims. She enjoyed revelling in the power she had over men. This would be like watching a mature lioness savage a stranded antelope. What theatre! "Hi," she called, from some ten yards distant from Andy.

Drawing closer, Andy could see that she had, not unusually, taken some time with her make-up that morning. Taking a brush out of her shoulder bag, she started to comb the back of her near-waist-length hair, only some of which was her own.

"Didn't know that you were keen on sport, Janey," said

Andy, his eyes subconsciously (but inevitably, following the breakfast-time discussion) focusing on her breasts.

Following his gaze, she also glanced at her breasts, then looked up, smiling, into his furiously flushing face. He might have been married for getting on for fifteen years, but a life that began as an only child, followed by a female-free, public-school life, had not really equipped him with the tools needed to relate easily to the opposite sex. "No, no. Not sport. Silly you. Just came for a quick sauna to get rid of all the toxins, and a massage from Chris to relieve the tension in my shoulders and back. Had a terrible headache this morning. Completely gone now, thanks to Chris. He's wonderful. I can fully recommend him. And of course, the place is so close to our estate… I mean house." Janey could never live on a housing estate even if it was an executive housing estate. "Chris was able to squeeze me in at the last minute."

I bet he was, thought Andy. *Tension? What on earth in Janey's child-free, work-free life could cause tension?* "Bad bottle or two of Malbec?" he teased rather meekly, having been joined by an immaculately dressed Sophie fresh from her dance lesson.

"Well, something like that, maybe." Janey smiled, her head turned slightly towards raised voices coming from the changing room.

"Right, OK. I suppose I'd better get a move on," said Andy. "I need to get Joshua and Rachel sorted," he said pointing to and turning towards the changing room door. But before he could take one step, Janey gently held his turning shoulder. He flinched at the unexpected human contact.

"Before you go, Andy." She caressed his upper arm, holding on for longer than was appropriate in a calculated move to make him feel just a little uneasy. It worked. "Graham told me last night about your dream. *Very* interesting. I will have to get my books out for that one, and we should meet up sometime! Anyway, must fly. See you, Andy. Bye." And that was that. Off down the stairs to reception and the exit went Janey, still brushing her hair.

"Bye, Janey," called Andy, raising a hand almost as an afterthought.

Dreams. At least they hadn't talked about camping holidays. In fact, Andy mused that they never would, and that it would all be forgotten soon enough – even by Ian, perhaps. Andy wondered exactly why he had grown up to be such an antisocial old bugger. Susan often wondered just the same.

Still shaking his head, Andy made his way toward the boys' changing room. With any luck, both Joshua and Rachel would have managed to dress themselves by now and all that would remain for him to do would be a double-check that nothing had been left behind and that Rachel's long hair would be sufficiently tangle-free when she appeared outside the girls' changing room to avoid Susan's displeasure upon their homecoming. Now to the next activity of Saturday morning: Advanced Microvascular Surgery for the Under-Eights. Or was it Basic Soccer Skills Two?

All that was left for Andy to enjoy from the remnants of his unfortunate Saturday ambush by his neighbours was a fast-forward to the evening's visit to The Raj, which could be found adjacent to the ludicrously named Metropolitan

Hotel. The latter was deemed enjoyable due to the opportunity it presented during the wait for the order to be cooked. This time was typically effectively employed by Andy in drinking up to the legal limit of stone-cold lager, so as not to imperil his drive home from the hotel's characterless bar. This evening he made a mental note not to overrun his drinking time allocation as he had some two weeks previous.

"I wouldn't use that Raj place again, Andy. This bloody dinner's freezing."

"All right, dear. I'll point it out to them next week."

Such is a typical Saturday for the residents of Malvern Drive. But all that is soon to change – at least for Andy.

JANEY

Janey, gone off on a Saturday-morning drive to clear her head? I don't think so. An oft-employed excuse to get out of the house, and a chance to meet others. The old, young Janey.

Compared to the rest of the cast living in Malvern Drive, Janey is an outlier, an enigma, even, which is why there is a whole chapter in this book just about her, even if it is rather a short one. Without her, this book and the police investigation would never have happened, and very few of you living outside Ulstown would have heard of Malvern Drive and its inhabitants. You won't find any chapters devoted solely to any of the other characters in this book. Not even Andy, who, after all, is supposed to be our hero, although many of you might arrive at a different conclusion, should you manage to get to the end of the story. Maybe; maybe not. Janey as the heroine? Probably not, but it will be interesting to see what you think. But that Janey – she is some character. Could well be that there is a little bit of me in her somewhere. I will let you be the judge of that. So, a chapter just for Janey, as do you really want to read through paragraph after paragraph revealing the lives of our other protagonists? I thought not. And, as they say back home, if truth be told, I could not be arsed to write them.

Janey the child. She was a little bit different right from the off. She was born in a Bournemouth hostel, to a drug-addicted single mother on a stormy autumn day. No time to get to the hospital. Within a month of her birth she was adopted and named Jane Middleton. The sickly but beautiful baby became the much-loved only child of the Middletons of leafy, very much upmarket Winchester City; a rather well-heeled couple in their mid-forties whose wish to pass on their impressive genes had slowly faded in a flurry of private-clinic waiting rooms and outpatient appointments. Much to their shared regret, that yearned-for ship had long sailed over the horizon, according to the results of the expensive tests that the even more expensive doctors had insisted upon. Adoption was their preferred way forward to become parents, and they were fortunate in that their wealth and good education could offset their age in the eyes of the powers that be. Experienced parents, including even their own, impressed upon them just how exhausting babies and children can be even when one is young. But no one could doubt the Middletons' commitment to becoming parents. Such was their passion that few were surprised when they soon navigated their way through the minefield that is adoption and welcomed baby Jane into their home.

The Middletons were able to buy their way out of sleepless nights and vomit clean-ups by hiring a succession of young and inexperienced live-in nannies, with new arrivals quickly replacing departing, burnt-out models. But, by and large, the nannies stayed for long enough to provide good-quality 24/7 care for a thriving baby Jane – and, in more than one case, a rather pleasant and discreet sex life for Mr Middleton, whose wife had rather gone off the idea of sex now that there was no longer any possibility of there being a deliverable product of such a union. The nannies – and, much to his angst, Mr Middleton's sex life – disappeared once Jane started primary school. Both parents were very concerned about the potential for her to be negatively affected by the absence of an on-tap nanny, but the girl seemingly took this major upheaval in her stride. It certainly wouldn't be the last time that our Janey showed herself to be resolute and in possession of a steely inner confidence.

Janey the girl. I suppose you now expect me to say that she excelled at school and was always top of the class. Not the case at all, I'm afraid. Jane was not exactly at the bottom of the class, but nor did she excel at any stage of her schooling, all of which came as a major disappointment to her adoptive parents, who were unable to improve her grades despite sending Jane to an expensive prep school. After school, home tutoring also failed to nudge the needle. Maybe a case where nurture could not overcome nature? But the Middletons did their best, and who knows how much worse it would have been if Jane had not gone to prep school, or had been deprived of her after-school lessons? That was the comfort blanket in which Jane's parents wrapped themselves as she moved through secondary school and towards exams, which became a fraught time for all as Jane's life-defining examinations coincided with her realising just how much attention and popularity a pair of tits, a pretty and discreetly made-up face, and a short skirt can attract. So, just picture the relief of the status-driven Middletons when a combination of the government's drive to grant degrees to all those in possession of a brain coincided with their daughter finally developing a semblance of a work ethic. The result? Jane was accepted by a London regional college to undertake a degree. Hallelujah! The Middletons had somehow managed to get her to the 'respectability' of being accepted onto a degree course, which made conversations with grandparents and friends on how she was doing so much less stressful. OK, it was only a degree in public relations, but it was, nevertheless, an honours-level degree, and much more than they had been expecting ever since one particular grisly parents' evening shortly after Jane's fifteenth birthday.

Jane left home for the first time just one month before her eighteenth birthday; a product befitting the care and attention the Middletons had devoted to their only child. Not to ignore the money spent, of course.

Janey the young woman. Janey was made for university and student life. Much to the initial disappointment of her parents, Jane became Janey in the summer before that first term. To Jane, it was her way of reinventing herself before going to university. Among her soon-to-be-dropped friends back in Winchester, it was universally viewed as just her latest affectation. And it was not just her old friends and clingy, on-off boyfriend who were dropped. Also left by the wayside was the opportunity to find out the identity of the person Janey referred to as "the woman who gave birth to me" which arrived on her 18th birthday. To Janey, that promiscuous drug addict (a truth that she found out from her adoptive parents) was no mother. "Why would I want to find out who abandoned me as soon as I was born?

Where's the upside for me?" she argued to her surprised but somewhat relieved parents when the subject was brought up. Sentiment and loyalty had to be earned as far as Janey was concerned. Her love and affection were reserved for the people who had lavished their love and affection upon her. Genetic similarity alone was insufficient to justify any real emotion or loyalty.

Janey the woman. Janey became a woman in the early hours after the college freshers' ball. The clingy boyfriend had been kept at arm's length for almost two years, but a combination of drink, her first experience of weed, and having her very own room away from prying parents led to her next rite of passage. And how very disappointing it had all been to an expectant Janey. Exciting? Yes, of course it was. He ticked all the aesthetic boxes that she was looking for in a lover, and she took no little pride in the fact that he was one of the most attractive boys at the ball that night. Hers had been far from the only pair of eyes lusting over him across the dance floor. But life-changing? No. Not even all that satisfying, she concluded when she awoke next to him the following morning. Despite him advertising that there had been several other lovers before her, Janey's experience of that early-morning rolling under the covers was one more of pleasure than of ecstasy. Where were the multiple orgasms she had read about in the glossy magazines and had rather been expecting? Further encounters in both his and her student hall rooms were no less enjoyable, but their shared frustration at Janey's never being able to reach orgasm meant that the relationship ended almost as soon as it began, and the beautiful couple went their separate ways: he to more responsive and appreciative lovers and she in search of one who could satisfy her. But that was not a priority for Janey in her first year of college. Her focus was making sure that she worked hard enough to progress to the second and third years of her course. She was going to make a success of her time at university.

Janey thoroughly enjoyed student life. Her own private room. Freedom to go where she wanted, when she wanted and with whom she wanted – and the money from her parents to do so. What's there not to like? Despite her priority being her studies, other lovers came and went over those three years, but they never stayed around for long. Janey made sure of that. Why should she be lumbered with the same body and the same conversations, week in and week out, when she could have her pick of whomever she wanted to be with, even though such promiscuity did bring with it an unenviable reputation? Even with that millstone around her neck, Janey clung on to a small, hard core of acquaintances who stuck with her throughout her college years. Her girlfriends were typically, similarly ephemeral. It took a certain personality to be able to warm to Janey's behaviours, which at the very least were often seen as selfish. Janey was well aware of this commonly held perception, but her own take on it was that she was not one to suffer fools gladly. She always had an excuse for her poor behaviour. Much easier than changing her headstrong ways. But she did work at her studies. She attended almost all her lectures. Her essays and a dissertation were without fail submitted before their deadlines. She was cute enough to cultivate good working relationships with her tutors, going as far as to rely upon some of the more gullible male ones to help her just a little bit more than they felt comfortable with. All of which led to Janey successfully graduating on a rather chilly summer's day in 2008, in the company of her small group of friends and a very pretty trophy boyfriend whom she had recently picked up to show off to her parents.

Everything was perfect in Janey's world. The latest boyfriend was soon dropped, and with her parents' money she was able to buy a small town house in London, with two of the rooms rented out to college friends. Her father used his network to squeeze her into a gofer job in a large PR agency off King's Cross. Janey's life was about to take off – and take off it did, both socially and professionally. Much to the surprise of family, friends and even Janey herself, she was quickly promoted through the ranks of the agency, as the very attributes that had stoked so much jealousy in her private life – force of personality, personal charisma, easy-going charm and attractive appearance – were in PR, valuable and highly sought-after assets. Not surprisingly, she revelled in her success. And although student life had been a huge step up from the social world of sleepy Winchester, a growing disposable income and a new circle of friends and acquaintances met through work allowed her to enjoy London to the full. This was where she belonged, and she thrived in all that the Big Smoke had to offer. She went everywhere, did everything and met everyone. If you wanted to host an enjoyable party, invite Janey. If you wanted a good night on the town, invite Janey. But if you also wanted to keep your boyfriend or husband, caveat emptor.

Perhaps most surprising of all the social groups Janey came across was a disparate collection of little more than a handful of well-to-do socialites whom she was invited to join some five years or so after she started working at the agency.

Her invite was courtesy of one of her colleagues, Lucy. Like Janey, Lucy was a rather forceful and energetic personality, and Janey got as close to her as she was prepared to get to anyone aside from her parents. This small group of twenty- and thirty-somethings was to have a significant impact on Janey's life. More to the point, perhaps, is what they did at their meetings. At best, this was a quasi-legal partaking in a motley assortment of alleged psychedelic substances. Each meeting was unique as it depended on who managed to find what drug, from where, and how. Whether from plants or the lab, from good friends or rip-off dealers, no one could be sure just what their next experience would be like. There were good days when euphoria, relaxation and self-confidence prevailed, and then there were bad days when the buckets were in use and arguments and even fights broke out because of frightening hallucinations. But the latter experiences were thankfully rare, and the group took good care of those who showed signs of distress. Janey's first experience coincided with the arrival of a 'fruity' batch of magic mushrooms – a uniquely euphoric experience for her, the memory of which lasted for weeks afterwards and ensured that she became a regular member of the group. "Food from the gods and better than any cock hot dog," was her considered opinion of that first experience. She was only too happy to contribute more than her fair share to the venture, as long as it was not she who had to go foraging for the stuff. She had a reputation to maintain, and hers was much more important than those of her new friends.

And so continued this important part of her social life: friendship bound together through the sharing of new sensations and an awareness of a spirituality beyond their normal experiences. All of which came as no little surprise to Janey, as she had shown little enthusiasm for drugs or drink when she was at university. She had tried and quickly dropped weed, and only very rarely drunk more than was wise for her to do so. She hated losing control, and so relishing doing exactly that with her psychedelic friends surprised even herself. The irresistible euphoria and the lasting feeling of everything being well in her little world provided, in Janey's mind, some rationale for this out-of-character behaviour. It was a controlled way of not being in control. She would never dream of telling her parents or anyone outside this tight circle of friends about these experiences. Nothing to gain from doing so. Only a downside.

Boyfriends? Janey so hated that word. She considered it a tacky description, the use of which made her sound like some hopeless, lovesick teenager. She never 'dated', nor even 'courted'. To her, the man she happened to be with was just a friend who happened to be a man, regardless of whether or not she was having sex with him. "Why should that be important to anyone but me?" 'He' would have had to be a man in a million to overcome her reluctance to embark upon a binding – limiting, in her lexicon – relationship at her age, or so was her conviction, and although there were many lovers, they did not number a million. Not that she didn't enjoy the attention and sometimes adulation of the men she met, but there was always another one who was that little bit more adoring. If I am a slut, at least I'm a classy one. And I do so love to dance, *she often thought with a smile after waking up next to her latest acquaintance. She sometimes wondered if this behaviour was driven by the search for approval rather than the desire to actually be with a man. She was not alone in that thought.*

Everything had fallen neatly into place to create a perfect life for a gilded young woman looking to make a mark on society. A burgeoning and successful career and a hedonistic social life that could only be imagined by most others. But – how did you know that there was going to be a 'but'? – then something started to happen which is all too familiar to those of us who know that good things never last. Slowly but surely, Janey's fulsome life as she knew it began to unravel.

It all started at work. Having breezed past her thirtieth year – and what a birthday party that was! – Janey was approaching the tenth anniversary of her first day at the agency. But instead of looking forward to marking that day with yet another celebration, she had more urgent and concerning matters to manage. The up-and-coming young woman who had swept through the company with one promotion soon following another was no longer that young woman but was now a highly paid, mid-level executive with onerous expectations to match. The eye-watering performance bonuses of her early years at the agency proved harder and harder to match, as she was struggling to even meet the steadily growing expectations the directors had of her. She was running hard to stand still. Not an unusual phase of a career plateau, many would opine, but Janey thought differently. "How dare they cut my bonuses? They can all just fuck off," was her usual refrain when others thought differently to her. She had also reached a promotion ceiling wherein further advancement could be achieved only through dead man's shoes, and there was not a single dead man (or woman) on the horizon, at least in her eyes. Now distinctly unhappy with her lot or with the surfeit of likely future opportunities, she began to look elsewhere, but that process took far too long for Janey. She even found it difficult to get interviews for the roles she felt her talents deserved. Seemingly, the prospective employers she had contacted did not concur with her assessment of herself. Who else, other than the company she was already with, would pay that sort of wage for someone with her skills and experience? She was better off where she was. But just you try telling her that.

And then came the one boyfriend too far. Finally, an affair that blew up in her face. An ever-so-important part of Janey's social life was to end, rather abruptly, upon her receiving a brief and uncharacteristically formal email from the broadly acknowledged leader of the supposedly leaderless drug-taking commune. Janey's presence at their meetings would no longer be tolerated on account of her adultery with one of the husbands in the group. He was the one who had broken the news to his apoplectic wife of an affair that had lasted for barely a handful of months. He'd thought it would be better for him to confess all before the news got back to her of a chance encounter with one of their friends who had seen him and Janey queuing for a hotel lift. A few weeks later, Janey was ushered roughly from the premises by more than one of the female group members when she turned up unannounced, prepared to give a gracious and fulsome (if not heartfelt) apology for her outrageous behaviour. It was not only the betrayed wife who was anxious to see the back of the bitch. The red-faced victim was joined by the 'There but for the grace of God go I' wives and partners who were only too keen to remove this threat to their own relationships. This was not a situation that could be easily rescued, even by someone with Janey's charm and charisma. For once, it was she who had been dropped and cast aside.

This turned out to be a seminal experience in Janey's life. Not just because she no longer had easy access to recreational drugs, but also because she finally realised that she could no longer afford to continue to be the arrogant and selfish woman she had become. No longer could she ignore and trample upon the perceptions and feelings of others if she wanted any semblance of a social life. The world, and Janey, needed and deserved a new Janey.

Her next reinvention necessitated a complete reappraisal of her work and social life. Word had spread of her indiscretion with the husband of a good friend, and she was no longer the first person on party invite lists. She had become a pariah, both within much of her social circle and also at work, thanks to Lucy's efforts to make sure that everyone at the agency was aware of her former friend's crime. Many had been waiting eagerly for such an opportunity for payback. Janey was confident that, given time, she could ride out this latest indiscretion and win back favour with those worth winning back, but why bother? Work bored her. Life bored her. Fuck 'em all. The London scene with which she had once been so enthralled was also becoming boring, as the few friends who remained drifted off into marriage and parenthood. Time to get out of the place was Janey's fix. A new place and a new life. The chance to wipe the slate clean and start all over again without a reputation hanging around her neck. And it was a kindly GP who lived out in the sticks who turned out to be the one to offer exactly that new life Janey was looking for.

Janey the wife. Dr Graham Robins first met Janey in a London hotel where she was organising a conference he was attending. It was a typically soulless venue with tinted-glass atria and synthetic carpets capable of delivering eye-watering static shocks to those wearing cheap shoes. Nothing that Janey or Graham needed to worry about, but it was the latter's worry about forgetting to bring any suitable ID that resulted in a lengthy discourse between the two and Janey ignoring a few red lines to present him with a lanyard, a conference bag, and entry to the event. With Graham not knowing anyone at the grandly titled International Conference on General Practice and Primary Care, it was Janey whom he approached for company at the evening reception of drinks and fashionable eats. He was certainly not the first and nor would he be the last to fall for Janey's approachable personality and good looks, which that evening were expertly enhanced with a smart business suit and a mid-length skirt – her 'number twos', as she liked to call them. Unfortunately for Graham, his interest was not reciprocated, although Janey at least found him good company, perhaps due to the intellectual snobbery that had been programmed into her by her parents. He was also far from unattractive, with the imposing frame and easy-going looks consistent with a character which could hold a room, although that was not something that he would ever wish to do. Grey hair, maybe, but at least it was a full head of grey hair, and few would have guessed that he was on the cusp of turning fifty. Many of his middle-aged women patients and even a few of his surgery's receptionists would, if asked, have said, "Yes, I will." If only he had bothered asking. When Janey finally gave in to the urge to fulfil her job description and mingle with her other clients, business cards were exchanged and both expressed hope that they would meet up again at a future conference.

They both surprised themselves: Graham by emailing her (though a few whiskies in the evening can impart considerable courage), and Janey by agreeing to go to dinner with a man who must have been at least ten, and maybe even fifteen years older than her. Still, he seemed like good company, And what's the worst that could happen? *she thought.*

The restaurant date turned out to be an unremarkable although pleasant enough evening for Janey, but Graham was smitten. There had been a few occasions since his wife had left him when he had roused himself to go out with women, but none of them had been followed up. This was different – different enough for him to end the evening with an offer to treat Janey once again.

"I'm often down here in London," he lied. "I would be delighted if you would accept an invitation to meet up again." He was disappointed by the way in which his last words faded to a whisper, no doubt in anticipation of his offer being rejected.

"I would love to." Janey beamed in the attractive way in which she could purvey positivity. "But next time, I will pay." She had not really made up her mind yet as to whether or not she would *meet Graham again, but why spoil the evening?*

"We'll see about that!" Graham stood up and helped Janey to put on her faux fur coat, and they walked out of the restaurant and into the chill November night. They parted with a warm cheek-kiss, then Graham floated back home

on a train while Janey took a taxi back to her town house worrying about the presentation she was due to give the following morning at work.

Maybe a little to her own surprise, Janey did agree to meet Graham again. Not that I have that many offers anyway, *was her take on the situation, but she was slowly coming around to the notion that he might just be at least part of the reinvention that she was looking for. A way out of the dying London lifestyle that she no longer enjoyed. A chance to start all over again, away from the relationships she had poisoned. A mature, provincial GP would likely provide stability, money, and no little kudos.* Let's just see where this takes me. *And Graham? He wanted a pretty wife before it was all too late. 'Someone to look after* him *for a change' was very high up on his wish list of what a partner should offer. Janey certainly fitted this criterion from what he had seen so far. Or so he thought.*

So, it suited them both to spend some time and effort exploring whether each of them could get what they wanted out of this potential relationship. A tad selfish, perhaps? Almost certainly, but few partnerships are made and stay in heaven; at least in my experience. Maybe theirs was more a case of mutual need and convenience. Although Janey represented everything Graham was looking for in a woman, he was far from the typical beau she had bedded. Nevertheless, he was not unattractive, he was kind and generous, and, most importantly of course, there was the money and the promise of a work-free, stress-free, relaxing lifestyle of a provincial GP's wife. Boxes had been ticked on both sides.

Over the coming weeks and months, through liaisons in Graham's Ulstown bachelor-pad apartment and various

London hotels and restaurants (Janey did not want her style cramped by her lodgers), they edged towards what they both wanted, even if they both wanted it for different reasons. And at their – hers, really – favourite London restaurant, just nine months after they had first met at the conference, he proposed with his grandmother's ring; one of the few things he had managed to rescue from his first wife. Janey accepted the proposal she had known all along would come sooner or later, and that night they made love with an intensity that had been absent at their earlier unions – or so Graham thought. Although he had seen far more genitalia than his new fiancée, there was little question as to who was the more sexually experienced, and Janey drew on that considerable experience to make sure it was a night (and morning) to remember, at least for him, although in many ways it was for her just like so many other nights and early mornings: exciting and comforting, but not satisfying. Still, there had been worse (some far worse), and she could certainly cope with waking up next to Graham every morning – maybe with an extracurricular change in bodies and venue every now and again, of course. She wanted to leave the door ajar for some more stamp-collecting, providing it didn't put her marriage at risk. Her quest wasn't just for sex, as that had never lived up to her expectations. Bizarrely, it was not as if sex had been an important driver even in her earlier promiscuity. But then again, Janey was nothing if not unusual. So what was the underlying reason for this approval-seeking behaviour? Ego? Reassurance of her worth? A substitute for the lack of real affection she had received as a child from parents who were more caring than they were truly loving? The genes she'd inherited from the wayward 'woman who gave birth to her'? Who knows? Certainly not Janey, as she's not the type to want to open up any unmarked boxes in her head, for fear of what she might find inside.

Graham suggested, but Janey apologetically declined the offer of, an engagement party, which surprised him given all the anecdotes she had shared about her life. Stories of a full social life; a busy and successful career which included travel and lavish parties. What she had not shared was that these were recollections of times long since passed; of relationships no longer maintained. With an engagement party turned down, Graham was not so surprised that his fiancée requested that only close family be invited to the wedding.

It was much to the delight of the Middletons that Janey married Graham early the following spring, in a modest ceremony held in a registry office near Ulstown. They would have preferred a lavish occasion during which all their family and friends could witness their successful little girl's crowning moment, but they knew it was pointless to argue against Janey's wishes. Their original concern regarding the fifteen-year age difference was soon cast aside when they met with the urbane GP over a wonderfully enjoyable dinner and overnight stay in The Dorchester, all at the expense of the man with whom Janey had chosen to spend the rest of her life. And anyway, Janey had made it very clear that the Middletons were never going to have the chance to be doting grandparents, so the disparity was perhaps not so very important, if it was not an issue for her.

Janey resigned from her job at the PR agency without so much as a goodbye lunch, although at her exit interview she thoroughly enjoyed giving both barrels to seemingly everyone and anyone. Not that what was said would go beyond the flustered, red-faced HR manager, of course. (Sorry, I meant 'talent acquisition leader', not 'HR manager'.) "And that is all absolutely fucking fine with me. I have never made a better decision," concluded Janey as she left the office for the last time, carrying her belongings in the largest cardboard box she could find. In her view, the pretence of the employees being the company's number-one priority could be seen for the obvious lie it was.

With little to occupy her days, now Janey's time was spent on finding the perfect new house in Ulstown, not too far from Graham's surgery. The start of her new life. Afternoons spent in estate agents' shops, long lunches, and no rush to get up in the mornings. What was there not to like in her new life? She had even managed to make a huge profit on selling her London town house and her parents were more than happy for her to keep the money from the sale of the property they had originally bought. Everything was coming up roses for Janey. Our Janey.

All of which, having just read through what I have written again, makes Janey seem like a rather shallow, selfish, even nasty person, and someone you would do well to avoid meeting. But au contraire. Although there are flaws in her behaviour and character – most of which Janey is perfectly aware of but consciously chooses not to change – she is a true force of nature who can light up a room with her mere presence. Men adore and lust after her. Women admire and sometimes fear her. What lies in store next for our Janey? Read on and find out.

Meet Janey Robins. A remarkable woman with the means to make or ruin your day.

part two

A LIFE LESS ORDINARY

FALLING

Another new day for Andy Jones of 6 Malvern Drive, Ulstown, England, the world.

Sitting at the breakfast table, he contented himself with watching raindrops merging, and then descending the kitchen window to the saturated, white plastic sill outside. He didn't really need to get up this early but had lately found it difficult to sleep, often waking at a ridiculous hour in the morning and being unable to get back to sleep. At least it wasn't another headache that had woken him on this particular morning. It wasn't as if he had excess energy to burn. Far from it. Much to Susan's disgust, he sometimes found it virtually impossible to avoid falling asleep in the evening, often even before dinner had been served. Similar fiascos in the pub had shown that this phenomenon was not necessarily restricted to the family home. "One of the typical signs of depression," would have been Andy's instant diagnosis, had the patient been anyone but himself. But Andy wasn't suffering from depression. "How could he be? Anyone who enjoyed such a privileged lifestyle as he could not possibly be depressed, was his reasoning. Sure, his job was starting to get him down, but he had a wife and family who thought the world of him, and he lived in a house the luxury of which he would have thought unlikely when he was at university. Depressed? No. Not Andy Jones. Never Andy Jones.

Today, Friday, he had elected to come downstairs rather than lie awake in bed and risk disturbing Susan. As the kitchen clock staggered towards 7am, Andy roused himself from the refuge of the table to prepare the school lunch boxes for his faddy-eating children. He was strongly of the opinion that none of the Jones children would see fifty if they continued eating the rubbish that he had been ordered to prepare for them. Susan always countered – equally strongly, and moreover successfully – that there was no point in giving them foods that they simply would not eat, and anyway, their diets were no different from their peers'. These discussions were usually ended by a request from Susan for Andy to join them in the real world and stop being his own father for once in his life.

Although some ten years deceased, Andy's father had indeed left a lasting impression on his only child leaving a clear imprint of a fastidiously conservative, old-school man; a chapel-going Welshman who, with Andy's mother, had easily blended into their new life in the Yorkshire village where they had moved a few years before Andy was born. It was a true home from home, and a town and society where the Joneses were made to feel very welcome. As was the case also for the birth of their new son, Andrew Bryn Jones, whose arrival was something of a surprise as his mother was in her early forties when he was delivered at home by a rather nervous young midwife. Andy became the centre of his parents' world and made up for the family's estrangement from relatives back in Wales; a black cloud and the real secrets of which they took to their graves without ever really telling him what had happened. It had been the subject of many frustrating arguments over the years, although Andy had slowly learned that his parents would never share those secrets with him, and so gradually got bored of asking. It was strange (if not bizarre) and not a little upsetting to Andy that he never got to meet his grandparents; nor was he even aware if any aunts, uncles or cousins existed. The family's collective absence at his wedding – and, even more remarkably, at his parents' funerals – was noticed but not mentioned, at least within earshot of Andy.

Andy granted that this rather less-than-radical upbringing could leave him open to valid charges of being somewhat old-fashioned in his ways and views, not to mention his fashion sense. *Maybe guilty as charged*, he concluded whenever he put on one of his several identical pairs of black trousers.

Andy had taken both of his parents' deaths very badly. His childhood security in their immortality had been cruelly exposed as yet one more myth. His father's twenty a day habit had killed them both: he from lung cancer and she from a heart broken by the passing of her husband.

Having placed the final Rocco vitamin-enriched, taste-free chocolate bar into Joshua's lunch box, Andy prepared the children's breakfasts experiences and called them all downstairs from their cluttered bedrooms. With the children safely corralled into the kitchen, Andy, mug of tea in hand, made his way upstairs to prepare himself for work, waking Susan whilst in transit.

It was almost 7.30am by the time the smart-casual, trench-coat-carrying executive closed the front door to Number 6 Malvern Drive and walked confidently towards his executive car. It was a nippy March morning, although not quite cold enough to warrant him searching for his always-missing ice scraper. Andy left Malvern Drive for the London-bound motorway and work. The move to the new house had increased his commute time substantially to almost two hours for the round trip, and longer still on a bad day. Although this was not exactly welcomed, he still preferred that option to buying one of the criminally expensive houses closer to his workplace that Susan had considered buying. The wisdom of this decision was certainly put to its severest test on Monday and Friday mornings. Having taken almost half an hour merely to fight through the queue of traffic wishing to join the motorway on this particular Friday morning, Andy allowed himself to relax and consider a topic somewhere in the subject of life, the universe and everything. A time to think. And this morning's object of contemplation was the not untypical topic of work.

It had all been so very positive, even exciting, at the start. Andy had joined Wright and Briggs Pharmaceuticals Ltd. immediately after completing his chemistry degree and graduating from Birmingham University. Initially apprehensive, he'd surprised even himself with the speed at which he'd familiarised himself with his responsibilities and the company working around him. His boundless enthusiasm for his new career, and his positive attitude, were noticed by many, but especially one of the older and more experienced section directors, Tony Adams. Dr Adams ensured that Andy was steadily promoted over the years, ultimately reaching the level of project leader.

Andy was thrilled at this appointment and delighted in announcing the wonderful news to Susan and his growing family. "What's more," he declared excitedly, "I'm the first person in the company without a postgraduate qualification to reach this grade." All of which sounded a little bit more grandiose than the reality, given how young the company was, but it suited his rhetoric.

Susan didn't mind too much the longer and longer hours Andy felt obliged to work, as he was clearly happy in his career and his ever-increasing salary suggested that the company appreciated his efforts and loyalty. She could cover for his understandable tiredness during weekday evenings.

And then it all started to go horribly wrong. It was almost imperceptible at first, but gradually the signs of what Andy considered to be a growing lack of respect for him and his work started to chip away at his self-confidence. What had he done wrong? Was he just imagining it all? He spent hours mulling over the reasons why his career had seemingly stagnated, and he was no longer considered the up-and-coming young scientist, and each time he arrived at a common conclusion: Tony Adams' retirement. Although there were undoubtedly a number of other contributing factors – not least of which were Andy's growing, time-consuming commitments to his busy family – the old boy leaving was the main one in Andy's opinion and had directly initiated the cascade of troubling events and negative perceptions that left him in his present predicament. With Tony gone, a thoughtful and reliable mentor, if not personal champion, had been replaced with 'colleagues' who had, at best, no particular interest in Andy's career aspirations, and at worst resented his fast-track promotions in the previous years. Although Andy still worked family-unfriendly hours and, in his opinion, made good progress with his assigned project, his far-too-regular performance appraisals deteriorated steadily to a point where worried memos were exchanged among concerned senior managers following the flurry of appraisals, feedback and management reviews instigated by the HR Stasi. Andy vehemently insisted that nothing had changed since the years in which his performance had been rewarded with excellent appraisals and subsequent pay increases. But those appraisals had been conducted by Tony Adams and only Tony Adams. Nothing had changed, in other words, apart from people's perceptions, which Andy considered were latterly driven by his new manager, Allison Emery, who he thought felt threatened by her new report's talent. The reality was that it was Andy who felt threatened by reporting to a woman and, moreover, one who was younger than him. People's perceptions of Andy having been promoted beyond his capabilities won the day, and he found himself more and more marginalised, to the point where his peers were now, for the first time, being promoted over him. What should he do? Senior management were clearly not listening to him. He couldn't afford to leave. No other company would pay as much for a mere graduate researcher. Taking another job would likely mean losing the house, the company car, the respectable neighbours (all of which would break Susan's heart), but how much longer could he put up with the stress of working all these hours for a boss and a company which clearly didn't appreciate his talents?

None of this angst had been shared with Susan. The tough Yorkshireman in Andy had once again prevailed, barring even his wife from access to his true emotions. And it was the tough Yorkshireman in him who also prevented him from building a good working relationship with Allison Emery and finding a way to turn things around. That was certainly not the fault of his new boss, who, despite her lack of managerial experience, had reached out to Andy in a genuine attempt to overcome his worries, although she could not ignore the reality that his performance did not match the levels boasted in the appraisals carried out by her predecessor. Perhaps Andy's difficulty in relating to her was actually more a reflection of his upbringing and his difficulty in accepting the authority of a woman.

So, to the big meeting today, mused Andy as his air intake unit sampled the aromas of the last of the deep-fat-frying motorway service stations he passed on his way to work. *Just who would want to eat a double cheeseburger with extra fries before nine in the morning? There surely can't be that many shift workers.* The meeting was scheduled to include a buffet for all the staff, followed by a live videoconference from the US-based parent company. Andy's excitement about what might be announced at this extraordinary meeting was tainted by the negativity he carried around in his back pocket. *But what's the worst that could happen?* he asked himself. With these thoughts uppermost, he joined the queue to leave the motorway. Not far to go now.

The slanting rain had turned into a dark afternoon and a reminder that winter was not quite ready to depart the scene. Finally free from traffic, Andy was able to join the motorway and turn home towards Ulstown. Coming to terms with the corporate announcement would take much longer to mull over than the dreary afternoon drive home. He felt himself struggling to prevent the tears gathering in his eyes from running down his cheek. His emotions ranged from worry for the future to anger, hopelessness at his inability to control events, and, probably worst of all, an overpowering feeling of being sorry for himself. "How fucking pathetic am I?" he shouted at his busy wiper blades.

He could see the logic underpinning the change in corporate strategy. The expectation of the company shareholders had won the day. There had to be a substantial commitment from the company to carry out groundbreaking research to meet the challenge of the ongoing fallout from Covid and its likely future sons and daughters. The vaccines were effective but there was still an obvious medical need for affordable drugs to treat the symptoms and keep people out of hospital. The shareholders wanted to see the company respond to the 'new normal' and, more to the point, make money from it. The internal meeting had been called to update the staff on the consequences – the fallout, from the staff's perspective – of how the company was proposing to meet this 'exciting challenge'. Through the remainder of the year, the neurology department in which Andy worked was to be wound down and its projects out-licensed to other companies where possible. The smaller virology team was then to be built up, with colleagues from neurology transitioning to virology if they had the appropriate skill sets.

"However, transferring to virology will not be possible for all our colleagues, and so I very much regret to say that this announcement should be considered as formal notice of discussions which will take place with some of you regarding potential redundancies. We envisage that efforts to out-license some of the neurology programmes will take us to year end, maybe even through into next year, and so some of our neurology team will be kept on as their expertise will be vital in our efforts to find good homes for the more advanced programmes. So, it is likely that discussions with those colleagues at risk of redundancy will begin to take place relatively soon in Q4 of this year or maybe even earlier for some of you. We will of course keep you all informed as the timelines are firmed up and as we progress through the year."

The intake of breath amongst those seated near Andy at the meeting had been palpable when the CEO, Dr Judith Meredith, had uttered the R-word over the video conference. No one had been expecting this. The excitement of any new announcements had turned instantly to fear and uncertainty for Andy and his fellow scientists in neurology. In many ways, Andy's skills as a medicinal chemist were potentially transferable to another discipline, and he was certainly in a much better position than some of his biologist colleagues, many of whom had only worked in neurology. However, even if he transferred to the virology department and clung on to his job, he would be very unlikely to remain a project leader given his lack of experience in virology research. Added to that, the project to which he had devoted himself for the past five years, and which was so close to producing a viable drug, was now going to end. But it was the uncertainty of whether he still had a job at Wright and Briggs that was front and foremost in Andy's mind as he drove home on autopilot in the gathering dark; an uncertainty which was guaranteed to be drawn out over a number of months by a litigation-fearing US owner.

Such was his dark mood that his appointment with Graham was only remembered after he had turned into Cambrian Way, despite it being the reason why he had left work early. Turning the car around in Mendip Road, he headed back towards the town centre, confident that he could reach Graham's surgery behind the High Street before it closed. This was not the day he would have chosen to discuss his health concerns, but he had not foreseen how the company meeting would transpire and he didn't want to have to make up an excuse for Graham as to why he was cancelling the appointment at the last minute. Besides, he was looking for reassurance; some calming words saying that he wasn't going to die. At least not just yet.

Within five minutes Andy was making the short walk from his parked car to the entrance of the Robinson Way surgery, whilst trying to hurriedly convert himself from pathetic hypochondriac to confident (albeit perhaps soon to be redundant) professional executive. He was confronted by a welcoming empty waiting room, with

Graham standing at the far end in discussion with what Andy presumed was an unseen figure behind the reception hatch. The sight of Graham reminded Andy of his concerns about disclosing his most personal health details to a neighbour and friend. *I should have stuck with my usual anonymous GP at this surgery*, he thought, but surely he could rely upon the confidentiality of a very experienced GP like Graham? *Does he ever tell Janey about his patients?* worried Andy.

The sound of the door closing behind Andy prompted Graham to spin balletically on his right foot to confront the intruder. "Andy, old man," he bellowed confidently. "Great to see you. Take a seat and I'll be with you right away."

Taking a seat somewhere towards the back row of the neatly assembled, matching yet uncomfortable chairs, Andy familiarised himself with the surgery which he had, thankfully, not frequented too many times, and more often in the company of a sick child than on his own behalf. He had forgotten the misery of such places. The bright streetlight managed to pierce its way through the grime covering the '70s-built skylight to cover half a dozen chairs in the poorly lit room. He could remember, however, the curiously inappropriate framed posters of precarious New York scaffold workers which were hung around the magnolia-painted walls, and a recollection of the disease-infested toy area in which his own children, much to his relief, showed little interest.

Having finished his busy conversation with the flustered receptionist, Graham walked briskly down the less furrowed side of the fading brown carpet tiles to greet

Andy warmly with a double-handed shake. "Sorry for the wait, Andy. Let's go through to my little emporium."

Following him, Andy once again attempted to establish that he was not imposing upon his friend. Reassuring comments from Graham were followed by him ushering Andy, almost childlike, into his consulting room and to an unfurnished plastic seat.

"And don't forget, Louise: make sure Mrs Johns sees me tomorrow before she takes away the prescription. You can go now; I'll lock up. Bye," called Graham to the receptionist before closing the door to his room behind him. "Sit down, old boy. Now, let's sort you out." He pulled up his chair, uncomfortably close to where Andy was seated.

What is it with doctors? You might argue in their defence that they only adopt their embarrassingly genial, overfamiliar "'And how are you today, Mrs Smith?' 'I'm fucking sick, Doctor; that's why I'm here'" persona in order to put their patients at ease. Well, maybe. Call me paranoid, but a less understanding viewpoint would label at least some of them as megalomaniacs bent on ensuring that they have an almost parent-child relationship with their patient – the patient, of course, being the child. Do you know why they do this? I'll tell you. With you safely installed as the child, they can get away with the most gratuitous of mistakes, as what grateful child would ever take their parents to court? The trust is too strong. Belief is everlasting. Very few question the opinion of the trusted local GP, and fewer still ever consider asking for a second opinion. Why do we Brits still put up with it? The Yanks don't. They call it as they see it.

Doctors may very well all be over six foot; have perfect white teeth; enjoy thick, dandruff-free hair until the day they die; and be able to drink the local rugby XV under their collective tables, but none of these enviable attributes should be allowed to excuse their patronising behaviour – and don't get me started on the male doctors. Their position of absolute power allows them to effectively conceal their almost frightening lack of knowledge and expertise. Believe you me, don't trust the buggers. Always ask for a second opinion. From your mother, your sister's friend, that nice Mr Lee at the late-opening store, your local mechanic – anybody but another bloody doctor.

But that's just my opinion, and please, please don't tell my GP what I think. She's such a nice doctor and so very knowledgeable.

During the short drive back to Malvern Drive, Andy attempted to put things into perspective by replaying in his mind the consultation he had just had.

"Probably nothing to worry about," Graham had announced, pointing to his own head, "but there's a very, very outside chance of something exotic going on up there. I don't think there is anything we need to follow up on right now, but if the headaches persist we can always arrange an MRI scan if we need to."

Not exactly the reassuring words Andy had been hoping to hear, as the clean bill of health was dependent on his intermittent headaches somehow disappearing, of which they had shown no evidence of doing to any great extent since they had first started some three months earlier.

"As I said when we chatted about this outside the house, Andy, there are so many causes of headaches, the vast majority of them being benign and transient. Mostly, we never know what's kicked them off, and they typically just go away on their own."

"But this has been non-stop since Christmas," was Andy's somewhat exaggerated pushback in the search for further reassurance.

"Any increased stress? Work? Family? Early waking? Tiredness?" was Graham's next angle of attack, with both understanding that he suspected depression to be the culprit.

"No more than my usual unbearable workload," quipped Andy. He thought he would bring up the D-word first. "Am I depressed? I don't think so, although I get the odd day when I just can't break out of a black mood, but I have always been like that. Isn't everyone now and again? And there's the rather disturbing dreams I have been having of late, like the one I talked about at the pub the other night." Immediately he regretted that last comment, realising how pathetic and weak it must have sounded to a GP who had, no doubt, seen it all.

"I have yet to make a diagnosis based on a dream," laughed Graham. "As I said the other night, Janey's your woman for that sort of diagnosis." And with that, he had unilaterally declared the end of the consultation by standing up and offering his hand to Andy. "See you down the recreation centre at seven. But one last thing before you go. I should add that it is rather frowned upon for a GP to treat a friend and I consider you and your family to be friends as I hope you do also with me and Janey. However,

I say frowned upon rather than illegal. So perhaps this consultation should not be discussed with, for example, Ian. OK with you, Andy?" There was precious little chance of that ever happening.

Graham's excellent bedside manner had failed to overcome Andy's worry about the offer of an MRI scan. *Why tell me what's on the table for the future if it's such a remote possibility that there's something really wrong with me?* thought Andy as he paused outside the front door of 6 Malvern Drive. He tried to concentrate on the positives as he searched his coat pockets for the front door key he had only placed somewhere in his jacket seconds before. Were there any? He still had the headaches – although, somewhat surprisingly given the trauma of this day, not at the moment he pushed open the door to be met by the reassuring aroma of steak being grilled and his usual Friday-evening banquet cooked by Susan. The consultation with Graham had managed to open just that little bit wider the door Andy himself had opened to the possible diagnosis of a multitude of various terminal brain disorders. This was not what had hoped for from the meeting with his friend. A hypochondriac's nirvana is a diagnosis of a mildly debilitating condition easily treated by drugs and the forbearance of which is sufficient to earn the sympathy and admiration of others. What they don't want to hear and, perversely, what they don't expect to hear, is that they may have a potentially life-terminating disease, but hypochondriacs also sometimes get ill.

"Kids upstairs in their rooms?" Andy asked his wife, who had yet to appear. The answer was of little interest to him, but any conversation would be welcome if it meant he could avoid having to tell Susan of the day's events. He *would* tell her, maybe on the weekend, but not tonight. He just didn't have the mental strength before he'd had time to himself to think it all through, consider the scenarios, come up with answers to the questions Susan was bound to ask, and regain some self-confidence and resilience.

"How did it go with Graham?" asked Susan, walking in front of her husband as they entered the smoky kitchen.

At least she had remembered his appointment, but Andy also felt ill prepared to discuss his imagined medical problems with her this evening. *No point in upsetting her as well*, he thought as an excuse for his dysfunctional emotions. "A bit of a waste of time, really. He just told me that it's probably just me getting a bit stressed about work and the headaches will no doubt pass soon enough," was the half-lie passed on to his wife.

Susan rotated mushrooms in a frying pan, seemingly happy with her husband's response, based upon her silence. Fine with Andy. Still, he could tell that there was something on her mind, and it was not his well-being.

"OK. What's up?"

"A couple of things, I suppose. Good and bad news, you could say," answered Susan, rather nervously and with her back still turned towards him.

"OK. Bad news first," sighed Andy, safe in the knowledge that there was nothing she could possibly say that would make this day even worse. Probably.

"No. I think I'll start with the good news, actually. I invited Janey Robins in for coffee this morning after bumping into her in town. Not something I really wanted to do, but better than me going around to their house, which is what she suggested. Didn't really fancy having the latest trinket being paraded in front of me. Anyway. What's all this about a camping holiday that you men have been talking about? I was really embarrassed. Graham had told Janey all about Ian's suggestion, but you obviously couldn't be bothered to tell me."

This is the good *news?* thought Andy. Perhaps he shouldn't wait around for the bad news. "Sorry about that," he replied, embarking on a search for appropriate cutlery to lay the table in the hope of distracting the attention of the enemy. "I didn't think there was much point in telling you as we had planned to go to your mother's caravan over Easter," interjected Andy, the mere thought of which made him shudder.

"I told you just the other day that that's very unlikely. Anyway, I told Janey we would *love* to go. We can borrow some equipment from Ian and Meera so you can't complain about the money." There. Susan had said it.

"What do you mean, you've told her we are going?! We haven't even discussed this. What if I – I mean, the kids – don't want to go?"

"I think you've said enough, don't you? We are not going to turn down our only chance of a holiday this year," answered Susan, finishing her sentence with an air of finality.

Fatally wounded, Andy took his place at the rectangular, distressed oak table in the dining room ready to enjoy the dinner Susan had served up to them both. The imagined pain from his backside as he sat down rather abruptly served as a timely reminder of his more serious worries. His wife slid her way onto the chair facing Andy. Dinner had been served.

"And another thing!" announced Susan. "What's all this crap about your dreams and Janey wanting to analyse them? Is there something I should know? Something going on between you two?" She stood up from the table she had only just sat down at in an attempt to find something that she wasn't looking for in a drawer of their reproduction Welsh dresser. By turning her back on Andy she could hide the teasing smirk on her face. She knew that he was just not in Janey's league, and so she had no worries there.

"Don't be bloody ridiculous," was his response, using exactly the words she had predicted he would. "We were all just talking at the pub about dreams, and I happened to mention some dreams I had long ago in the past," he lied. "I can't help it if Graham invites me to talk to his dream guru. Nothing will come of it. All just talk."

"Au contraire, my darling. Janey is very keen to make a date with you, which I took the liberty of doing. Round to the Robinses' house at 5.30pm next Friday. Me and the kids will be out of the house that evening at a kid's party and then at my mother's. All sorted for you." Susan smiled sarcastically. "And she also mentioned your job again, which, as I said before, is a bit bizarre. What's all that about? What could she possibly find interesting in your job?"

"Well, at least someone seems to show some interest in my career," was Andy's riposte.

His wife did not rise to the bait. "I said to Janey that I would tell you, and now I have. Up to you what you want to do about it, and anyway, just exactly what are these dreams which are interesting enough to tell people you have only recently met, but not interesting enough to tell the person you actually sleep with?"

"To be honest," which he wasn't, "I can't remember what I said or even anything about the dreams the others talked about. Trivia. Not worth remembering."

Susan was willing to let the matter lie and spare her blushing partner any more teasing – *Why does the man blush at the drop of a hat?* – as there were far more important items on the agenda. "Now the bad news," she breathed nervously. She was staring at the condiment set in the middle of the table which had been given to them as a wedding present by a long-since-forgotten, mutual university friend. "Brian rang up today and wants to come and visit us next Saturday." The last sentence was uttered with admirable speed, and quickly followed by Susan skewering an overripe tomato from the salad bowl. *There, I've gone and said it,* she thought.

Andy returned his knife and fork to his dinner plate in exaggerated slow motion. His blush had vanished. "You are *joking*! Was it not you who said that Brian will never be allowed within one hundred yards of our kids?"

"Things have changed," pleaded Susan, staring at her dinner with no little embarrassment. "My mother promises me that he has been clean for over six months now, and he has kept his new job for a few months."

With the paper-thin case for the defence having been rested, the Crown wished to interject. "Well, whoop-de-doo. So you believe your mother, do you? The poor bugger he took the most money from? You think it's worth exposing our kids to a convicted drug pusher, a chronic addict, thief and complete arsehole? Again? No way is he coming round here. No way. I can't believe that you have changed your mind so completely." Its point having been forcefully put, the Crown felt at sufficient ease to return to its dinner.

"He is my brother, Andy. Everybody deserves a second chance – even somebody from my family, believe it or not. He only lives just up the road on the other side of town since he moved." This fact was emphasised by a wildly inaccurate pointing fork. "You know I wouldn't do anything that might harm the children. He's only coming for the day. Anything strange and I will personally chuck him out of the house, I promise."

"You won't need to because I will have already done it."

Susan could sense victory. "Just promise me you will give him a chance," she pleaded, her face now raised and her eyes trained imploringly on her husband. "That's all I'm asking of you."

"If he comes – and I mean *if* – he is not to be left alone with any of the kids at any time. We'll see," was Andy's final comment.

This seemed to satisfy Susan, who sliced into two her mini cucumber.

Andy had far more pressing things on his mind and was certainly not prepared for all-out war on this occasion. Given a fair wind, and a combination of the kids' Saturday classes, shopping, and some soon-to-be-invented errands, there was every possibility that he could manage to completely avoid meeting his untrustworthy brother-in-law. There was a side to Andy that almost looked forward to a visit from Brian as no one could deny that he was good company, but that was not something he was ever going to disclose to Susan. Once again, he'd managed to lose an argument with her, although admittedly he hadn't tried too hard on this occasion. Two in one night. Why did they ever bother discussing anything at all? He could save an awful lot of time and effort by just conceding everything, regardless of the subject matter.

Andy comforted himself by cutting and eating a particularly large piece of fatty steak. Stress? What stress?

Tricky blighters, relatives. My golden rule is to treat them as you would a fresh joint of red meat. One finds that after about three days hanging around your house, both red meat and relatives start to go off and emit an unpleasant odour. At this point both the red meat and your relatives should be ejected from your household forthwith. Works every time for me. Try it yourself sometime. On second thoughts, maybe you should keep the meat for a little longer given the current price of beef.

THE SECOND TIME

The two friends sat at the end of the table underneath the largest window of the company cafeteria, which overlooked a neatly manicured garden enjoying the first signs of spring. Weak sunshine filtered through onto their lunches, which competed fiercely in their frugality. Such was a typical lunch for Emily and Li.

"Regardless of your opinion of him, you have to feel sorry for the man," started Emily. "That project team meeting was terrible. Terrible. Andy was terrible."

"He looked so pale," added Li. "I'm sure he was close to tears on several occasions, which I suppose you can sort of understand as he has put his life and soul into that drug project, and I suppose it has barely been a week since that big company announcement, which I suppose must have really hit him hard." She made a mental note to try to find an alternative English word to 'suppose'. "Have you ever met his wife? Such a nice woman, without any of the airs and graces you get with some of the partners around here."

"And we were so close to getting that drug candidate approved. WRT743 could have gone all the way into the clinic by the end of the year given a fair wind, after that fantastic data in the anxiety and depression assays. Could have been a game changer for the company and for patients, although that hint of hyperactivity we saw in the rats was a red flag that needed to be sorted out. You could see the disappointment etched across his face, and of course we are all shocked and disappointed that we won't be working on the project for much longer. I've been on this project for nearly two years, and it's been the same for you as well, Li," pointed out Emily. "But he didn't do himself any favours with the way he behaved in front of all those senior managers listening in. You have to wonder what was going on in his head, as that was not the Andy we know."

"But I suppose you and I should be fine with all this upheaval, Em, as we both came out of virology and so should be welcomed back with open arms." Li flashed a reassuring smile to her friend whilst pushing a distressed-looking gherkin around her eco-friendly, ostentatiously obvious cardboard plate. "And the chemists should be fine too, but Greg and Steph have no experience outside of neurology biology. Not good times for them."

"And although Andy is a chemist, I wouldn't be too sure of getting a job in the virology department if I was him, at least not at the grade he's at now. And he just moved into that lovely big house on the new estate with, no doubt, a big mortgage to match. Talk about stress." That was exactly what Emily *was* doing. "It's the uncertainty that kills. Take my word for it. I've been there and done it, and I certainly don't fancy going through all that again, I can tell you."

Li nodded in agreement back to her lunchtime friend. "There but for the grace of God go we, I suppose. But it would have been nice to have been invited to the free lunch all the senior scientists have just gone off to. Perhaps a few drinks, a slap-up dinner and the afternoon off will improve Andy's mood. I know it would improve mine! Yeah, sure. Come and join us. Pull up a chair." Li signalled to a colleague whom neither of the two friends particularly wanted to join them.

I get all types in the back of my cab. From overpaid city gents to borderline tramps, with more than my fair share of drunks sandwiched in between the two extremes. Do my clientele have anything in common? A shared characteristic, or even a theme? Now that you ask, yes, they do. Stress. Too much stress. Not everyone, of course, as your top guys – I mean your really, *really* top people – actually get off on stress, which is, I guess, why they are where they are. And not many of my happy Saturday-night drunks come over as all that stressed, either. Two ends of the spectrum, I suppose. But it's difficult to escape the reddened, sweating faces of the not-quite-so-important 'executives' swearing into their expensive mobile phones, or the pinched features of those minion employees of some godforsaken multinational who are travelling to meet someone they would rather not, to talk about something of which they know very little and in which they have even less interest. These are the ones who get shit showered upon them from above and unsolvable grievances passed up to them from below. Middlemen indeed, regardless of gender.

Now, don't get me wrong. I'm the first to argue the importance of a good, stable job, because we all need something to give to those awfully nice people at the supermarket checkouts on a Saturday morning, don't we? But there has to be a limit. A balance between human relationships and work, if you like. A nice, comfortable middle ground between just about being able to pay the mortgage on a nice little pile of bricks in the country and living in a shithole. I hate that 'work-life balance' phrase we hear all the time these days, because the people who use it seldom achieve it, and I bet you all the cash in the wallet of the fella sitting behind me right now that you would not get a straight answer from anyone if you asked them exactly what that phrase means to them. And where the fuck is this so-called 'tipping point' between work and life? But what I am really trying to say is that the person who puts work before everything else has very much got it all arse about tit in my humble opinion – which, I grant you, is, I suppose, a tip of the hat to this work-life balance bollocks. Sort of. If you are grinding yourself into the dust for kudos and respect, then forget it. This is class-ridden Britain, for Christ's sake, where money and status are much more sources of anger and resentment than they will ever be positive aspirations. If it's the money that turns you on, then please explain to me how you are going to get the benefit of your profits if you have to work all the hours God grants you to get it? The only ones who will get to enjoy the proceeds of your labour will be your hands-out begging kids, who will be contemplating with barely hidden glee your premature, work-stress-induced death.

The sooner all of these people – maybe even you, perchance – realise that they are just a number among so many other (usually much bigger) numbers, the better it will be for them, if not, maybe, their dependants. The trick, you see, is to realise this blindingly obvious fact before it is all too late and live for the hour, the day, the year… yourself. You don't have to conform to the life 'they' have to offer. The life that is chosen for you by others, whether they be your family or your employers. The life that is devoted to, and then ripped away by, those same others. But not many of us have the cojones to do what *we* actually want to do with our life, do we?

Take this latest fare I have in the back now. Jones, I think his name is. Whoever he is, it's a nice little earner for me, taking him all the way to Ulstown from Harlow way. Ker-ching! But the man does not look good. Sweating like a pig but deathly pale. Like most of my punters, he finds his phone unputdownable. 'Smart casual' is, I think, what they call it, and he might well have dressed like that when he left the house this morning, but he ain't that now. Poor bugger. The weight of the world looks like it's on his shoulders, based on the way his brow is furrowed, despite the skinful he has clearly enjoyed with his Friday lunch. You know what? He can keep his nice house with white plastic pillars, his membership of the golf club, Tuesday night playing mixed-doubles badminton at the sports centre, and whatever else his money has bought him. Life is too short to have to go through what these people suffer at work. Maybe it's time for our Jonesy to choose his own life rather than the one others have chosen for him. Give me a cab, the choice of when to work, enough money to afford getting bladdered with my mates on a weekend, and a couple of weeks in Magaluf with the family in the summer. Nuff said. Roll on the summer.

The votes had been cast and the result was in. Today was officially confirmed as the shittiest day of the shittiest week. Andy was struggling to find more elegant prose to define the week that had just passed, but 'shit' and 'shitty' pretty much described it perfectly. Here he was being driven home in a cab by a mercifully silent driver after a very wet company lunch which had been arranged by the CEO's top skivvy for the senior scientists. "An opportunity to lift morale and look at the bigger picture," was how it had been sold by Dr Judith Meredith, which could no doubt be considered good management practice. A suggestion from HR? A chance to get pissed on company money and forget for a few hours all the looming trauma was how it was perceived by many of Andy's reports, especially given that free taxis had been offered to take everyone home should they wish. A shocking waste of company money and time was the viewpoint of the uninvited junior staff, whose views would no doubt have changed had they been invited. How Andy had wished to be one of those junior staff, as he had no particular yearning to socialise with anyone after recent events, and least of all with his colleagues, several of whom were annoyingly bullish about the future; at least their own futures. But he had to go. He had no choice, as not going would not paint a nice picture for his employers of his commitment to the company, and, as unattractive as staying at Wright and Briggs might now seem to Andy, it was better than being on social security. So, if he had to go, why not eat and drink away the misery?

The Friday morning before the lunch had started with heavy-duty project team meetings for those non-virology projects that were to be pulled, with Andy's being one of them. And what an event that turned out to be: as ill-prepared and shambolic a meeting as any Andy had ever been responsible for. His passion for this soon-to-be-terminated (or maybe out-licensed) programme had now vanished, and he took an almost childish pleasure in making it clear that he no longer had any interest in it, despite the meeting being an opportunity to showcase his leadership skills to watching senior management and maybe get a stay of execution from potential redundancy by leading any out-licensing activities. This car-crash behaviour was very un-Andy-like, and he knew it, but he just couldn't help himself. In the days and weeks that followed he would come to regret his impulsive and petulant actions on that Friday morning, and the way in which he let down himself and, much to his shame, the scientists working on the project who had given just as much to the cause as Andy had. It was inexcusable. His biggest mistake at work, and not one that he made any attempt to overcome at the company lunch that followed.

The function in a private room of a local hotel saw an uncommunicative Andy make close friends with white wine, red wine, port, and even a 'celebratory' flute of champagne to toast the future of the company; a toast he struggled to acknowledge. He managed to get to his taxi under his own power when the time to sneak away from the car-crash lunch had arrived, but only just. He could feel the stares of those he had left drinking at the free bar boring into his back as he used the door frame to finesse his exit, and knew that he would be the subject of chatter, derision and maybe even pity.

"Fuck 'em. Fuck 'em all." The drink reassured him that he didn't need Wright and Briggs and the incompetent tossers who were in charge of it, and anyway, as a company it was going absolutely nowhere other than down the toilet. The drink wrapped its arm around his shoulders and told him that this was the best thing that could have happened to him, as to stay at Wright and Briggs would consign his ambitions to the graveyard. He needed to leave, and leave now. What a shame that his bestest new bottled friend wasn't around in the weeks and months that followed to help him put back together all the things that he had broken on that shitty Friday.

By the time he was deposited at the bottom of the driveway of 6 Malvern Drive by a smirking taxi driver, Andy had sobered up to the extent that he could at least find his house keys. But he couldn't find anyone at home, or at least no one willing to answer his calls as he hung up his coat in the hallway. His first port of call was the kitchen and the calendar on the back of the door, which required him to switch on the strip of lights above the dining table. March was a gently reassuring photograph of a picturesque Cornish village, not that Andy felt all that reassured.

"Shit. Shit, shit," he said loudly to the empty kitchen. In the box labelled Friday 23rd Susan had written, 'Kids birthday swimming party. Mum's 4 till about 10', and underneath that, 'Janey dreams 5.30'.

Andy resisted the temptation to blaspheme, and was a little surprised at just how quickly one could sober up. He had completely forgotten that his wife had taken the liberty of booking him a 'session' with their neighbour when the two of them had bumped into each other in a coffee shop in town. As much as Susan and Meera would have preferred to have had a quiet morning between themselves, they really could do nothing other than invite Janey to join them when she happened to walk in just as they were about to leave. At least they had been able to enjoy a free cup of coffee with extra chocolate, courtesy of the late arrival.

"Nearly four. Well over an hour before I have to go over the road. Bugger it. I'll cancel," explained Andy to the kitchen table, but he knew that would not look good given how widely advertised the chat about dreams had been. "Bugger." He could really do without this right now. A damage limitation plan ran through his mind as he climbed the stairs whilst undoing his shirt buttons. *Painkillers to head off the headache which is in the post. A quick shower. Mouthwash. Fresh clothes, and maybe even a little lie-down if I have time. An hour talking about dreams should be long enough to avoid looking rude. I can handle it. Back here pronto, slump in front of the TV, and then woken up by the hordes when they come back. Job done. Should I take a bottle? Bit too early in the day for that? But I should take something.* All these thoughts served as excellent displacement activities and he had completely forgotten about the disasters of the day; at least until the cool shower – *Can't blame Susan for not putting the water on* – brought up a reprise of the day that had been. *What the fuck have I done?* It was a rhetorical question.

Andy had never been one to be late, and he left 6 Malvern Drive at 5.25pm with a bottle of the best white wine he could find in the house. He couldn't face the thought of drinking a beefy red wine tonight. There was nothing else he could think of that was in the house and would be anywhere approaching appropriate, although he did briefly consider stealing the vase of daffodils perched on the kitchen windowsill. *Susan would have found something to take.* The alcohol was still to completely leave his body, but his status had been downgraded from embarrassingly drunk to what his mother would have called "a little bit squiffy". He brought down the heavy brass knocker twice on the door of Number 4. *Nice pillars*, he thought as he listened to the increasingly loud (but still quiet) footsteps of someone he presumed to be Janey. A quick double-take of the driveway alerted him to the absence of Graham's car. He decided to be nervous.

"Andy!" announced Janey through a beaming smile. "Come on in. You know, I thought you would make some excuse to cancel."

"So did I," was Andy's attempt at humour which also happened to be true.

"Come on in." Janey beckoned once again, waving him through into the hallway.

Andy was relieved at not being offered a cheek, as he somehow always managed to approach the cheek that was not being offered. And anyway, they didn't really know each other that well.

Once in the hallway, he paused to allow Janey to lead him through into what he presumed was the main living room. The house was not dissimilar to his own in dimensions, but the decor was in a different league. Unrecognisable (at least to Andy) contemporary paintings and sculptures were obviously the preference of either Janey or Graham. The spotless soft furnishings and table surfaces, and an impressive piano, bore witness to a childless couple.

"Do you play?" asked Andy, his head gesturing towards the piano near the doorway.

"Me? Oh, no. I'd love to learn but I can never seem to find the time," replied the woman with all the time in the world on her hands. "Graham brought that with him from his grimy old bachelor flat that he ended up in when his ex left him. He's quite good, but I can't remember the last time he spent any time on it. A pity, don't you think? Do you play?"

"Definitely not," countered Andy, suddenly remembering why he was carrying a bag in his left hand. An understated chandelier was not switched on, the soft lighting instead provided by scented candles placed with some thought about the room. *Very New Age. Very Janey*, thought Andy. "No Graham?" he asked weakly, producing the bottle of white.

"You really didn't need to, but thanks awfully anyway," replied Janey, taking it and glancing at the label. "Very nice," she lied. "Graham? One of his usual meetings with partners at the practice, no doubt followed by a taxi home after a boozy farewell in The Prince of Wales. You are very unlikely to see his car in the driveway tonight." She walked over to the drinks chiller and bent to place Andy's gift on the bottom shelf. "Maybe something we can try a bit later once you have helped me finish off this bottle of Argentinian

Malbec," she suggested, picking up a bottle perched on top of the chiller, although there didn't seem to be that much to finish off based on Andy's view of the bottle. Janey topped up her glass and filled a fresh one for Andy without feeling the need to ask if he even wanted a drink. Similarly, it did not feel appropriate for Andy to refuse the unspoken offer, despite all the alcohol he had already consumed this Friday.

Janey ushered her companion to the edge of a large L-shaped sofa decorated with cushions which she had carefully arranged prior to his arrival. She sat down on a sumptuous armchair opposite him and placed her glass on the low, antique wooden table between them. "*Cin-cin*," she pronounced, offering her glass to her guest.

"Your good health," was the counter-toast.

Both sat back and relaxed into the soft furnishings. Andy appreciated the effort Janey had gone to in spending so much time in trying to appear that she had not spent much time preparing for the occasion. She wore a simple, figure-hugging but demure, knee-length, floral-patterned dress, immaculately accessorised with a belt and jewellery including a modest pearl necklace. Her hair was left long. *That woman could look immaculate dressed in supermarket carrier bags. But maybe more Waitrose than Aldi*, thought Andy. Her complexion belied her age by at least five years, and was no doubt aided and abetted by the regular application of the most expensive, AI-designed, high-tech face creams one could buy.

"So," announced Janey. "Dreams." She waved towards a modest stack of books on the subject of dreams, carefully arranged on a nest table next to her chair. "Tell me something interesting."

Andy swallowed heavily. "Well, to be honest, I'm not sure I've got much of interest to tell you. This was all Graham's idea… yes, Graham's idea to come and talk to you as you… well… you seem to be the expert."

"Nonsense. All dreams are interesting to me. They provide an insight into the soul." The latter statement had been lifted verbatim from and without acknowledgement to the author of one of the few books she had bothered to read, *Dreams: An Exploration of their Meaning.*

"Ah… OK then. Where to start? All a bit gruesome, I suppose. A bit grisly," commented Andy.

"My favourite!" Janey rubbed her hands with overstated glee.

"The dreams usually end with an unnatural death. Sometimes mine, but not always. Murder? Now and again, I suppose, but there's some supernatural stuff mixed in there as well. Some really dark stuff and, I guess, something that started since Christmas, for some reason," he added, starting to get into the swing of things. "An example was that dream I told Graham about."

Andy then went on to describe that dream, adding invented bits and pieces to try to make it (and him) as interesting as he could manage, but he could see that this particular New Age healthcare practitioner was starting to lose interest. *I thought she was supposed to be interested in this stuff? The expert?* thought Andy. Consequently, he ended his tale rather abruptly, signalled by him reaching for his glass of wine and taking a large mouthful, rendering him momentarily speechless.

Janey recognised the cue. "Very interesting," she lied. "What does it all mean? A tricky one, I would say. Maybe there is something going on in your life which you are not comfortable with, and that started around Christmastime? Perhaps even something that you are unhappy with? Could be that you are not even aware that you feel unhappy." All of this was rather obvious to them both. "Not that I would wish to pry into these sorts of things, of course," she lied once again before moving to bring the subject to a close, rather forcefully and with an air of finality. "I tell you what. Give me a chance to do a bit of research in these books and maybe we can catch up in a few weeks' time and I can give a better answer as to what's going on in that complicated little head of yours." This was punctuated by a gentle smile and a finger pointing gently to her right temple.

Is that it? thought Andy. Not that he'd really expected any great insight, but she didn't seem any more informed as to the nature of dreams than anyone else interested enough to provide a blagger's view of the subconscious state.

"That OK with you, Andy?" asked Janey fully knowing what the answer would be.

"Of course. Looking forward to a… another session," came back Andy struggling to find the most appropriate terminology to describe what had just taken place.

"A refill?" offered Janey, although there was precious little room left in Andy's glass. "Graham is a member of one of those internet wine clubs. I expect you and Susan are too."

They weren't.

"We had this lovely Malbec which Graham ordered a case of. Not many left," she remarked whilst uncorking one of the 'not many'.

The bottle of white that Andy had brought seemed destined to remain untouched on this occasion, and, perhaps, never to see the light of day again in polite company. *Maybe a Christmas present for one of Graham's nearly dead aunties*, was Janey's default position for the unwanted gifts which they received from time to time, and a concept that usually benefited all. Aunty Phyllis had never before owned such a fine set of avocado-green bathroom towels. "Matches our bathroom suite perfectly. Thank you so much, Janey. How very thoughtful you are." One less wedding present to worry about finding space for.

Janey wanted to talk about something else. "Susan tells me you make drugs in your job."

Rather a dramatic change of subject, thought Andy. *I wonder where this is going?* "Well. Sort of. I work in research for a small pharmaceutical company just outside Harlow. We are trying to find drugs that work on brain diseases." He had no wish to delve into what had happened at work in recent weeks.

"How interesting," responded Janey in a tone which suggested that she genuinely was more than a little interested. "I suppose you get your hands on all sorts of mind-bending drugs that could kick off an interesting dream or two." And that's why, of course, she was not just a little interested in Andy's career.

"Not really, although we do test known drugs as a control in some of our experiments, but that's what the biologists do. I'm a chemist and so I just make new compounds to be tested," explained Andy, trying to avoid any discussion about drug abuse, which, he assumed, was the topic Janey was now heading towards. And he was correct.

Janey leaned over to take another drink. Andy followed her lead.

"Fascinating. And I tell you for why." She paused to consider more carefully what she was going to say next. "You might well be surprised to learn that I dabbled a bit in drugs, back in the day."

He wasn't.

"More *after* uni than when I was *at* uni. None of your hard stuff, I didn't touch anything around the dance scene, and I hated the smell of that nasty weed, which I found all rather tawdry. Sure, a little bit of coke, but my real fascination was with psychedelics. You know – magic mushrooms, mescaline, all those three-letter-named drugs I have forgotten the names of. Have you ever tried them?"

Andy hardly needed to shake his head. They both knew he hadn't.

"Anyway. All rather illegal back then, but great fun. We took them as a group of friends and, I suppose, got off a bit on seeing each other move into a different world. And that was what it felt like. A parallel universe. You have never experienced such a complete feeling of relaxation; of being at one with the world; a world where all the bad things happen miles away. You have no worries. You just don't know what you have missed, Andy." She took another drink as a small compensation for no longer being able to enjoy the good times. "But of course, that particular avenue of enjoyment has been closed down for me."

"Graham?" suggested Andy.

"No, no. Not Graham. He knows about my past and is understanding, I think. At least, that seems to be the case. I just lost touch with that group of friends, and I am not the sort of person to hang around street corners to get a fix. One has one's reputation to consider," joked Janey. She didn't feel the urge to tell Andy why she had lost touch with her friends. Too much detail. "And now I read that these drugs are all the rage. How times change."

Time for Andy to show off his knowledge. "Absolutely. Very much back in fashion these days, with lots of clinical trials going on to find out how we can use them to treat neurological disorders such as depression and PTSD. And they could well be the next big breakthrough in neurology, from what I've read," he finished, congratulating himself on his impressive knowledge by taking another drink.

"Do you work on those sorts of drugs?" delved Janey.

And now Andy could see exactly where all this was going. "Oh, no. Would be fascinating, but not something the company is interested in, at least for the moment. So, nothing for you to try out, I'm afraid," he bantered in the hope that Janey would see it as the joke it was intended to be, and maybe change the subject to something a little bit more comfortable.

She did pick up on the joke. "Perhaps you know me better than I thought you did," she said in a tone to reassure him that she too was joking, although she would certainly not turn down anything that might be offered. "One day we will all be on these. Take my word."

"Maybe you are right. Time will tell," answered Andy. "There are some big players in this area, so who knows?"

And then an idea came to him that would have unforeseen outcomes which would dramatically affect both his life and those of the people around him. Not that he was aware of the consequences of this epiphany when it appeared. They would not become clear for many months. Here was the perfect human guinea pig to find out if WRT743 had the same effects on her as it had on him when he'd first taken it before Christmas. A guinea pig who had, no doubt, been on all that there was to take, and knew perfectly just what 'good' felt like. And better still, a guinea pig who could actually tell you what she experienced, rather than the researcher having to anthropomorphise based on how an animal reacted with its peers. Could Andy's drug, the one on which he had toiled for so long, actually be a useful compound? He was going to seize the moment regardless of the consequences.

"Listen. Just a thought, and please, please say that you are not interested if any of this scares you, as it certainly scares the bejesus out of me." Andy could barely believe he was saying this; that he had chosen to go down this avenue that was as far out of his comfort zone as he could contemplate. But they were only words, and he could find a way out of this if Janey reacted negatively. What do mere words mean when you have had more than a few drinks?

A stretched out "OK," was the rather tentative answer of a clearly intrigued Janey. "You have my full attention." Once again, she went to top up their wine glasses.

"Might be sensible for us not to drink any more if you are going to agree to my proposal," added Andy, who was a little concerned that they, and especially he, had drunk too much already. He began his pitch. "Has Susan ever talked to you about her brother, Brian?" He had assumed not, given who he was.

She answered no.

"Good, and probably best not to repeat anything I have to say about him. In fact, can I trust you not to say anything to anyone about this conversation we are having now? Susan, Graham, anyone?" For the first time that evening, Andy felt that he had her full attention, which excited him. A beautiful, sexy woman was listening to his every word.

"Of course," she answered, although such promises never really counted for anything with Janey.

"Well, Brian is very much the outcast of the family. In and out of jobs for years, and the only thing he has been successful in doing is keeping a network of customers for his drugs." Andy, at least, appreciated his own wit. "Anyway, to cut a long story short, we were out on the piss a few months back. Got talking about this and that – he is good company, despite his problems – and he offered me his latest product, which he said was going down a storm with his punters. Of course, I refused, but when I was rummaging around in my coat pocket a few days later I found a few packets that he must have slipped in, probably when I went to the toilet or something like that." Andy was committing the cardinal sin of over-explaining a lie. Would Janey believe all this rubbish? Maybe she wouldn't care?

"Given that you are telling me all this, I'm guessing that you didn't immediately throw the drugs away as you should have done, and that you still have them for a reason that would be interesting to hear about," interjected Janey, who had already guessed where all this was heading. *Just get on with it, man*, she thought.

"Good point," he answered, trying to buy time to conjure up a good argument for not doing the 'right' thing. "Truth be told," was the phrase anticipating his next lie, "as I said earlier, I have never dabbled in drugs, but I thought I could hide them away for some rainy day in the future. Never-say-never sort of thing. They are safely tucked away in the attic. Susan knows nothing about this, so please, our little secret. In fact, our *big* secret."

"You mean to say that you spent three years at university and never tried anything? What a good time you must have had," laughed Janey, reaching for her glass of wine and then returning it to the table untouched in deference to Andy's earlier advice. "So, what are you waiting for?"

"Sorry?" questioned Andy, feigning ignorance as to what Janey was alluding to.

"Aren't you going to run across the road and bring your free samples back here to give me a go? And what better time for you to have a go as well?" She had taken the obvious bait he was dangling before her. "You can rely upon me to tell you whether Brian was telling the truth or not."

"Ah. OK then. I'll get them. But only for you. I have had too much to drink today."

"We'll see," answered Janey, rising to usher her guest to the door. *This has all turned out much more interesting than I imagined*, she mused after closing it behind him. *Boring, old before his time, suburban Andy. Maybe I've got him all wrong. Let's find out for sure.* She toyed with the idea of leaving the door on the latch to ease his return, but the sensory memory of the sort of 'locals' she often saw in Graham's waiting room made her reconsider. *Can't those people afford deodorant? Maybe they should rethink their priorities before buying the latest iPhone.* The door was closed and locked. Her real reason for inviting Andy to her house had clearly not been an interest in the unconscious, but an intent to start a long game to work on him as a potential source of soft drugs. A huge, long shot, of course, and even in the unlikely scenario that her plan actually worked, it would no doubt take months of coming on strong to Andy to bear fruit. But Andy was such an easy mark: as ordinary a man as you could ever meet, and so surely very susceptible to some heavy-duty flirting. She would be a fool to at least not give it a try.

"So, what happens from here?" whispered Andy to himself as he crossed the road, almost breathless from a mixture of excitement and nervousness. "Neither of our other halves will be back home for a while, and so any effects from the drug should have peaked long before they appear, based on what happened last time," calculated a hopeful Andy. He was not a fool and could sense that he was being used; his company likely only humoured because of the chance for her to get high. As would he, and in the company of a beautiful woman. *So, what is there not to like? What's the worst that could happen?* Being teased and played by a beautiful woman was far from the worst that could happen in Andy's eyes, and he would also benefit from finding out how someone else reacted to taking WRT743. All very well as long as no one else found out what he and Janey were now contemplating.

It took less than ten minutes for Andy to barge through the front door of his house, pocket two vials of the experimental drug stolen from work which he kept in the tea caddy in the attic (he assumed that he would be forced to partake, and actually quite looked forward to repeating his pre-Christmas experience), pick up a half-full two-litre bottle of diet lemonade from a kitchen cupboard, and cross the road back to Number 4, looking up and down the close in fear of an undercover police sting. There was none. Janey again opened the front door and led Andy into her kitchen, which smelled of cinnamon. *But why?* thought Andy.

"Glass vials? That's unusual. I thought you said that Brian had given you packets," observed Janey. "I'm rather more used to grubby little sandwich bags and dirty brown powder, not white drugs in a screw-top glass vial. Very upmarket, Andy. Please pass on my compliments to your brother-in-law."

This attempt at humour made Andy feel more than a little uneasy, not least because Janey had already picked up on an inconsistency in his story. Glass vials were what was typically used to store chemical samples at his workplace. Not sandwich bags. Perhaps he should have thought that one through before taking them across the road. Many unanswerable questions raced through his mind. Did she not appreciate all the risks they were taking? How would she react to knowing that she would be just the second person to have ever tried this drug? Would she not try it if he disclosed that little fact? Then there was Graham and Susan to worry about. But the events leading up to Andy showing Janey how to dissolve WRT743 in lemonade made him fully aware that he had started an unpredictable fire which was really now being controlled by her. No way back now without looking pathetic in front of her, and he had had more than enough of being made to feel pathetic for one day. This was his time.

"So, you have absolutely no idea what these are?" asked Janey once again.

Andy shook his head.

"Ah, well. What's the worst that could happen? *Cin-cin*," was the repeated toast as Janey clinked her glass on Andy's and downed her non-alcoholic cocktail in one. "A bit metallic?" she offered.

If only she knew, thought Andy. He followed suit, placing his emptied glass on the table and filling it and hers with some more lemonade. "Maybe this will take the taste away," he suggested. It didn't.

"Why don't we sit down and enjoy the moment?" said Janey, leading him back to their seats in the living room.

Andy was thankful that no more wine had been consumed as both glasses remained full, but they had probably shared well over a bottle already. Not so good.

"How about some music to soothe the nerves?" That was more notice of what she was going to do anyway than a question for Andy to answer. "Because, I must say, you do look a bit on edge, Andy." She didn't know the half of it.

Unrecognisable jazz. Not that Andy would have been able to recognise much jazz anyway, *but not a bad choice*, he thought, *for our current situation and circumstances. So why not?*

"Graham's music really, but nice background noise, don't you think?" pondered Janey. A rhetorical question.

A mention of Graham! A streak of nervousness passed through Andy's body. Were his hopes of keeping this evening's events confidential too ambitious? That was all down to Janey, as he would certainly keep to his side of the bargain.

Janey returned to her armchair and slumped back into the soft leather. "Sit back. Close your eyes. And bloody relax!" was the order. "No police will be turning up tonight. Or any night."

But Graham might, worried Andy silently. Still, he did as he was told, trying to remember a mindfulness afternoon he'd attended at work several years previously. That was something he really had not wanted to do. "New Age crap," was the feedback he'd given to Susan when he got home that evening. *Terribly earnest and gratuitously pleasant tutors battling against sniggering children*, was a phrase that came to mind when he'd taken the time to take in the scene.

But now might be a good time to put his learnings into action, as it was clear that Janey had no intention of discussing the state of the world or, for that matter, anything else. Her eyes were closed. Her arms rested gently across the high sides of her chair. She was waiting for the buzz; the kick. The advantages and disadvantages of Brexit could wait for another time. *Feel heavy in the chair. Sink back. Deep breaths. Concentrate on each breath in, and then exhale. Focus on the toes. Move up to the ankles. The calves. The knees. And so on. Easy.* Andy felt he was drifting in and out of consciousness, although he couldn't be sure. How long had it been since he had taken the drug? He really couldn't be sure. Then those sensations he remembered from the last time, the first time, started to materialise. The tingling down his spine. All feelings of tension (of which there were many, despite the so-called mindfulness and consumed alcohol) started to leach out of his body. His neck and shoulders relaxed. He began to enjoy his situation: being comfortable with being drunk and high in the company of a beautiful woman. He liked who he was. Andy was a good person. A nice man. Confidence. Time to become conscious; to talk and enjoy the evening. But the room and Janey he saw was still a dream. He couldn't quite manage to rouse himself to full consciousness. No bad thing. This twilight zone was certainly no bad place to be. Now he was walking around the room, looking intently at the paintings. But he wasn't. He opened the patio doors to look out onto a beautiful garden on a breezy summer's day. But he didn't. He had not left the comfort of the sofa. His movements were all a dream.

In this dream, Andy felt a hand being pushed softly through his hair. An unseen presence of someone sitting next to him on the sofa, gliding their hand across his leg. In this dream, he slowly opened his eyes to watch this woman pull him down to lie across the sofa. She straddled him. In this dream, she leaned forward to push back his hair. Kiss his cheeks. Unbutton the top of his shirt and stroke his chest. He did nothing other than become aware of the erection that was pressing against his trousers. In this dream, she pulled away from his supine body, stood up, and started to loosen his belt. She pulled down his trousers and boxer shorts to his knees. He didn't object.

In this dream, she straddled him once again but this time his erection was guided into a warm and already moist haven; a movement that made them both gasp for air. She placed her hands on his chest and started to rock forwards and backwards, slowly and gently. He remained motionless. In this dream, she continued her gentle exertion, with the only communication between them being selfish sounds of enjoyment. He grasped her waist through the floral dress spread around them and pulled her down onto him, guiding her up and down his body. In this dream, she pulled away, stood up, and then lay down on the floor next to the sofa, her hand pulling him down onto her. She gasped as he entered her once more.

In this dream, the lovemaking began to increase in intensity and speed. It was never frantic. He could sense that she was close. So was he. The final few minutes of their love making passed in seconds as his final, most penetrating thrusts brought them both to orgasm and exhaustion. He pulled off her to lie next to her.

Only, of course, it was not a dream. He was now lying on the floor of the living room of 4 Malvern Drive, struggling for breath, having made exquisite love to the entrancing wife of a friend. *How did this all happen? What did she think she was doing? Why didn't I stop her? Why? Wasn't it all so very wonderful?*

Time passed.

"What… er… what now?" Andy asked the chandelier above him, not wishing to turn his head towards his new lover and read the anticipated disappointment in her face.

"What now? You go home and I stay here. And then, please God, grant us just a few more hours in the company of this unbelievable drug so that we can both make beautiful love to our spouses. They at least deserve that."

"And after that?"

"And after that, you track down that sweet little brother-in-law of yours and get hold of some more of that fucking drug!"

Andy awoke suddenly to experience an immediate feeling of nervousness. He really didn't know where he was, other than lying in a bed, staring up at a nondescript bedroom ceiling. He was conscious of someone lying next to him but all he could see was an unrecognisable head prominent above the covers. He assumed it was Susan, but he had no particular interest in finding out who it was. Without realising he had even got out of bed; he was now staring out through a curtain-less window to the garden below. It was his garden, but where was the children's swing? Where were the young roses that Susan had planted that first autumn when they had moved in? Perhaps this was another house after all. Past the boundaries of the garden, where he expected to see the neighbours' properties and suburbia beyond, was a total, funereal blackness. Some of the blackness was starting to escape, with darting, morphing shapes sliding across the garden and then back into the refuge of the black mass. A mass which seemed to be edging ever closer to the house.

Andy looked back at the bed to urge his companion to come and see what he could see; to confirm the unlikely. But there was no one in the bed. There was no longer a bed; just an empty room, aside from the far corner, from which the same black shapes slithered across the floor and then back to their sanctuary of the blackness. He looked outside again. Now he was certain that the blackness was coming.

For the house. For him. He turned into the room to try to find a way to escape the blackness. There was no door. *One last chance to escape. Open the window, jump down into the garden and run around the house to the front and safety from the blackness*, thought Andy. But the window had no way of being opened. It was just glass. He turned back to face the room and the slithering blackness was at his feet, rising slowly like a faceless cobra ready to strike. He tried to kick it, but his foot passed through it without disturbing its shape. He retreated to the far corner of the room stepping backwards while watching the blackness follow him making its way across the room in a side-to-side motion. As he reached the corner, more black shapes appeared from under the skirting boards, joining forces with the faceless cobra, which grew in height to tower over him. Nowhere to run. No escape. But maybe there was. At the far end of the room, the floor was starting to fall away. A crisp white light shone through this growing space. It was getting brighter. A chance to escape?

The jolt which brought Andy to consciousness raised his head above the pillow and sent a spasm of pain from his neck through into his temples. He risked turning his head marginally to the right to find out that it was almost 7.35am on Saturday 2nd April, and it was ten degrees Celsius. What a nice Christmas present that digital weather station from his mother-in-law was. He was back in the master bedroom of 6 Malvern Drive. The real 6 Malvern Drive. Turning his head slightly to the left further confirmed his location, as lying next to him, her hair tied up in a knot, was his wife, whose face was, typically, submerged under the duvet. Susan's way of avoiding having to confront the real world for as long as possible, or so Andy often thought. But all this comforting familiarity came at the cost of a head that was being clamped in a vice. Pain coursed through his neck and into his pulsating forehead. This was a headache that was not going to go away any time soon.

He used his right leg to feel for the bedroom floor and his left side to provide the momentum to sit up on the side of the bed. Phase one completed. Next, the gentlest of walks to the not quite fully decorated en-suite bathroom, where he had stored emergency medication for just this sort of emergency. Two ibuprofen and two paracetamol tablets were pumped out of their blister packs. He toyed with the idea of making it three ibuprofen tablets. This headache was a really bad one. *Maybe in an hour if this doesn't work*, he concluded. Head under the tap. Tablets taken. Very small steps back to the sanctuary of his bed, and the relief of avoiding waking Susan. Talking was out of the question when in this sort of pain. As slowly and gently as he was able to, he lowered his head onto his two pillows. The vice should begin to relinquish its grip by about nine, when the children would start to sound like there were more of them in the house than there actually were. And the brain fog? Well, he could live with that.

And then he remembered the day just passed. A Friday, the events of which would dictate his life from this day forward, although it would take many months for Andy to realise fully the consequences of his actions. Despite the work calamities of the day before, his thoughts quickly turned to Janey. Of a uniquely pleasurable and emotional experience; an unforgettable adventure that would be replayed over and over in his mind for years to come. It had not just been sex with a beautiful, unobtainable woman (although by itself that would be remarkable and a moment to cherish); it had been the sensation of two bodies acting with perfect timing, each doing what the other craved. No fruitless fumbling. No unwanted moves. No wish to focus on either their own or their lover's needs. Instead, a breathless and unspoken encounter in which orgasm was effortless and mutual. Andy had never felt more like a man.

But, as he gently turned his head towards his still unconscious wife, nor had he ever felt such guilt. Susan was far from deserving of an adulterous, drug-taking husband. It was not as if sex with her was anything other than enjoyable. Maybe not quite as enjoyable as in those first few months of pure hedonism when they had both cashed in their virginity and explored the pleasures their bodies could provide and receive, but surely few couples could maintain such excitement in the years to follow, or would want to as their lives together took on new priorities and outlooks?

But this 'thing' with Janey was just a one-off. A life-lifting, energising and ego-affirming one-off, but a one-off nonetheless. His guilt would, given time, pass, and surely Janey would never breathe a word of it to anyone? Why would she? How would she benefit from doing so? And even if she did, who would believe her? Who would ever believe that she had opened her legs to welcome someone as ordinary as Andy? She was, after all, way out of his league. This was how Andy reassured himself that the events of the night before would not go beyond his private memories of a one-night stand; a home-made DVD, to be played again and again in his mind, of a moment in his life which would not threaten his marriage, his family or his home. For the time being, he chose not to concern himself too much with Janey's parting request to "get hold of some more of that fucking drug". An attempt at humour in the heat of the moment? He did hope so.

It was Sophie who beat the 9am alarm and asked her abruptly awoken parents if she could make the cereal breakfast for her brother and sister. This was a treat she looked forward to on a Saturday morning, and one her parents encouraged as it gave them another half-hour in bed now that she had passed her probationary period.

"Of course, Sophie, but please try not to make any mess, and please give Josh what he wants rather than what you want him to have," advised Susan, who was yet to raise her head off her pillow. When Sophie had gone, she added, "And thus another small lie-in was engineered for Mr and Mrs Jones of 6 Malvern Drive. Isn't Mrs Jones awfully clever? Just as well, given what happened last night."

Within a heartbeat, Andy switched from a semi-conscious state to full fight-or-flight mode. "What do you mean, 'given what happened'?" he replied with rather more urgency than he'd intended.

"You don't remember? I am surprised." Without leaving the comfort of her pillow, Susan turned her head to face her husband. "You were all over me like a rash. Couldn't wait to get me into bed. You actually undressed me. Don't know where you got the energy after such a busy day. You even put a wash on before we got back from my mother's. And there's me thinking you didn't know how to use the washing machine." She gently stroked Andy's head in recognition of the shared experience of the night just passed.

Washing machine? Then Andy remembered that he had first showered and then changed his clothes when he'd got back to the house to remove any evidence of the perfumed Janey and their lovemaking by washing all the aromas away, even if he had used fabric conditioner instead of washing powder. The thought of murderers washing away the blood from their crimes came to mind.

"Not that I am complaining, of course. What a night! Sort of reminded me of that time before Christmas. Do you remember?" Susan looked closely into her husband's eyes to see if he did remember.

Last night. Both Janey and Susan in one night. And the night before Christmas that Susan was referring to. It must be the drug. "I think I remember. But isn't sex with me always that enjoyable?" Humour to avoid answering questions he would rather not entertain.

"Of course, dear," she lied. "But sometimes the same wine can taste so much better on some nights than it does on others."

A clever answer, thought Andy. "I'm glad that you are happy. Happy enough to give me a few more minutes in bed to recover from my exertions?" A further attempt at distraction.

Another "Of course, dear" from Susan, who kissed her finger and placed it on Andy's forehead. "You have a little lie-in. I'll sort out the kids." And with that, she crept out from under the covers and disappeared from the room to the kitchen below, just in time to moderate the argument about cereals that was starting between Sophie and her brother.

Andy spread out to cover both sides of the bed in the hope that the extra space would hasten the annoyingly slow retreat of his headache.

Time passes. Lie-in enjoyed, and the pain receded sufficiently for the man of the house to embark upon the checklist of activities and responsibilities of a normal Saturday morning at 6 Malvern Drive. Andy had just completed loading the dishwasher with the breakfast crockery and cutlery, and had listened attentively to Susan's tutorial on the different roles of washing powder and fabric conditioner in the modern household, when he heard a ping from the company phone he had, through habit, kept in his shirt pocket. *Who the hell would want to bother me on a Saturday morning, and isn't it now time to stop keeping this with me night and day, given what has just happened at work?* he thought. It was Janey. *How the fuck did she get hold of this number? I must have given it to her last night. Of course. So that she could contact me to follow up on those stupid dreams.*

"Everything OK?" Susan was drinking her coffee at the breakfast table. "You seem to have gone awfully pale. Problem at work?"

"No, no. Everything's fine. Just got a stinking headache again. Some idiot at work looking for a phone number. Someone else can sort it out. Delete text." He didn't. He walked into the hallway to get the peace and space to collect his thoughts and read it.

How about a quick coffee in the recreation centre this morning when you are there for the children's swimming lessons? I will be finished with Chris before 11. See you there. XXX

'XXX'? What did she mean by that? Although Andy suspected that that was how she ended all her texts, and it did not mean that he was anything special to her. But what should he do? His immediate thought was not to do anything immediately. He had long learned the lesson of not rushing important decisions. Shower, shave, get dressed, and use that time to make a call and reply. He really didn't need this today. But still, the thought of meeting his new lover again energised him.

The shower managed to shift the nastiest remnants of his terminal headache, as well as providing the time to decide how to answer Janey's text. He towelled himself to relative dryness, picked up his mobile phone (which he had left just outside the shower, having decided in retrospect that it might be better to keep it close to hand), and typed his reply: 'OK.' He had no idea what she was going to say, but at least it would provide him with an opportunity to remind her that the events of the previous day must be kept secret and never leaked to anyone. He wanted to cling on to at least a semblance of control over the situation. The downsides of them sharing a coffee in the recreation centre and being seen together were minimal. They were neighbours, so who would be surprised to see them together? The downsides of an uncontrolled Janey constituted the greater risk.

A more than averagely flustered Andy ushered his young reports past the showers and on to the swimming pool beyond. An hour of relative peace for him, but this morning he was not going to be watching them. His nerves were jangling, as he was going to meet the enigma that was Janey. The night before seemed so long ago.

He walked into the recreation centre café through a door held open by a rather pungent blue-belt member of the ju jitsu club, who hardly reached the height of Andy's chest. *Maybe the young man should have had a shower after his class.* Andy could see Janey watching him from a table she had commandeered near the window looking out over the car park. With a beaming smile borrowed from the night before, she waved him over to join her.

"I took the liberty of treating you to a latte, as I'm sure I remember Sue telling me that you're a coffee drinker. Is that OK?"

Andy gave a discreet shudder at the mention of his wife's name by the woman who was, at least in part, responsible for his adultery. "Yeah. That's fine," he replied, searching frantically for change in his jacket and trouser pockets and wondering why Susan had told someone that he drank coffee when he drank tea competitively for Yorkshire. He assumed that it was Janey who had remembered incorrectly or had just guessed.

"Sit down, Andy. You can buy the next one."

He pulled up an attractive but uncomfortable cane chair and sat down opposite her at the small, green plastic table. "So, anything in particular you wanted to talk about?" he prompted, partly in humour and partly as an attempt to control the conversation.

"Well, what do you think I would like to talk about?"

Touché, thought Andy. "How about something along the lines of what a jolly nice time we had yesterday, but that will be the end of it? Our little secret?"

"A nice time? I thought it was more along the lines of a great fuck."

Andy looked quickly to his left to see if their nearest neighbours had overheard her profanity. They hadn't, or at least they acted as if they hadn't. The word and the memory of the act sent a shiver down the back of his neck and into his shoulders. "It was." He paused for reflective thought. "It really was, and it's something I will remember for a long time. But my marriage – *our* marriages… As much as I would love to… you know… we can't do that again. We just can't."

Janey sat up straight in her chair and a smile appeared across her thin lips. "Who said anything about repeating last night? Rather presumptuous of you, perhaps?" she replied in full prick-teasing mode. "Don't panic, Andy. I've no intention of leaving Graham and certainly not of breaking up your home. I'm simply not the overdramatic, falling-in-love sort of woman, and definitely not after just one night of rolling under the covers. But look." It was now Janey's turn to glance across at the occupants of the neighbouring tables, but they were all too busy boasting about the sporting excellence of their children to pay any attention to whatever she was planning to say. She pulled her chair closer to the table and leant over to move closer stilll to Andy. "I have had my fair share of lovers in the past. Perhaps more than my fair share. But I just love to dance." She could see from the expression on Andy's face that she had confused him. "Look, I'm not talking ballroom here. I love to *dance*. To enjoy myself. The thrill of saying 'I will' to someone for the first time. To get fucked. And how we danced last night!" She moved her hand close to his, which rested on the table, but did not make contact. "Tell me that you didn't find last night special. Look into my eyes and say that to my face."

Andy was silent.

"It's not often that men bring me to orgasm. At least not with penetration. Graham doesn't. Although he tries his very best, bless him, and we do enjoy ourselves in bed."

Andy struggled to picture them together, naked, in the same bed.

"But you did last night. A wonderful, deep, everlasting orgasm. Now, you tell me. If neither of us has any intention of leaving our partner – neither of us betrays our 'little secret' – then why should we deprive ourselves of enjoying such pleasures again? Why? Tell me, Andy."

It was the drug. It must have been, thought Andy. Had she not considered that? A combination of any prick and the drug would have provided the same result. But no one else could provide her with that combination, as only he had access to the drug. Yet, although their conversation had veered far from how Andy had envisaged and planned it in the hours before they sat down for coffee – as a grateful and gracious signing off on a one-night stand – Janey's offer, almost insistence, to 'meet' again made him feel wanted. His virility was being approved by a woman many men could only dream of bedding. Still… "Anything you have missed out here, Janey?" he asked, attempting to take back the initiative.

"I don't know what you mean."

"Really? Is it the drug or me that you are looking to have another go with?"

The tight smile reappeared. Janey had anticipated that Andy would be just as aware as she of the likely contribution the drug had made in bringing her to such an overwhelming orgasm. "Are you sure that drug you brought to the party wasn't some sort of psychedelic? It certainly felt like we had taken something like that last night." She hoped she had nimbly sidestepped articulating what they had both independently assumed: that if he ever wanted a repeat of that Friday night, he needed to supply the drug.

"Like I said, I don't know. And I'm pretty sure Brian doesn't either," lied Andy. But perhaps she had a point. Maybe there were some psychedelic properties to WRT743, properties they had not picked up in all the tests they had carried out on it, because they hadn't been expecting and thus had not tested for a psychedelic.

"What can I say? Sometimes one needs a little push to get up on the dance floor. A drink or two. Maybe even something a bit more hard core. But one still needs a partner to dance with. Wouldn't you like to come dancing with me again?" teased Janey, looking intently into his eyes. "Just think what you could be walking away from. The chance of another night like last night." She sensed that if she pushed him for an answer now she might not get the one she wanted to hear. Andy was not just another boyfriend looking for a quick jump. "Just promise me that you will at least think about it, Andy. Take your time. No need to decide right now. I know this is not easy for you.

But one thing to remember when you are thinking all this through…" She paused for dramatic effect and placed both her hands on the table just inches from his. "Last night was truly special for me."

Andy just didn't have the experience, nor the skill set to tell whether or not she was being genuine. She had bewildered him. Confused him. Enchanted him. He was a lovestruck, excitable teenager all over again. A rabbit caught in the headlights, unable to escape from the lights of its tormentor. "I can't do this, Janey. I really can't, and I apologise for what happened last night."

"Apologise? Keep your apologies to make to yourself, should you decide to walk away from ever having the chance to make some more wonderful memories. Just think about it, Andy." And with that, she gently stroked the back of his hand, looked around the room at their oblivious fellow coffee-shop customers, stood up, picked up her tiny handbag and walked to the door leading out into the reception area, which was being guarded by members of the archery club wondering why their coach had yet to turn up. She did not look back.

Andy was left sitting alone at the table, with a full plastic cup of cold coffee and a mind buzzing with excitement, trepidation, worry and guilt. He had said the right things to her. He had been honourable and courteous. But nothing he could contemplate doing came close to just how much he wanted to take Janey up on her offer. At least she had given him time to not have to make a decision. Not just yet.

Andy had been given special dispensation from going shopping that Saturday afternoon, which was just as well given how physically and mentally draining the past twenty-four hours had been. Susan would go to the supermarket on Sunday. He wondered what the quid pro quo would be. He did not have to wait long to find out.

"Teabags or loose tea?" asked Susan of her husband, who was trying to stay awake in front of a newspaper spread across the kitchen table.

"Whatever we have the most of." Andy thought he was trying to be helpful. He looked forward to the surprise.

Susan pushed a mugful of hot something towards him through an avenue between the newspapers and sat down almost opposite him. "So. How was your night with Janey?"

Andy had anticipated this not unreasonable question, and had already rehearsed both his answer and his demeanour. "What a strange woman she is," he started, pretending to still be reading the newspaper. This opening statement was calculated to take any discussion away from what had happened and instead focus on the woman herself. Align himself with what he thought was Susan's view and then let her monopolise the conversation.

"Pretty much what me and Meera talk about, really. A very strange set-up they have over the road. Could Graham find anyone more different from himself?" Susan picked up her cup and set it back down without drinking. Too hot. "But as long as they are happy, I suppose. It takes all sorts. What on earth did you talk to her about? Just the dreams?"

"Yeah. Mostly just the dreams," lied Andy. "Lots of New Age stuff about well-being, and a tour of the living rooms and kitchen. They have – or at least one of them has – good taste. Lovely garden."

"So, how long were you over there?" pried Susan.

"Didn't really notice, but it couldn't have been more than an hour. I took that bottle of Bourgogne, but we didn't get to drink it. Bit of a waste, really. Ho-hum. As for the dreams, she will have to think about it a bit more and get back to me," finished Andy, thinking ahead about a valid excuse to see Janey again, should the need arise. "In fact," he added hurriedly, "I bumped into her in the rec this morning and bought her a coffee." He was covering himself in the unlikely event that someone who'd been at the recreation centre knew Susan and reported back to her on the glamorous woman whom her husband had entertained.

"I suppose we should try to get to know our neighbours a bit better. It's not as if we have an address book full of friends since we moved here," lamented Susan, edging to move on to another, far more important subject. "And don't forget that camping holiday that Ian and Meera keep banging on about – which, by the way, they have pushed back to after Easter, when it should be warmer given the Easter weather forecast. We might end up in the next tent to Graham and Janey, for all we know."

Andy very much doubted that, as did Susan. He relaxed back in his chair and felt brave enough to confirm that she had made him a far-too-milky tea. Well, his fault for letting her make that particular decision. More importantly, the immediate danger had passed. His shocking, guilty secret remained a secret. At least for the time being.

"Anyway. At my mother's last night," announced Susan.

Andy could sense the imminent arrival of something he would prefer not to arrive.

"She was very appreciative of the olive branch you offered to Brian. She thought you would never let him back into our house. So, well done, you!"

Andy was worried as to where this narrative was heading. "I'm sensing a 'but' here," he interjected.

"No. Not really. Not a 'but,'" said Susan. "A good suggestion from my mother, I thought. A halfway house which ticks all the boxes." Her coffee had now cooled sufficiently to excuse a pause in her report of her visit to her mother, during which Andy tried to imagine the worst that could happen. "Instead of Brian spending a few days here, Mum suggested that we all spend a few days with her up in the caravan. The Easter weekend. Make it into a real holiday. I thought it was a great suggestion. A cheap holiday, and God knows we all need a break, especially the children." She was struggling to imagine how Andy might react to all this, but hoped that she had finished on a strong point.

Andy was not sure just how many boxes this proposal of his mother-in-law's ticked, but it was certainly not the worst that could have happened, and it would probably do him good to get away from Ulstown for a few days, given what had taken place at work and with Janey. Time and space to think, and a night out enjoying a few drinks with Brian on neutral territory, might actually be something to look forward to.

Just then Joshua came careering around the corner and into the kitchen, pushing a rather battered British racing green toy Aston Martin under Andy's chair.

Andy reached down to ruffle his son's hair. "Not the worst suggestion in the world, I suppose, and certainly something for the kids to look forward to. Why not?" He smiled.

His smile was mirrored by the CEO, Susan Jones, who looked fresh and energised after getting approval from the chairman of the board. "I'll let Mum know. And I'll let you break the news to the children."

This was going to be a good weekend. *And about bloody time*, thought Andy. It was not a time to think about work or Janey. But he would. And he knew that.

HOLIDAYS!

Well, that wasn't so bad, thought Andy as he sat at a table in The Golden Fleece, just yards away from the quay at Wells-next-the-Sea. Brian was queuing patiently at the bar of the rather crowded pub, the busyness consistent with it being late in a Good Friday evening. *Too many children. Shouldn't be allowed in a public bar*, fumed Andy. Still, the drive up the A10 had been much quicker and easier than he'd feared. Maybe the heavily forecasted wind and rain had had something to do with the hesitant appetite of holidaymakers for travelling to the rather bracing Norfolk coast. Fine with him. And a couple of hours to ponder a rather quiet week just passed.

Not unusually for the week before a national holiday, work had been quiet, which was just what Andy needed after the tumult of the preceding week. It had become painfully clear to him that an uncomfortably high number of staff were treating him differently, at least in his eyes, to what he had been accustomed to before the company announcement. There had been nothing overtly malicious, but an undeniable reluctance from some to engage in anything more than the briefest of functional conversations. The warmth that typically came with good working relationships was missing with at least some of his colleagues. *And who could blame them*, thought Andy, *after his self-centred behaviour?* Fences needed mending, even if he was to leave Wright and Briggs by either the company's decision or his own. The industry was too small to withstand enemies or even a poor reputation. Post-Easter would provide the opportunity for him to turn the ship around and not exactly reinvent himself, but at least make good the damage he had done. A plan was needed, but a plan that could wait to be born until after this holiday.

As much as he had thought about work throughout the week before Easter, what was really front, foremost and all-enveloping in his thoughts had been, of course, Janey. Would he ever be able to forget the scent of her perfume? Her soft, welcoming thighs? The touch of her dress on his skin? The excitement of a simple kiss on his neck, and so many more erotic and beautiful memories? But why hadn't she texted him? He had checked his phone at least once every waking hour, to the point that Susan had picked up on this change of behaviour. "Work! There aren't half some bloody idiots there, considering all the years most of them spent at university," was Andy's excuse for his new telephonic vice. "Some of them are just looking for reassurance about their jobs. As if I can provide that!" Being texted by a mistress was probably at the very bottom of Susan's list of guesses as to why Andy kept his phone with him constantly, and his very next action after excusing his behaviour was to once again take the phone from his shirt pocket to check for new messages. Nothing. No new blue circles. Not even from the excuse that was work. *Will she ever get back to me? Perhaps I put her off too much when we met in the recreation centre. I didn't mean to say no. It was a no I said, but really it was a maybe. But would I really say maybe? Why am I so fucking crap with women?* he asked himself rhetorically.

"Andy," announced Brian loudly, whilst placing a pint of still-unsettled bitter on a beer mat to the right of his brother-in-law and trying to divert Andy's attention from something seemingly far in the distance, "you look as if you are miles away. Bloody nightmare at the bar. Much easier to get served when we all had Covid!" In front of Brian were his usual pint of lager and whisky chaser. *Some things never change*, thought Andy.

"Cheers, anyway," replied Andy, waiting for Brian to finish his chaser in one and then rush to raise his pint glass to meet Andy's.

"Your good health, and hopefully it won't be as long until we get to meet up next time. Cheers," was Brian's sincere hope.

We will see, was Andy's silent thought, but tonight he was happy to be where he was and with whom he was with.

"Anyway. How is my favourite brother-in-law? Mum tells me that things are not all going to plan. Some shitty things going on at work, or whatever Sue told her."

Andy had no wish to spoil both of their evenings by telling Brian the truth about what was going on at work. "Well, no shittier than what routinely happens from time to time. Managers not being able to manage, leading to them making staff redundant before realising that they then have to recruit to make good the skills and experience of the scientists they sacked. The usual merry-go-round."

"But I'm sure Mum said something about your job being at risk as well," countered Brian, who had never really bought into recognising people's sensitivities.

"Very unlikely," lied Andy, trying to keep up the line he had also spun to his wife in the rather-too-painful conversation he'd had with her in the week leading up to Easter. Susan had seemed even more worried about what might happen at Andy's workplace than did Andy himself, but he could not have wanted for a more supportive wife. She'd made it clear that she was there for him, and that they would find a way through this whatever might happen in the months to come. "I'm a chemist and so could be put on any project in the company. I'll be fine. But it's not looking so good for some of the others I work with." He was a little perplexed as to why Susan had passed on a different message to her mother, given how hard he had tried to reassure her of his position at Wright and Briggs. Perhaps she hadn't been completely taken in by his patter. It wouldn't be the first time. She could read him like a book.

"That's good to hear," replied Brian, who was already close to finishing his first pint.

Noticing this, Andy tried to catch up, taking an uncomfortably large gulp of his own drink. This could get messy. "But never mind about me. Susan tells me that things are going well at the bookmakers. Well done to you, Brian," he said, raising his glass to his drinking companion.

"Thanks, Andy." Brian smiled, planting his pint glass on the table. He had left a small amount of lager in the bottom to allow Andy to catch up. "But hats off to my good friend Ryssy. He has really gone out of his way to help me out. Really gone out on a limb to take me on at his bookies. Not many would take the risk he has. A good man." Once again Brian raised his glass, this time finishing what little was left in it. "And it has been really helpful and reassuring to move closer to Mum – and, of course, to you and Sue."

Andy shuddered. "Same again?" he asked, having rushed down what remained in his glass.

"If you insist. Cheers, Andy."

Queuing at the bar, trying to gain the attention of the clearly flustered bar staff, Andy pictured in his mind the bookmaker's where Brian worked. A notoriously seedy establishment on the very edge of town, nestled amongst the more down-at-heel charity shops and where shop rentals were cheapest. But fair play to the man, and indeed to the manager who had taken a risk on his friend: Brian had managed to hold down a permanent job for once in his life. What neither Andy nor many others knew, however, was that Brian was using the venue to push drugs from which his manager friend was taking more than a healthy cut from the proceeds.

"So. No need to risk dealing drugs now that you have a steady wage coming in, I imagine," suggested Andy, innocently enough, having rested his round of drinks at the table and taken his seat.

Brian downed his second whisky chaser of the night and took on board a healthy portion of his lager. "Have to be honest with you there, Andy," he replied dishonestly.

"A bit of a yes-and-no answer to that. Absolutely yes to not selling drugs. A mug's game, is that," he added, as if he were delivering a startling revelation. "But I am, if I am being totally honest, still partaking myself from time to time in the safety of my own flat. Just can't kick the weed, I'm afraid. So relaxing and it's not as if I'm causing any harm to anyone, but please don't tell Sue or Mum as they are bound to give me a hard time if they find out. Is that OK with you, Andy?" He added a full stop to his less-than-honest confession by draining his pint until it was half full – or, in Andy's eyes, half empty.

"Look, I have absolutely no experience in taking any sort of recreational drugs, so to speak," lied Andy. "So it's not as if I am in a position to pass judgement on you or anyone else for that matter, but I do agree that you should not tell Susan, as she is bound to tell your mother. Your secret is safe with me, Brian, as long as you don't go smoking that stuff in front of the kids."

"Cheers, Andy, completely understand," trilled Brian, raising what was left in his glass towards his drinking companion.

Andy clinked his glass rather clumsily. "But all bets are off if you fall back into your old ways. That really would be overstepping the mark in my view, as I would not be happy for our children to be around a drug dealer. You do understand that, don't you, Brian?" Andy finished with his serious face on.

"Absolutely. Absolutely, Andy. I can promise you now, hand on heart, that will never happen again. Same again?"

Andy still had almost half a pint of warm, flat real ale left in his glass, but he agreed to another so as not to appear too much of a lightweight. *He seems genuine enough*, he thought as he watched his allegedly reformed brother-in-law join the back of the throng around the bar. *But then again, he always did.* He resigned himself to giving Brian the benefit of the doubt this one last time, and also to the rather heavy night of drinking that no doubt lay ahead of them both.

The perverse thought that came to Andy towards the end of their session was undeniably a complete contradiction to the guidance he had given his brother-in-law just a few hours earlier. *Perhaps there's some serious money to be made here. Passing on samples of WRT743 for Brian to sell? Something to think about*, he mused as he used the door handle of the pub to steady his descent down two steps to the pathway. *Definitely something to think about.*

A good time was enjoyed by all that Good Friday night back in the family caravan. Even Susan was a little taken aback by Andy's bonhomie shining through on a night when the children were allowed to stay up long after their usual bedtime, and when her mother took centre stage retelling all her memories of Susan and Brian's childhoods. He also took with seemingly good humour the ridiculously cramped sleeping arrangements to which he usually took vocal exception. "Us two in a bed not big enough for one, and all three kids jammed into a one-bed hovel of a room. How will any of us get any sleep?" had been his more typical rhetorical question on such occasions in the past.

Retribution for an enjoyable evening arrived early the next morning for Andy, who very nearly didn't escape through the caravan door before vomiting up the previous night's enjoyment just shy of the Calor gas cylinder. Brian, who was sleeping on a reclining chair in the caravan's 'lounge', acknowledged the safe return of his rather sheepish-looking brother-in-law, but was unable to fully suppress a knowing smile.

Never again will I allow myself to get in such a state. Never, was Andy's fervent pledge to himself as he returned to his bed and lay staring at the flimsy ceiling, which was far too close to his still-toxic, supine body.

Ulstown, 27 Miles –

What's there not to like? mused Andy, listening to his choice of music in an otherwise quiet family car. *A bright and sunny Easter Monday morning, and within the hour I will be back at home, sitting in the garden and enjoying the sun. I will start off by doing absolutely nothing, to be followed later by some more nothing. No chores, no work, no even thinking about work, although I might just spend some time thinking about that woman who lives just across the road.*

For all, the Easter weekend had been a great success. All in the car were in good moods, and even the children had behaved well, despite spending the holiday having to take it in turns to sleep on an inflatable bed which refused to stay inflated. Maybe it had something to do with some not-so-subtle bribery involving the supply of Easter eggs. The outcast of the family had once again been good company, and had gone the extra mile in entertaining the children on a very wet Saturday. Even the mother-in-law had kept her waspish tongue confined to a locked drawer buried very deeply somewhere in her mind. So it was with this relaxed feeling of being comfortable with his world that Andy indicated left and gradually steered into the inside lane of the dual carriageway with the intention of coming off the A10 at Junction 6 and the road to Ulstown.

It was Susan who was the one to spoil the moment. "Oh! And I forgot to say," she said, in a tone of voice which suggested that she had not forgotten anything at all, but had rather been waiting for the best moment to break the news. Andy in a good mood. All the family locked up together in the car. "Here goes," she announced, almost audibly. "I bumped into Janey early last week, outside the house. She looked immaculate as usual, and I looked as if I had been dragged through a hedge after the effort of running down to the shop to buy bread which I had forgotten to buy on the Sunday. Anyway. She said how much she'd enjoyed talking to you about dreams – but of course! – and that she and Graham are very much up for the camping trip. What a turn-up. I couldn't see her ever wanting to go on such a holiday, but I suppose we don't really know her, do we?"

Andy was both glad that he wasn't blushing and relieved that he was not expected to answer a rhetorical question.

"So, of course, I said we'd see them there if the dates work for us." Susan was expecting some sort of negative response to this from Andy.

He paused for careful thought. "I must say, although I really don't know Janey very well – at least, not as well as you know her – I do find it difficult to picture her in a tent." (Although that was actually what he was doing at the end of his sentence.) "And, I would add, the same goes for Graham, although perhaps to a lesser extent."

Susan had been expecting something along the lines of 'Never in a million years' or 'More fool them, but we won't be there.' "So are we going or not?" was her not unreasonable question. "What should I tell Meera so that she can sort something out with Ian?"

"Depends on the dates, I suppose."

"You are happy for us to go if the dates work?"

"In principle, I suppose," was Andy's less-than-definitive response.

"That sounds pretty much like a 'yes' to me," said a visibly surprised Susan. "I'll sort it out with Meera, then." She gave Andy time for a right to reply. None was forthcoming, which she took as recognition that the decision had been made and the discussion was over. "Job done." Anyway, she doubted that Janey would stick to her word, and suspected that they would probably end up going camping with just Meera and Ian, which was absolutely fine with her. At worst, Janey and Graham would end up staying in some nearby hotel and thus avoid any perceived hardships. Again, absolutely fine with Susan.

Meanwhile, Andy was grappling silently with Janey's surprising willingness to go camping. An ulterior motive? Almost certainly. He couldn't decide if he should be excited or absolutely terrified at the prospect of going camping with both his wife, his lover and her husband, one of whom would likely pester him for drugs.

The thought of blackmail had now first appeared in Andy's consciousness.

WORK

Don't you just hate going back to work after your holidays? You work just that little bit harder before your holiday to clear your desk, and so arrive a tad bit frazzled on your first day at the beach. It takes you a few days to relax and get into the swing of things – Yeah! This is the life. I'll have some more of this, thank you very much – *and then all of a sudden, you are back at work again with a pile of paper in front of you. The back of the tosser who sits in front of you all day long has become even more annoying. The screaming, high-pitched voice of Debbie from accounts has gone up at least a semitone, and Roger from sales is still seemingly unable to quite clear all the dried-up snot from his nostrils.*

Welcome back to work! Next holiday? Only another four months to go.

Andy was not just a little aggrieved that the good weather had extended through to his first day back at work. "Where were all these blue skies on Saturday and Sunday?" he asked an empty car on its unerring way to Harlow and work.

No one replied. Still, might be a good omen for the start of a working week in which he was going to start afresh and rebuild all the fences through which he had crashed through just a few weeks before.

Harlow, 32 Miles —

It is the way of scientists to design experiments to affirm or cast doubt upon proposed hypotheses. Scientists in business, with bosses and shareholders to satisfy, are also expected to deliver on objectives within agreed budgets. At Andy's level, this boiled down to proposing goals and timelines that senior management would approve of and be willing to fund. So his world was one of lists, agendas, minutes, PowerPoint presentations, and action points. And he loved it! To him this bureaucracy represented empowerment and accountability. To senior management it was a tool to provide clarity as to whom to blame when it all went wrong. *What better way to start afresh than to come up with some new personal objectives?* mused Andy as he carefully overtook a police car travelling marginally under the speed limit.

Objective one: turn the other cheek. He'd do a bit of growing up and ingratiate himself with reports and senior management alike. This would take time, but it was important. It was also important to stay in this job for as long as possible, if only to be able to look for another job whilst still in employment.

Objective two: re-energise the WRT743 project. Making that a success with the goal of being able to out-license the drug to another company would not only contribute to objective one, but add to his CV. Even more important, if through his illegal drug-taking he had been fortunate enough to stumble across a compound which had the beneficial effects of a psychedelic drug but not the hallucinations or bad trips, it could potentially represent a breakthrough drug in neurology and a sure-fire ticket to a successful career whatever his next move might be. So, he would carefully steer the project team around to carrying out the experiments that might prove that WRT743 had psychedelic properties. That was very important.

Objective three: a personal objective. Success with objective two would provide a justification for synthesising more batches of WRT743. That would mean more vials for personal use – if ever, whatever and whomever that might involve.

Probably best that I don't write all that down. One for the internal hard drive only. Andy smiled and congratulated himself on the clarity of his thought. *Sounds like a good plan, although perhaps the last objective should be considered a stretch goal.* Pushing the button on objective three was something that he was far too nervous to contemplate at this time. It was not just another objective on which to deliver, as achieving it would reach far beyond any work consequences and change his life forever. He was just not sure if he wanted to make that decision just yet; to risk criminal activity. *But if not now, then when?*

Harlow, 12 Miles —

His phone made a sound. Andy glanced over to the central armrest to see who was the sender of the text.

Janey! Involuntarily he swerved towards the phone, only snapping out of switching lanes following a blare from the horn of a car travelling in the inside lane, whose driver was doubting the competence and parentage of his fellow motorist that morning. Andy regained his composure and lifted up the phone to view the message through the corner of one eye; something he hated doing, but there was no way he was going to wait until he parked up at work to find out what Janey had to say.

Hi. So I hear we are all going camping. Who would have thought that little old me would ever go camping? But I would do anything for a chance to go dancing! Don't forget, you still owe me that answer to my offer. See you soon. XXX

Andy could feel his heart pounding. Was this the heart attack he considered inevitable? *Don't be so stupid, you pathetic little man*, he told himself. She hadn't forgotten him. She hadn't run away. And there was no threat of blackmail, at least not yet. But what the bloody hell was he going to say in reply? He pulled up sharply in a parking space as far from his office as he could find.

Hi. Speak to you soon. Andy.

It had taken him the final twenty minutes of his drive into work to come up with a six-word reply, but the words and thoughts swirling around his mind – *Yes, No, Maybe, I don't know* – didn't really read very well.

DEATH

Maybe now would be a good time to introduce myself, and for you to find out just who has been writing all these bloody italics.

My friends and family call me Mary. The junk mail and bills you will find near my front door in the morning that are addressed to me will be labelled Ms Mary Elias, and now and again will be more accurate: Mrs Mary Elias. Professionally I am known as Detective Sergeant Elias; DS Elias for short, although my work colleagues often use alternative nomenclature. But you don't need to know all these names – too much information. My most important role in life is as the mother of my two grown-up daughters – not that they much need a mother these days – and the grandmother of my adorable little Alex. Oh, and I nearly forgot: I am married to Twm, who retired far too early – in my view – and now spends his days pretending to do things to our lovely semi in a quiet village just north of Harlow. But of course, I am not being fair to my dear husband, as I have a lot to thank him for, even if that does not include the arch in the garden, which is still not straight. Aside from the stresses that visit me at work from time to time, ours is a good life.

What do I look like? Well, if such things are important to you, I'm quite tall, I suppose, at nearly five foot ten inches, which can sometimes be useful in my job. Please do me the favour of not asking what my metric height is. Or even my weight, as I seem to be running a little to fat these days. Maybe I am looking forward too much to joining Twm in early retirement. Hair? Never liked it. Straight, greasy and lifeless. It wouldn't be unreasonable to call myself a brunette who, these days, chooses to keep her hair pretty short; something that is getting harder and harder to achieve with my legs these days, I can tell you. You will usually find me in trousers and comfy shoes. Well, I won't see fifty again, don't you know? Could you pick me out from a crowd based on that description? Probably not, which is absolutely fine with me.

Despite my arguing to the contrary, the editor-cum-agent of this little book I have written (with myself in a starring role) has suggested that I say something about my past, as it apparently provides important context as to what unfolds in the chapters to come. And I suppose she is right. But please don't blame me for having to read my life story if you choose not to skip the below.

Janey might tell you that she had an unfortunate start to her life, but my misfortune did not arrive with my birth but much later, and, looking back, was really no one's fault but my own, as much as I argued to the contrary at the time. I was born in a hospital in a Welsh Valley town to respected and responsible parents. As the firstborn, I suppose I had a pretty typical upbringing and was a pretty typical child as a result.

Wholly unremarkable. That was, until all those teenage hormones started swirling around, which made me take exception to the boundaries set by my chapel-going, strictly religious parents – or so they appeared to me at the time. Not so much as a 'bloody this' or 'bloody that' was allowed to be spoken around our house, and may God strike you down where you stood if ever the F-word passed your lips. Those boundaries were meant to stop me hanging around with my smoking, drinking and fornicating friends; guidelines in which any responsible parent would wrap up their children, as I have since done with my own offspring. But rebellious Mary Jones was having none of it. Few, other than my selfish arsehole of a boyfriend, were surprised when I became pregnant at just seventeen. Surprised or not, my parents could not cope with the shame of housing an unmarried teenage daughter and I was packed off to the other side of the world to spare them their blushes – times were very different in those days. Off to North Wales, to the spinster sister of my seemingly cold-as-ice mother. And, you know, as harsh as it all sounds now, it was the best thing that ever happened to me.

My Aunty Rose was the sweetest woman you could ever wish to meet. Some ten years older than my mother, and long past her men-chasing days. And, boy, did she have some stories to tell about her men! But there was no husband to show for her troubles, nor even a live-in lover. But there were no regrets; no tragic, long-lost loves. She was as content with her life as my parents were bitter and twisted about theirs. She owned her own little, chaotic house and meandering garden leading down to a spring stream. A job as a curator in a local museum was as much for social reasons as it was for earning money. Rose was the saviour of my life and that of my new daughter Ruth, with my aunt being the first person Ruth got to meet, as she was the one to hold my hand at the birth.

Thanks to Rose's wisdom, boundless energy, and optimism, our unconventional little family thrived. I became a police community support officer – yes, a plastic policewoman! – and we managed to find a way for at least one of us to be at home to look after Ruth. Before we knew it, Ruth was crying through her first day at school and I, much to the delight of my hopelessly proud aunt, became WPC Jones. Whatever would my old friends down south have said about Mary Jones being a rozzer? But they never did get to find out what happened to their once-upon-a-time close friend, because I had deliberately lost touch with them all, as I had with my parents. They never met Ruth. Why should they be granted that unearned privilege?

And after all that, I got to meet and then marry my man, Twm Elias. Or, should I say, Police Sergeant Elias. My aunt gave me away at our wedding. We were nothing if not unconventional. And I cried for weeks when Twm, Ruth and I followed my husband's new posting and left for a new life in England. It might have been a four-hour drive to my old home by that spring stream in North Wales, but it would have had to be much, much further away than that to stop me going back to see my dear old Aunty Rose as often as I could. Which I still do to this day, but now to tend to her grave and tell her stories about my life in Harlow. About how her little wild child became a successful career policewoman and is now a detective sergeant – and she's not stopping there! About how her family has grown with the arrival of another daughter, Bethan, and, more recently, a grandson; the little whirlwind called Alex. How Rose would have doted on him, and he on her.

So you see, I have been so very lucky in my life, and all thanks to a little old lady who lived by a stream and gave so much of her life to turn around mine. Thank you, Aunty Rose. You will never be forgotten.

"Do you think we should offer them tea and biscuits?" suggested Susan, who was busy cleaning a kitchen surface she had cleaned not an hour earlier.

"Maybe offer them tea and coffee, but not biscuits. This is not a coffee morning with your friends. And anyway, why do you think there will be more than one of them?" answered Andy.

Susan turned to face her husband, waving a dishcloth in the air. "Well, you always see two of them visiting houses on the TV."

Andy considered this remark unworthy of a response, and instead peered intently through the kitchen window to see if their expected visitor(s) would appear on time. He could not see anyone, so they were both surprised to hear an urgent knock on the door, not least because they had a doorbell. Andy opened the front door.

"Good morning. I'm DS Elias. You should have been contacted as to my coming along this morning and the reason why I am here. My apologies for being a little late." ID was presented, albeit with insufficient time for anyone to have been able to validate the profession of the owner.

"Not a problem. Please come through." Andy waved the alleged policewoman into the living room and then directed her to the lone armchair.

"Would you like some tea or coffee?" asked Susan, transfixed by the sensible shoes worn by at least this particular law enforcement officer.

"No. That's fine, but thank you," was Elias's stock answer to such offers. She had a bladder unbecoming of a police officer and so avoided any beverages. However, she always accepted a biscuit or two. But none were on offer today, it would seem.

"How did you get here? I didn't see a police car. Do you live locally?" asked Andy, trying to make small talk.

"I parked just up the road at the entrance to the estate. Nothing more likely to get the net curtains twitching than the arrival of a police car, so I thought I would spare you the awkward conversations with any nosy neighbours you might have. My usual car is out of action and I had to use a marked car, unfortunately."

Susan and Andy took up seats on the sofa facing Elias and smiled at the gentle humour.

"Before we start, just to confirm. You are Andrew and Susan Jones of 6 Malvern Drive and, Mrs Jones, you are the sister of Brian Tyler of 37A High Street, Ulstown?"

Andy was pretty sure he could pick up a Welsh accent. Maybe North Wales?

"Yes," answered Susan. "The children are with my mother this morning." Immediately she wondered why she had offered such superfluous information.

"Thanks. And apologies for not shaking your hands. We have been advised not to, for obvious reasons." Elias adjusted herself in her seat, pulled out a small notebook from her briefcase and adopted a more serious expression. "This must be a very troubling time for you both and I will do my best to avoid adding to your grief, but I'm sure you understand why I'm here."

"Do you have any idea who killed Brian?" interjected Andy, rather jumping the gun. "It's been nearly three weeks since he died."

"We have some strong leads that we are following up, but I'm afraid that we can't disclose anything until someone is charged."

"Of course. Completely understand," replied Susan, keen to stop her husband talking and let the officer do her work. A firm look was sent over to her husband to reinforce her wish for radio silence from Andy.

Elias paused and adjusted her body to directly face Susan. "OK. We understand from the statement that your mother, Sylvia Tyler, gave that you were also both with Brian over the Easter weekend and last saw him on the morning of Monday the 18th April. Is that correct?"

"That's right, isn't it, Andy?" replied Susan, now seemingly keen to involve her husband in the conversation.

He nodded silently in agreement.

"And you did not have any contact with Brian after that morning, whether through meeting him, or by phone, letter or social media?"

"Nothing at all from Brian that we are aware of," answered Susan.

Similar answers in the negative were given to further questions regarding whether Brian had shared with them any concerns or fears about work, friends or money issues. Elias scribbled in her notebook.

"Brian did tell me that he was very happy in his new job at the bookmaker's. His boss seems to have been a big help," said Andy, remembering their discussion at the pub.

"Were you aware that Brian was using the premises to sell drugs with the approval of the owner, Mr Ryszard Ivanov, who was taking a share of the proceeds?" asked the detective.

The shocked expressions on Andy and Susan's faces suggested that this news came as a genuine surprise.

Susan was first to respond. "Well, no. Not at all." She shared a sideways glance with her husband. "I – well, we all thought that he had turned a corner after getting out of prison. New flat. New friendship circle far away from all his troubled friends back in Birmingham, and, of course, the new job. He certainly fooled us, then. But whatever he did or didn't do, what possible justification could there be for anyone to break into his flat and murder him?"

Susan was doing her very best to manage her emotions, but she was now clearly struggling. She reached for a tissue which she had tucked into her long cardigan sleeve which had been put there precisely in anticipation of becoming upset. Andy rubbed his hand gently across her shoulder and neck as a sign of support and recognition of her grief. He had gone out of his way to comfort her since her brother's death, which was something that did not come easily to him, but he was genuinely concerned about how distressed Susan had become over the past few weeks at random moments and seemingly harmless events.

Elias had come to know how to anticipate and manage such difficult meetings, often through resigned smiles, nodding in sympathy, and soothing hands placed on arms regardless of the non-touching directive they were supposed to be working under. She was grateful that she was not allowed to share the details of the horrific scene that the forensics team had helped her to construct of the most likely way in which Brian had met his death.

At this point in the investigation, the evidence pointed to Brian letting at least two people into his flat just before midnight on a Tuesday – the 26th April, to be precise. The assumption, therefore, was that he knew his assailants. The state of both his living room and his body suggested that he had put up a concerted struggle. He had been stabbed several times with two small blades, the fatal injury likely being the severing of a femoral artery, leading to dramatic blood loss. That Brian's death was violent was borne out by two neighbours independently calling the police to report worrying sounds coming from Brian's flat. Officers arrived some ten minutes later to find an open front door and Brian's body lying next to a broken sofa bed in a large pool of his own blood. Enquiries in the neighbourhood had failed to provide any information as to who visited Brian's flat that evening.

"I am so sorry for your loss, Mrs Jones," was Elias's attempt to comfort Susan. No need for any touching on this occasion, she reasoned. "Our suspicion at this point in our investigation is that Brian's death was drug-related but, of course, that remains to be determined. We will keep you informed as our investigations proceed."

What Elias could not disclose at this time was that forensics had been able to place both Ryszard Ivanov and his brother Alexander at the scene of the murder through fingerprints and blood DNA, although the latter was still to be confirmed. The current thinking in the investigating team was that Brian had not been handing over what the Ivanovs thought they were due. An argument had presumably followed, which Brian lost. The brothers had form, with previous convictions for drug-related violence, and so the police were pretty convinced that they knew who had killed Brian. How the detective wished she could share this encouraging news.

"Is there anything else you would like to say that might be relevant to the case?" asked the policewoman.

Silence from both interviewees and a shake of the head from Susan confirmed that there was nothing else they could think of.

"Well, if something comes to mind later then please feel free to contact me directly," prompted Elias, handing her card to Susan. She then closed her notebook, returned it to her briefcase and stood up. "Thank you for your time this morning and, once again, sorry for your loss. As I said, we will be in touch when we have something worth updating you with. I can assure you that we are throwing everything into this investigation."

"And thank you, officer." Susan smiled. "Yes, please do keep us informed, and of course we will be around if there are any other questions you would like to ask."

Andy and Susan walked behind the detective to the front door, which Andy opened to allow their visitor to leave. The Joneses then retreated to the sanctuary of their kitchen and eager fortification with alcohol. There were very few mornings if any when Andy treated himself to a measure from his bottle of ten-years-old-and-counting Irish single-malt whiskey, and rarer still was Susan breaking into her pink grapefruit gin from many Christmases past.

"She seemed to know what she was doing," suggested Andy to his wife, who was managing to get two hands around a small tumbler. They were seated facing each other across the kitchen table.

"Who knows?" answered a rather resigned Susan. "I just can't get over that he lied to us again. I wonder if my mother knows. Perhaps she knew all along. I will let her bring up the subject. Nothing we can do or say is going to change anything, anyway. How did we allow ourselves to be taken in by the little bugger yet again?" She sniffed and reached again for her sleeve and the now-tattered tissue.

"Who are we to try to understand what your brother was going through? He was still addicted, both to drugs and to the easy money that could be made through them, although clearly this time it turned out not to be so easy." Andy was trying to reassure her, but feared he was actually making things worse. "Come on. Let's go down The Royal Tavern for lunch. I've got the whole day off from work and your mother has the kids until two. We've got over two hours to spare before we become parents again."

"What a good idea. Is Brian really worth all this pain after what he has done to himself and to us? But I suppose he was my brother."

Andy could not and did not provide an answer.

The first time I got to meet the main man! Our hero. And I must say that he seemed like a very nice gent indeed. In fact, a very pleasant couple altogether. Who would ever have guessed that everything could change so very quickly?

So sad to hear of your news. Sue must be devastated. I guess that means we won't be going dancing again any time soon. Maybe meet up again in the recreation centre for a coffee? XXX

That was the early-Saturday-morning text Andy read just before he put on his second sock. Janey was fishing. He was relieved that Susan had left the bedroom to mediate in the usual Saturday breakfast arguments. Time to ruminate on the thrill and anxiety of receiving a message from his lover.

He had used the not unreasonable excuse of his brother-in-law's death to avoid contacting Janey as promised in the text he'd sent her soon after the Easter holiday. Much to his relief, she had been the one to overcome the impasse. No need for Andy to torture himself with taking the initiative and making a decision. But here was a decision that was, unavoidably, his call: agree to meet Janey, or make his excuses and walk away for good. The nagging thought that she could 'out' him to Susan convinced him that it would be sensible to at least maintain good relations with the woman who had the power to make things very uncomfortable indeed for him. *Whatever happens next, I must keep her sweet. But would she really risk two marriages and his family to get hold of some mystery drug?* Probably not, but Janey was unpredictable enough for him to at least tread very carefully. *What the fuck have I done?* was his rhetorical question once again.

OK. See you there.

Too cold thought Andy.

Great. Nice to hear from you again. Sorry I have not contacted you before.

Too submissive.

Why not? See you about 10.30.

Which was the text he sent.

He didn't expect a reply, but that did not stop him checking his phone continually, right up to the point at which he shooed the children off to their swimming lesson and walked down the recreation centre's main stairway to the café. He could see Janey smiling at him from the same table they had shared earlier that month. He sat down, relieved to be able to place his freshly purchased tea opposite her coffee and avoid any further pain from holding onto the cup containing the superheated floating teabag.

"I thought it was my turn to pay?" were his first words, having noticed that Janey had already bought her coffee.

"Like I said last time, you can pay next time," was her quick-fire reply.

She was not quite as perfect as his memory of her from that night. How could she be? No one could be as flawless as the woman in the memory he had replayed time after time in the weeks since they had last met. He was sure he could see some downy hair under her nose. There was an angry spot on her cheek which she had not quite managed to hide with a combination of concealer and foundation.

Her scent was more high-street chemist body wash than expensive perfume. But the body was still all there; the body that he had imagined beneath him whenever he had made love to Susan since that adulterous night. Janey was the personification of Andy's ideal of what a woman should be: a wholly unrealistic expectation born of inexperience and ignorance, and one to which Susan was not held up to, as she was the obtainable girlfriend and wife, not the perfect, unobtainable woman.

"How's Sue now? Must have come as a great shock to you both," commiserated Janey.

What does she care about Susan, given what she has been doing with her husband? thought Andy. "Good days and bad days, I would say. Can't see her getting back to something like normal for a good while yet, at least not before the funeral. But proper closure? Maybe not until someone is locked up for this. You can imagine her thinking she could bump into his killer just by walking through town. Not nice." He risked taking a first sip of his tea. Not a good idea.

"How terrible. Only time can heal, I suppose – not that I have ever experienced anything like that, of course. I have had a very fortunate life."

Something they could both agree on. Andy smiled. *OK. Get on with it. What have you got to tell me? Why have you invited me here? Please tell me you have found a guilt-free way for me to shag you stupid every week without risking my house, wife and career*, were his impatient yet silent questions and wishes.

"So. Andy. Let me start by being very selfish and also, maybe a little callous and thoughtless. Being insensitive is one of my worst faults, or so I have been told. But I'm afraid I can't help asking you this question. With Brian now having passed away," how much nicer is that phrase than having to say that someone died, "I am assuming that there is no longer any chance of us going out dancing again." Janey surprised even herself by feeling a twinge of embarrassment at how self-centred, how very selfish her question was.

Andy had anticipated this question coming up, although not so early in their conversation. "Well, you have asked me two questions there, haven't you? First, does Brian's death mean that there are no supplies left of that drug we tried a few weeks ago?" He could sense her impatience building. She had expected a straight 'yes' or 'no' rather than a rambling monologue. But he was not going to rush his well-rehearsed script. "Second, are we going to go out dancing again?" He paused to make sure he could remember all of his lines. "As for the first point, I sort of lied. Brian actually put nine vials in my pocket." He thought an unusual, odd number sounded more believable. "God knows what he was thinking of. Maybe he was high. He was certainly pissed. Now for the second point." He thought it best not to let Janey in on the reality, which was that he had given her an untested drug which he had stolen from a pharmaceutical company. He paused again. This was the difficult one. The impossible one to answer, at least for Andy.

Janey continued to smile thinly at her hoped-for new drug pusher.

"I told you before when we last met how difficult this was for me to decide on. Nothing would give me greater pleasure than the chance to repeat that evening we spent together. It was really that special. But—"

Janey cut him off. "Yes, yes, yes," she responded rather impatiently. "I know all the buts and the why nots and the terrible regrets. You told me all this over the last cup of coffee, and they are some of the buts I have as well. This is not all one way, you know. You are not the only one with something to lose. I would be taking risks as well, although – and I do at least appreciate this difference – Graham and I don't have kids. Still, the bottom line is that we would both be taking a big risk. We both have something important to lose if we're ever found out. Which we won't be, I hasten to add. If you like, we have each other's balls in our hands. It is not as if one of us is single with nothing to lose. What am I trying to say?" Janey paused to gather her thoughts for a concluding statement. "It is not in either of our interests to tell anyone what we are doing, and it is in both of our interests to be as careful and discreet as humanly possible to stop anyone finding out. Am I being clear here, Andy? This is not love. This is not even an affair. We are just going dancing on our very own private dance floor."

She makes it sound so easy. So guilt-free. Sex without consequences. No strings. At least she has not threatened me with the B-word to get what she wants. Not yet, thought Andy as he quickly reconsidered his options. In his mind it came down to three very basic choices. He switched his mind to bullet-point mode.

Bullet point one: drink his tea quickly, and say thanks but no thanks in the politest way possible, and walk away.

If she attempted blackmail, then he would just deny everything. She had no proof and who would believe that beautiful, precious little Janey would ever lie down with the likes of him. Not Susan. Surely not Susan. But could he be sure?

Bullet point two; he could just supply her with the drug without the sex as a quid pro quo. But what would be the benefit to him for taking up that option other than getting her off his back and keeping her quiet? No sex and still the chance that he could be blackmailed if he stopped supplying her with the drug.

Bullet point three: just agree to her wishes and go along for the ride whilst pushing the guilt into the bottom of his stomach and crossing his fingers and toes in the hope that they'd never be caught and Andy not rumbled at work when taking out the drug.

So really it came down to two very basic choices: walk, or agree to her wishes. Still, he wanted clarification on bullet point three. "OK. Hypothetical question. Let's just say, for argument's sake, not committing anything here…"

Could the man be any wetter? Janey asked herself. *Is he going to need even more reassurance than I have been able to provide so far? What more does he bloody want? A legally binding contract*?

"If we did carry on what we have started," he wanted to avoid having to use the word 'sex', "where would we… uh… Where would we do it? Surely not round your house?"

"Why not?" answered Janey, trying to adopt a bewildered expression. "Graham is often out in the evenings with his work and golf, although perhaps we might want to use the bed next time," she added, trying to lighten the tone of the conversation.

Andy's subsequent smile wasn't convincing anyone. "Around your house? What will the neighbours say when they see me going in and out of your house all the time?" he worried.

"We are neighbours. What could be more normal? If you want a cover story for Sue, just say that we are talking about dreams. Better still, what about this for a plan?" urged Janey, becoming very pleased with herself at the idea that had just arrived in her mind courtesy of the caffeine infusion. "We both would like to learn the piano. Why don't we get Graham to teach us and, as only we have a piano, you could then come round and practise when Graham's not in? You're unlikely to learn much about the piano but there would be other benefits." She could see that she was wasting her time with her attempts at humour. "Sorted." She was making it as easy as possible for Andy to make the hard decision. "Unless they catch us with your pants around your ankles and my legs in the air, no one will ever know. Everyone can say what they like but – let's be honest here, Andy – who would ever believe that you are shagging me?"

Andy looked around nervously to see if anyone had heard Janey's latest profanity and maybe actually believe that she would open her legs for him. *Bloody hell. That woman can be convincing*, he thought. After listening to her hastily drawn up plan, it almost felt like it would be insulting for him to turn down her offer. Sex for drugs was going to be their verbal contract.

He felt someone pulling at the shoulder of his jacket. "Dad, Dad. Josh and Rachel are waiting for you outside the changing rooms. Hurry up," pleaded Sophie.

The colour drained from Andy's face. "Sophie. Is it that time already?" A glance at the clock directly above the untouched vegan sausage roll and pasty display counter confirmed that it was indeed. He struggled to collect his thoughts and what he should do now. "Silly Daddy. Can you run up to the changing room and tell them I will be up there in a minute? Two minutes. Thanks for helping out Daddy."

Sophie, as ever, did what she was told, but the moment in which Andy had felt convinced and reassured enough for him to say, "Yes, I will," had passed, and both he and Janey sensed this. Nothing more likely to interfere with extramarital sex than children.

He stood up in front of his still-full plastic cup of tea. "Janey. What you say sounds so convincing. So easy. So without consequences. All rather like meeting for coffee in the recreation centre. But whatever you have and could say. However straightforward you make it all sound, there will always be risks. And we haven't even talked about the guilt." *Not that the latter is likely to be of any great concern to Janey*, he thought.

There was no smile from Janey on listening to Andy's thoughts. He even thought that there was a hint of anger in her eyes.

"Look. As you can see, I have to go. I'm not saying yes, but I'm not saying no either. Give me a little time to think all this through – after all, this is the first time I have heard about this piano excuse; if you really mean that, of course. Give me some more time and I will get back to you."

"How much more time do you want, Andy?" asked a clearly impatient Janey, who managed to avoid swearing but clearly revealed that anger had now displaced a reasoned, persuasive approach. "We fucked over a month ago. In fact, it was so long ago that I think I have forgotten if it was any good or not." The very temporary swearing ban was breached. "I'm sorry, Andy," she added quickly, moving her head from side to side in an attempt to reinforce her apology. "No excuse for me to have a go at you. It is a big decision for you to make. I do understand that. I really do." The unspoken inference was that it was not a big decision for Janey. "But I am so frustrated. So frustrated that we can't have another night – and another night, and another night – like we had last month."

Andy waited patiently for her to make the next move. He wasn't going to swallow the line that she wanted another night with him. It was the drug who she wanted to be with for another night and another night.

"I tell you what, Andy. We are all going off camping in a few weeks' time. A few weeks to make up your mind. I'm sure we can find a quiet space to talk it all through, in some muddy field or riverbank." She wondered again if it would have been better to exchange the camping holiday as a chance to screw some more drugs out of him for a meeting in a more normal place. "I hope I have been able to convince you that there's not much of a downside to our deal, but plenty of upsides. Lots and lots of upsides. For us both."

Andy's answer was a wordless smile and nodding, almost resigned, agreement to Janey's suggestion. He unconsciously maintained the former whilst walking up the stairs to the changing rooms. *Have been rather backed into a corner there. But perhaps she really has found a way for all this to work. At least she didn't bring up the B-word, although there is no doubt that she has a temper. But then again, what is there for her to blackmail me with? Pregnancy? Fuck! We didn't use contraception.* "Fuck, fuck, fuck," he muttered to himself as he neared the entrance to the boy's changing room to see Joshua with his hair sticking out from his head at right angles from using too much shampoo.

SAYING GOODBYE

Everyone agreed that it was rather a good turnout. A surprising number of the Tylers from the Midlands had made the effort to travel to Ulstown Crematorium, together with some old friends of Susan and her mother from when they'd lived there. Sylvia was particularly grateful for the respect shown to her little family, and was understandably emotional throughout the day. The child should not perish before the parent. It was not supposed to happen that way.

Susan kept it all together for most of the just over half hour-long ceremony, up until the point when Brian's coffin was lowered through the floor and, presumably, sent off to the furnace. "Why do they have such medieval contraptions in these places? It's as if he was being taken to hell," she gently sobbed to Andy, who held her close enough to prevent others from witnessing his wife's distress.

Andy dared to think that, if there was such a place, it was surely where Brian was going. They were both relieved that the children were at home with a babysitter whom the Stevenses had recommended.

The mourners filed slowly out of the chapel, nodding their thanks to the minister for a respectful and mercifully short service. They then reassembled in the covered passageway adjacent to the chapel, to be immediately replaced in the pews by the next funeral's entourage. They kept a tight ship down at Ulstown Crematorium. Here was a chance for Susan and her mother to meet all who had come to say goodbye to Brian. None of his old friends from Birmingham were there, thankfully. A few whom Susan did not recognise turned out, when she took the time to talk to them, to be local friends. She preferred to think of them as friends from outside of his drug-addiction circle, but was content to simply not know. A few of her and Andy's old friends from Harlow had made the effort to attend, and Susan was genuinely delighted to see them. All of the time that they were in the passageway, she darted glances around to see if her mother was coping with both the occasion and being in company. It was not often that Sylvia got out of her apartment these days. The Tylers from back home were taking good care of their own, which reassured Susan. Her only disappointment was that there were none of her close friends from her university days. Perhaps now was the time to consider those days long gone. She was no longer a young woman.

And Andy? Busy shaking hands and thanking all those present. Every short conversation was ended with an invitation to join the family in a room they had hired in the church hall. "There will be nibbles and drinks," he announced many times. As he finished saying those very words to someone who had announced, to his surprise, that she was Susan's Aunt Joan, he noticed *her* for the first time. Standing next to Graham, who was towering over a congregation of grey-haired old women who seemed to surround him, was someone who made Andy's heart skip a beat. Spectacular. Mercilessly sexy. Dressed in black, and a magnet for the eyes of every straight man who could risk staring. And she knew it. Yes, Janey knew it all right. She loved playing to the gallery. *And I am walking away from that?* wondered Andy to himself. He thought it not unreasonable for him to approach the Robinses and thank them for making the effort to come to the cremation.

"But of course we would be here," gushed Janey. "Meera came around to tell us the date and the arrangements, and here we are. Such a sad occasion, given how young Brian was. How is Sue bearing up?"

"Not so bad, all things considered," was the pat answer Andy had used each time he had been asked that very same question today.

"Yes. So sorry for your loss, old man," whispered Graham, stepping behind his wife to shake his friend's hand. "Not good times."

"Will you be coming over to the church hall for nibbles and drinks?" asked Andy of his neighbours.

"I'm afraid I can't, old man. All hands-on deck back at the surgery, but Janey's planning to go, aren't you, Janey?" said Graham.

"Of course, as long as you can drop me off, dear." Janey smiled, to her husband. She then turned on her smile to Andy. "I will see you there, Andy."

He shook both of their hands, as he had done with the rest of the congregation. Provocatively, Janey pulled her fingers gently across his palm as he relinquished his grip. "We'll talk later," whispered Janey to her prey taking advantage of Graham being accosted by two of the grey-haired women.

Andy smiled and nodded, seemingly incapable of talking.

And she kept her promise. Up to that point at the nibbles-and-drinks reception, Andy had busied himself by making hushed small talk with as many people as possible, including Ian who, much to the obvious disgust of his wife, had turned up without socks and wearing an untucked shirt which dropped below his beaten-up jacket. That was probably the most difficult conversation Andy had experienced that day, trying to engage separately with a husband and wife who were clearly not talking to one another. *Isn't marriage just great?* he reflected as he walked away from the feuding couple and into the path of the black-stockinged Janey. He hoped that she had not noticed him staring at her slender ankles and how they introduced the legs that rose up to disappear beneath her knee-length, tight-fitting black dress. But she had noticed. Women always do.

"A very pleasant reception, Andy," she observed. "I must say that I am not just a little surprised at the quality of the food. Didn't think that the caterers you have used was up to this sort of thing. Not drinking?" she asked, raising a glass of white wine as evidence that she was.

"Not exactly the best day to have a drink, being one of the hosts and all that."

The sunlight shining through the window behind Janey picked out the gentle curve between her long neck and the start of her paper-thin shoulder. Her skin almost glowed as it should do given the price Janey paid for her creams. She glanced to her left and then to her right. "I know we agreed that we would wait until the camping holiday for you to make up your mind, but have you given it any thought at all? Taken a few minutes out of your very busy schedule to give little old Janey some thought?"

Andy could not work out if she was trying to be funny or just sarcastic. Softly, she glided a palm down the length of his left arm, sending electric shocks running up through to his shoulder. He glanced around the room to see if anyone had noticed the caress. Susan was busy loading up her paper plate with fluffy food, and looking elsewhere.

"Um. Lots to think about, you know," he apologised. That included a conversation about contraception that would need to be had, although now was not the time or place for it. "But I will – I promise you I will – have it all sorted out one way or another for when we go camping, just as we had agreed. It's less than a couple of weeks away – I mean, the camping holiday is less than a couple of weeks away. You have my word. My word on my decision." Immediately he regretted sounding so indecisive and weak. Almost pathetic. *My word?* he thought. *What the fuck is that supposed to mean?*

Janey thought likewise but she could see that his nerves were shot. Time to move in for the kill. She flashed him her most intimate smile, her thin red lips parting to expose her expensively maintained teeth. She brought down her right hand across her left breast, pausing over her waist, and turned her hips sideways on to Andy. “Do you like this dress, Andy? You do seem to have been paying it rather a lot of attention today. I don’t just wear it to funerals, you know,” she laughed. And with that, she waved to Susan, who was stationed across the far side of the room, and walked the ten yards between them as seductively and slowly as she could manage.

Andy’s were not the only eyes watching a perfect arse commandeer the room, even if the performance was meant for him alone.

WHO'S A HAPPY CAMPER?!

"The plan for tomorrow, lads," announced Ian, in a louder voice than he had intended and loudly enough to elicit a disapproving glance from the proprietor of The Royal Oak. "The plan for tomorrow," he repeated, sotto voce. "Arrive at the campsite at around 4 or 5pm. I have sent you both an email with the best route, and you should allow yourselves at least three hours if you don't plan on stopping. Personally, I would give it more like four hours, as it is a holiday weekend, and the route is hardly as the crow flies." He drew a representative, meandering route with his finger between the pint glasses on the small table separating the three drinkers.

"So, *that's* the way to the New Forest," chuckled Andy to himself.

"We can all have lunch at home before we leave, which will save us some money. Not looking at you here, Graham," said Ian, looking at Graham. "The Stevens clan will be leaving pretty early on Monday to get home around lunchtime – and again, saving some dosh – but the rest of you can stay on the site until midday if you prefer."

It appeared simultaneously to both Andy and Graham that the sole reason for this holiday was more to save money than for it to be enjoyed.

"I have pre-booked three adjoining plots. We have been before; and it is a lovely site and I just couldn't find a better option when I last looked online at the weekend. Really well-kept place with its own stream the kids can mess around safely in." Ian had shared the latter fact with his friends on at least a handful of previous occasions. "We'll all pay individually when we get there. Your family's tent is already packed up safely in the trailer, Andy," was the reassuring news from Ian. "As I said, not quite the spec of our new family tent, but the one you have has served us well over the years despite the large tear in the groundsheet," was the not-so-reassuring news. "And the courier emailed me to say that the brand-new, Russian-oligarch-style tent I ordered for you was delivered safe and sound to your house last week, Graham. Check, Graham?"

"Check, Ian," replied Graham, with not wholly convincing enthusiasm.

"You should be able to squeeze that into either of your German-mobiles, given that there are only two of you. Which one are you going to drive down in?" asked Ian.

"Janey hasn't – I mean, we haven't decided yet." Graham wasn't fooling anyone, least of all himself.

Ian glanced between his friends. "You'll love it, I promise. This is not the camping you remember from back when you were kids."

Graham had no recollection of ever going camping, as a kid or otherwise.

"This is proper glamping," announced Ian.

Glamping, my arse, thought Andy. Graham preferred to just think forward to when this ghastly business would all be over.

"Cheers, boys. See you in the New Forest tomorrow," were Ian's parting words as they all disappeared into their houses at the end of their boy's exercise-and-drinks Friday night. Each of them had very different thoughts as to what he hoped to get out of the long weekend camping holiday that lay ahead of them.

"Just what the fuck do you think you are doing?" Ian asked his wife. "We only have room for two cases of clothes. There's no more room in the trailer because we have to take along our new tent and the old one for the Jones lot. If you want to take that suitcase you will need to put it on your lap in the front. Don't you ever fucking listen?"

"Piss off," was the best comeback Meera could think of, given that she knew that she was in the wrong this time. She walked out into the hall to see if she could squeeze the contents of her banned suitcase into the two suitcases which had already passed through customs. "Twat," she whispered, to the sound of her husband failing to pass through the front door without scraping the door frame with a cooking gas cylinder.

Jessica, Uma and Jake had been stationed in the back garden during the always-stressful process of packing. At such times Ian often wondered if their holidays were worth all the aggravation of packing, unpacking, and then repeating it all to come back home a few days later. Only Jessica seemed to be in reasonable humour, which was all the more surprising since she had the most stressful job of them all; namely trying to prevent Jake from killing either himself or someone else with one of the garden tools Ian never quite got around to putting out of harm's way. Happy times.

Ian slammed the boot of their ailing people carrier and walked back into the hallway to make his usual call to arms. "Everyone ready?"

No one answered as no one was ready. They never were. What Ian really meant was that they would be leaving in about thirty minutes. Otherwise, he really would be angry.

Packing in the Robins household was altogether much less stressful, even though it took longer than it did for their more down-to-earth neighbours. But not because of Graham, who had managed to collapse a weekend's worth of clothes into a modest sports bag in the time it took for his coffee to cool to a drinkable temperature. He had already paid his regular handyman to load the newly purchased tent into the back seat of his car and pack all the things they were likely to need on a camping holiday into the boot. Graham had absolutely no idea what one might need on a camping holiday, but his handyman did and so had been given the run of Graham's laptop so as to order whatever was required. (Rather careless of Graham to leave open the email inbox of the laptop he shouldn't have taken out of the surgery in the first place. Seldom had the handyman had such fun, reading about some of the more exotic ailments from which his neighbours and friends suffered.) It took the Robinses longer to get on the road than it should have because of Janey, of course. Few could take as long to dress down for a camping holiday than Janey. But, as always, she did it with a certain style, and it was not exactly her fault that Graham had fallen asleep in his chair by the time she reached the bottom of the stairs.

"Come on, Graham. Have you seen the time?"

It remained for Graham to squeeze Janey's two full suitcases into the boot and balance his sports bag on top of the tent. A nervous spasm fired down his spine as he closed the door and climbed into the driver's seat next to Janey, who was busy adjusting the tilt of her sunglasses. *How the devil am I going to put up that tent without looking a fool? I do hope that Ian will help*, he worried.

The Joneses? Aided and abetted by a comprehensive list compiled by Susan, they were the closest to leaving at the scheduled time. In fact, they left 6 Malvern Drive almost ten minutes before the time Susan had written at the top of the list in red biro, and this despite Andy having to walk around the house twice to double-check all the locks. The house was locked. Official.

It was Andy at the wheel of their people carrier, with an unspoken agreement that Susan would take over should her husband start to flag. Flagging was typically represented by head-bobbing and -weaving behaviours, whereupon she would have to take on what she hated with a passion; namely, driving a full people carrier. But it should not be a long drive, so she was looking forward to a relaxing few hours of catching up on her latest classic novel, *The Catcher in the Rye*.

How nice it must be to have time to read, thought Andy as he pointed the car towards London and the inevitable spring bank holiday traffic jam. With Susan at least pretending to be engrossed in her latest piece of culture, and all three children genuinely absorbed in various forms of electronic media, the silence was now in place for Andy to think.

London, 35 Miles —

Priority number one. What to do about Janey? Decision time for Andy had arrived. All his excuses had been used up. His first reaction was to wonder why he was wasting his time thinking about it at all. Surely it was a no-brainer? How could a quick jump with a neighbour ever justify risking his family and career? It just made no sense. The risks far outweighed the benefits. The rational course of action would be to tell Janey once and for all that theirs would only ever be a one-night stand. If there was any fallout, any blackmail, then he would just have to deal with it. At least she was not aware of where the drug had actually come from. Easy. All decided. Not a problem.

But then again…

London, 12 Miles —

Stationary traffic. Here was an opportunity to experience a life he had never before experienced. The hedonism seemingly enjoyed by everyone else in their youth had passed him by, blotted out at far too young an age by responsibility, expectation and loyalty. But that had been his choice, even if that life decision had been framed by the lifestyle and expectations of his parents.

Would the rest of his life be one of duty and putting the care and happiness of others before himself? Devoting most of his daylight hours to a career that was unlikely to get any better than it was now, and would very probably get worse? More of the same, year after year? Did he have a choice? Was the choice his to make?

Just imagine being able to rerun that night again and again for real, rather than merely in his mind. A woman and an experience that were beyond his dreams. And he was going to turn her down? To walk away from the hedonism that he believed had passed him by? An opportunity to finally put himself first; an opportunity that he was highly unlikely to ever be offered again? Surely only a fool would say no?

M3, 15 Miles —

Heavy traffic, but moving. The benefits were clear. It all came down to risk. He could easily swing it at work to pretty much guarantee a regular supply of the drug for himself and Janey. They were taking a relatively low dose and, as the project leader, he could order more batches of WRT743 to be synthesised without arousing suspicion, providing Wright and Briggs kept the project alive for out-licensing. It was not unusual for a project leader to sign out small quantities of a drug for experiments, and in doing so he could 'accidentally' take more than he had recorded. And anyway, few would agree that the compound-tracking process at Wright and Briggs could be considered as an example of good working practice. So getting the drug should not be a problem and should present relatively little risk. The affair being discovered by Susan was, by far, the greatest risk that Andy would be taking if he decided to push the button. How great was that risk? Janey had certainly come up with a good cover for their future meetings, and, of course, he could comfort himself with the knowledge that few would ever imagine that Janey would offer him a place in her bed. So, if they were careful – very, very careful – then was the risk manageable?

Southampton, 43 Miles —

Light traffic.

"Dad, can we please stop at the next services? I really need a wee," pleaded Josh.

"And can we get some sweets while we're there, Dad?" pleaded Rachel.

"And some Coke? I'm really thirsty," pleaded Sophie.

"Good idea. I could do with finding another book as I've nearly finished this one. Can you pull over at the first services we get to?" pleaded Susan.

"But there's no traffic at the moment, and stopping will just slow us down. Can't you all hang on a bit longer? All the traffic we have been through has added a good hour to the drive, and I am starting to feel a bit tired," pleaded Andy.

"Not me, Dad," replied Josh, thus bringing the discussion to a conclusion and a decision in favour of the pleading of the majority.

Lyndhurst, 7 Miles —

Never in my life have I ever tried to be something I wasn't. Maybe this is the time to change.

Despite being the first to leave Malvern Drive, the Jones family, much to Andy's annoyance, were not the first to arrive at Fairview Farm campsite. Once he had checked in at a rather unkempt Portakabin office, he was given a map which was no more than a colourful interpretation of reality and directed to a plot almost equidistant – in Andy's parallel world filled with sarcasm – to Ulstown. His annoyance at arriving after the Stevenses, who he could see were busying themselves with putting up their tent as the Joneses pulled into the adjacent plot, was tempered by a realisation that he needed Ian to help him to construct their own accommodation. On the plus side, the Joneses all agreed that the campsite was indeed as attractive and spacious as had been advertised by their neighbour. Their field was fringed by a mixture of large oaks and pines, and the grass was no taller or shorter than it should have been. Both Andy and Susan commented that it could have been a lot worse, although the final judgement was to be held back until the toilet-and-shower block had been experienced in the flesh.

"Andy!" cried Ian, as if meeting a long-lost friend. "Glad you could make it. Car break down?"

Andy needed to come up with a reason why he should not be labelled as Malvern Drive's slowest driver. "We would have been here over an hour ago if it hadn't been for the kids wanting us to join a long queue at the services, wouldn't we, dear?" he asked Andy to his wife's back. He didn't expect her to answer, and she didn't.

"Whatever," concluded Ian. "Give us a hand with finishing off putting up our tent and then we can crack on with yours. No sign of Graham yet." Both men stared at the entrance to their field as if their friend's arrival was imminent.

It would be almost another three hours before the Robinses turned up on the site not least because Janey had insisted that they stop off at a "lovely little restaurant I know" near Ascot for an early dinner. "Anything to avoid having to eat dinner at the campsite," she'd argued to a husband who remained bemused as to why his wife insisted on going camping at all when it was far outside his comfort zone and, he imagined confidently, hers as well. The still evening was drawing in when they finally arrived at the entrance of Field Number Four and spied their neighbours sitting around a table, balancing variously coloured drinks and surrounded by the aftermath of a dinner laboriously cooked but eagerly eaten. Janey was not alone in being comforted by being able to see only the youngest of the hordes of children with whom they would be holidaying.

"Red or white?" asked Meera of their newly arrived guests.

"Never mind red or white," snorted Ian, pointing to the Robinses' car. "We need to get that bloody palace of yours up before it gets dark."

"But not me," smiled Janey as she pulled up a chair newly vacated for her by Andy. "Why, thank you, Andy. I owe you one. Red, please, Meera. Start as I mean to go on."

Andy raced to the distraction of what became a rather heated hour of erecting chez Robins.

"Worst set of fucking instructions I have ever come across." Ian was sweating.

His marginally useful wannabe civil engineers nodded in agreement. Both took a swig from their bottles of cheap, home-brand supermarket lager in sympathy with his frustration.

The day, evening and night had been tiring for all, but exhausting for Susan and Meera, who had done the bulk of the painful preparations for and clearing up of dinner for ten as well as the childcare. Both women made their excuses not long after ten, retiring with their broods to their uncomfortable berths and leaving the men and a daisy-fresh Janey to drink away the night.

First it was cars: what they were likely to buy next and what they would really like to buy if money was no object. Then an appreciation of each other's tents, with Graham graciously accepting Ian's delusion that the Stevens family would be enjoying the most comfortable holiday. They touched upon Covid before Ian dragged them into politics; a subject of discussion which Andy and Graham always tried to steer clear of when in the presence of Ian. Although not exactly a fanatical socialist with strident views readily imposed on others, Ian was close enough to the real thing as far as they were concerned. The increasingly silent friends were almost relieved when a clearly bored and borderline drunk Janey decided to enter the discussion.

"Don't you gentleman ever get bored with your cars and your toys and your own opinions?" was Janey's observation.

Ian had also had more than his usual intake of alcohol, and was ready for some banter. "Bored of our own opinions? That coming from a woman!" he laughed.

Graham started to feel nervous. *Does Ian know who he's taking on?* Andy also decided to keep his head down.

"Why do you men automatically assume that your

conversations are any more erudite than the ones we girls enjoy?" Janey smiled and refilled her plastic glass with what remained in the bottle of red.

Ian made an educated guess as to what 'erudite' meant. "I don't, but is there anything wrong with men and women being interested in different things?"

"Of course not. But don't just assume that we poor women don't have anything up here," responded Janey, tapping her head in support of her statement. "And you know what, Ian, I bet you would much more enjoy a conversation with us girls."

"Try me!"

Graham was genuinely fearing what might happen next. "I don't know about you lot, but it's been a really long day and I'm ready to get my head down. Coming, darling?" asked Graham of his wife.

Janey didn't respond, but instead formulated a comeback to Ian. "OK, Ian, OK. Never mind about cars – what does your perfect woman look like?"

"Open the door to that tent and look inside. You will see what my perfect woman looks like," replied Ian, satisfied with his rapid response.

Too easy a question to evade, thought Janey. "So, if Meera is the personification of your perfect woman," she said, "one can only assume that you would marry her again in a heartbeat if you could live your life again."

"Of course I would. *Fuck her!*"

The laughter was heartfelt and mutual. But loud.

"Keep it down, guys. My perfect woman might not be so perfect if we managed to wake the kids up," added Andy.

The holidaymakers paused for thought and another drink.

Janey turned to face Andy. "I know what Graham's perfect woman looks like as he is sitting next to her, but what about yours? And please don't repeat Ian's almost witty line."

Graham was now starting to panic. "Come on, Janey. Early morning tomorrow."

"In a minute, Graham, in a minute. Andy, your thoughts?" teased Janey.

Andy blushed throughout a stammering description of someone as close to Susan as would convince the others that he had married someone reasonably adjacent to his dreams without making said description obviously fake. He thought that he had got away with it; answered Janey's question well enough to avoid any embarrassing follow-up questions. But he was wrong.

"I'm not your type, then. What a great shame. Too small? Too slim? Wrong clothes? Too intelligent, maybe? Not sure I will be able to get over this." Janey smiled at her prey.

"Right. Come on, Janey. Time to call it a night. I think you have managed to embarrass Andy more than enough for one night," joked Graham, who was now standing. He hooked one hand underneath her arm.

"Bedtime it is, then, guys. Or so I have been told. You know I'm only teasing, Andy. All harmless fun. Now perhaps you can see how much fun we girls have, Ian. See you all in the morning." Janey waved to her drinking partners before being guided into the luxury of the Robinses' new tent.

"What a fucking handful that woman is," whispered Ian to a slowly recovering Andy. "But she does have a cracking arse."

Andy could only nod in agreement.

"What the hell were you playing at last night?" Andy whispered urgently to Janey, who had rushed up to stand next to him in the queue for greasy barbecue handouts.

"Just having a bit of fun, Andy. Lighten up. At least Ian was up for some playful banter even if you and my husband weren't."

They shuffled forward by one space.

"But… you know. Us. What happened. Others getting suspicious," worried Andy.

"If we really were up to something then surely that would have been the last thing I would have said."

Andy admired the counterargument, but it was a high-risk strategy.

"And we aren't up to anything anyway, are we Andy? So what do we have to hide? But I do recall that now was the time when you were going to let me know if we are going to have anything to hide in the future?"

Andy was now within touching distance of the large bowls of dried-up salad. "They really do a good barbecue on this site. Great value," was part of the conversation he overheard from the two middle-aged men in front of him. As attractive as the trees were under which the barbecue and barbecuers were sheltering, in retrospect it might have been better to avoid the favourite playground of the local flying insect life.

Andy chose to focus on the fly-covered food laid out

in front of him. "I know. And I will let you know. But we have only just arrived."

"I'll be waiting," threatened Janey, wearing her best mischievous smile.

But she didn't wait long before making her next move. "At the back of the toilet block in one hour," was her order as they parted company, lunch in hand.

Andy's excuse to his family was that he was going for the shower he had not had time to have in the morning. Janey's excuse to Graham was that she was going for a walk in the woods behind the campsite to clear her head after the excesses of the night before. No one suspected that they were going to do anything other than what they had described. A sun-kissed day when everyone was keen to do what interested them most, whether it be an afternoon nap for Graham, lager refills for Ian, a chance to chat in the sun for Susan and Meera, or the children enjoying the boundless things to do around a shallow stream. It was the towel-holding Andy who was the one left waiting beside the toilet block. But he didn't have long to wait. He could see her moving purposefully towards him, looking around for any spies. She had changed her clothes since they had stood in the queue for the barbecue. Her trousers and blouse had been replaced with a sleeveless white summer dress which showed off a hint of the figure that lay beneath. It was only when she was within smiling distance that he noticed that she had also applied fresh make-up and perfume. She was just gorgeous. But he already knew that.

"Come on, Andy. Let's take a walk into the woods. Some privacy." And with that, she took the lead, with Andy following her first over a stile and then along the bank of a stream that was almost dried up. They were alone. After no more than a minute of silent walking, Janey pointed to a gap between the trees and led the easily led into the woods.

"And just where are we going?" asked a concerned Andy.

"Just a bit further. Trust me." Janey smiled, turning her head momentarily towards her too trusting companion. She looked around and stopped beneath a large oak. "Peaceful here. Time to talk," announced Janey. Time for Andy to talk was what she really meant.

"I have given it a lot of thought. I really have," insisted Andy. "It was a good idea of yours to use the piano lessons as a cover. I was thinking, perhaps we could really ask Graham to help us learn the piano and we can see how it goes from there. Sort of a probationary period where we don't actually do anything and sort of just see what happens. Take it all slowly to start with."

Janey didn't answer but just stepped up closer to Andy, who had backed up against the tree. He could hear her deep breathing. He was close enough to be able to almost taste her perfume.

"What do you think, Janey? Does that work for you?"

If she was thinking anything, she wasn't saying anything about what those thoughts might be. Instead, she took Andy's hand and guided it slowly between her legs, moving it up her thighs whilst pulling up her dress with her other hand. She pushed his hand towards her moist crotch and beneath her satin panties. She closed her eyes and raised her head as his fingers entered her. She opened her legs a little wider, and at first moved his hand up and down before relinquishing her grip and letting him continue what she had so expertly started. His full concentration was on watching her face contort with pleasure and her body writhe under his sensual touch. She rubbed his erection through his trousers, massaging it gently, keeping rhythm with his movement. Her breathing became shallower and more urgent; her massage more distracted and random. She adjusted her leg to push up against his erection, and pressed her breasts against his chest. She massaged his body with hers. He judged correctly that she was getting close, and increased the tempo and his depth. Her body tightened next to him, and her mouth opened to emit a low, guttural murmur in harmony with the motion of his hand. Her orgasm was sudden and quiet. At once all the tension disappeared from her body. He stopped and withdrew his hand. She took one step backwards and rearranged her attire to better resemble how it had appeared when she had left the tent.

She smiled and swept her hands through her hair. "I'll take that as a yes, then."

part three

A BETTER LIFE THROUGH CHEMISTRY

PIANO

There are many, many views out there, but Mr Irvine Welsh had some intriguing thoughts about how one should live one's life. What again was it that he wrote? Something like choose us, choose our life. Our lifestyle. Choose a career that fucks with your mind and consumes all of your waking hours. Choose mortgage payments the Bank of England decides on houses you will never own. Choose Sonos sound systems, AGA cookers, and radio-controlled lawn mowers you don't understand how to use. Choose overpriced German cars which depreciate viciously in value in front of your eyes as they sit on the driveway. Choose falling asleep on the couch in front of embarrassing reality TV cabled into a seventy five -inch HD screen which will end up getting stolen. Choose living with the same people in the same house next to the same neighbours for year upon year upon year until either you or they die. Choose mentally and physically decaying in a care home paid for with all the money you scrimped and saved for throughout your life and with which you had hoped to enjoy your old age. Choose our lifestyle. Choose us.

All of which was absolutely fine with Andy. Or at least, it had been up until now. He had bought into it all: ambitions of career success and kudos; a family neatly arranged in a home fully equipped with all the labour-saving devices and soft furnishings one could wish for; a life in which hedonism was defined as having three drinks instead of two on a Saturday night, or being the last to leave the garden centre on a Sunday afternoon; a future of more of the same followed by even more of the same, and in which his life's destiny had already been determined before that life had even started. But had the time now arrived to choose a different lifestyle? Could Andy really turn into a person he had never been and was not ever likely to be? Was he really going to choose a different path; one to a destiny which even he could never have contemplated? Time to find out.

'*Have you talked to G about him giving us piano lessons?*' texted Andy, having parked up in his usual space in the main car park at Wright and Briggs.

He had not yet entered reception when his phone pinged.

Am on the case. Will try to sort something out for later this week. After all, one can't dance without music. Will get back to you soon. XXX

Andy shivered in anticipation of the meetings yet to be enjoyed. *XXX? Dancing? Probably time to come up with some code words if we are going to communicate through texts.* He smiled as he climbed the stairs to his first-floor office. It was unlikely that Susan would ever read his texts because she did not know his PIN, but it was better to build in some extra security, just in case. Something to discuss with Janey sooner rather than later. But now it was time for Andy to focus on work.

The next project team meeting was in less than two hours and he needed to finish his PowerPoint presentation. He felt energised, motivated and committed. This was a fresh start and he needed to get this sentiment across to the team. Build back the bridges he had ripped up. Encourage the team to follow and support him in his quest to take WRT743 into clinical development and into humans through finding a partner who would acquire the programme. In merely attempting to meet that goal, he would provide a steady supply of recreational drugs for himself and Janey – or, more to the point, sex for him and drugs for her. What could possibly go wrong?

Based on his few experiences with the drug (as well as that of his rather more seasoned collaborator), Andy was convinced that WRT743 shared at least some of the more typical properties with known psychedelic drugs. If he could demonstrate that that was indeed the case, and that the compound was safe, WRT743 was very likely to be of interest to large pharma companies looking to add to their drug pipelines. And what a boost being the head of a programme that was out-licensed to a major player would be to his career, regardless of who he ended up working for. But what did Andy need to now do to go about achieving this? The plan was going to be the essence of the presentation he would give to the team later that day, and featured two key objectives: determining the drug's activity on serotonin and dopamine receptors in cell lines (which would help determine its true mechanism of action and its profile as a potential psychedelic), and synthesising larger batches of WRT743 to be able to carry out further profiling of the compound, including its suitability as a manufacturable drug. As an important afterthought, he included some additional toxicity assays just to make sure that WRT743 was as safe to take as he and Janey had found it to be so far. He fully understood the risks both he and Janey were taking, even if she didn't. The synthesis of new and larger batches of the drug was, of course, a perfect cover to ensure a steady supply for both him and his new lover and the personal angle to his renewed enthusiasm for this project.

After his own experience of taking the drug, Andy had started to do some background reading around the topic of how psychedelics impact sexual function. The literature was complex but there was a reasonable body of evidence to suggest that drugs like LSD could boost both libido and sexual performance. His belief that Janey's obvious enjoyment of the sexual aspects of that special evening had been driven by the properties of this new drug had thus been substantiated. *No big surprise there, then*, he mused as he placed this latest scientific paper on top of a growing pile of publications on just that subject that he had already trawled through. He was a little bit surprised that this hypothesis did not make him feel less of a man, but this was supplanted by a dose of realism. The realism that Janey desired him and needed him, even if because he had access to a drug she could not find elsewhere. So be it.

“What a great project team meeting. The man has got his mojo back.” Li beamed as she slid her dinner tray across the table next to the seated Emily. She often wondered just how much longer she could continue going home after work feeling so very hungry.

Emily had already started pushing her Caesar salad to the far edge of her plate. “Back to the old Andy, I would say. In fact, maybe even better. Some real passion and commitment. No one there this morning could doubt that his heart and mind are not back in the 743 project. And what about his thoughts about 743 acting as a psychedelic? It would certainly explain why it was so active in the tests for depression. Maybe we have overlooked something. Fascinating, I thought.”

“Just what I was thinking,” agreed Li. “Just imagine if he is right. That would really put the cat amongst the pigeons, especially given all the latest press on psychedelics being useful in treating depression. You could just feel the enthusiasm around the table for following this up. I wonder what made him come up with the idea?”

“And some good comments from Mike about adding some other profiling tests,” added Emily. “Even Liz was helpful for once, saying that if you are going to make a hundred grams of 743 then you might as well make 250 or even five hundred grams given the lead time to synthesising the drug and the cost of the starting materials. Did you see Andy’s smile when she said that? Must have been because he could see that even Liz, the ultimate devil’s advocate, had bought into the concept. I think there’s a really good chance that senior management will want to try to out-license this project, which will be good news for us all, but especially for Andy. And here comes the man of the moment!"

"Can I join you, ladies?" enquired Andy. "Don't know about you, but I am absolutely starving after our project team meeting going on for so long after time. What a shocking project team leader," joked Andy.

"But of course," replied Li who was worried that she would start dribbling at seeing Andy's tray struggling under the weight of a plateful of battered cod and chips and a bowlful of chocolate gateau smothered in fresh cream.

He pulled up a chair and settled himself at the table. *Forgot to get my bloody drink*, he seethed silently.

Emily felt that she should cover for her clearly overwhelmed colleague. "Very engaging meeting, I thought, Andy. Wherever did you come up with the idea of profiling 743 as a potential psychedelic compound? It certainly wasn't obvious to me."

"Nor me," added Li, who was trying to mentally morph her carrot into a fully greased up, oversized chip. *If only I could get my hands on a hallucinogenic drug right now*, she wished.

Andy paused for thought and to repeat the rationale that he had introduced at the meeting and which these two particular team members had either misunderstood or forgotten. "Really, it just came out of some extra bedtime reading about aspects of neurology I really should have known about in the first place," he lied. He was too polite to say that he had already explained this not two hours earlier, but maybe he should see how he could explain it more clearly in future presentations, especially since it was a cover for the real reasons why he thought WRT743 could act as a psychedelic.

"How was your holiday? Weren't you down south somewhere?" asked Emily.

"Camping in the New Forest," replied Andy. "Never thought I would enjoy camping at my age. I guess you have to have the weather, though, and we were pretty lucky given what it's like out there right now," he added pointing his knife towards the window behind Emily. "Beautiful part of the country when the sun is shining. You can almost touch the serenity."

"It would take more than a touch of serenity to get me under canvas, I can tell you," laughed Emily.

"All depends on who you go camping with and what you get up to," said Andy, trying to suppress a smile.

"Well, I must say," chortled Graham (Graham liked to chortle), "I always did enjoy a challenge. And I've certainly got one on my hands here," he announced eyeing up his wife and her aspiring fellow classmate across the low sitting-room table stocked with three full glasses of red wine.

Janey looked to the heavens in mock annoyance. Andy smiled back at his drinking partner and GP.

"Neither of you has played an instrument in your life. You don't know a piano from a flute. Written music is a foreign language to you both. But good on you for wanting to learn. Janey was telling me that you came up with the thought at that dreams chat you had a few weeks back, Andy."

Andy was replaying that scene from a few months back, which had taken place on the sofa on which Graham was now sitting. "Well, I saw that wonderful piano over there and said to Janey that I've always wanted to play but never got round to learning, and I think you said exactly the same thing yourself, didn't you Janey?" He had kept rigidly to the script he had pre-agreed with Janey.

As did she. "It's always nice to listen to you playing, Graham, but you never seem to play much these days, so what better way to get you up and playing again than to have a couple of students?"

"Indeed," smiled Graham. "But where to start?"

"How about showing us just how good our new teacher is?" was Andy's challenge.

"I never thought you would ask, old boy," replied Graham, who finished off his wine, stood up, and walked over to the piano near the doorway of the Robinses' grand living room. His students dutifully followed and stood to attention behind him as he tried to get comfortable on the spartan bench seat.

Andy couldn't fail to be impressed by the selection of jazz and blues numbers that Graham was able to play from memory. *How did such a busy professional ever find the time to learn to play as well as that?* he thought in genuine wonderment. *No excuse for me not to learn.* At some point during the recital Janey tugged at his sleeve and slipped him a knowing smile. A smile of knowing what had happened between them in this very room, and a smile knowing of what was still to come. And it wasn't learning how to play the piano. The final bars of Graham's version of 'Autumn Leaves' finished off An Evening with Dr Graham Robins, and was met with an enthusiastic and genuine round of applause from his students.

"That was really fantastic, Graham. Brilliant. Why didn't you ever tell us you could play?" asked Andy.

"Not something I recall ever coming up in our Friday-night discussions, old boy. For all we know, Ian might well be first violin in the London Philharmonic," answered Graham.

"Good point. I will ask him that very same question when we meet next."

All those around the piano laughed, to varying degrees.

"So. What do we start you two off with?" was Graham's rhetorical question. "I'm afraid there's nothing better than starting off with the scales, as they will teach you basic music theory as well as where to place your fingers and thumbs on the keyboard. Scales are what every music teacher will ask you to recite as a warm-up to your lesson. Very boring, but very useful and good discipline."

With nothing useful they could think of to add, both students nodded.

"Let's start with the C major scale."

Which is exactly what they did – first Janey, and then the rather more competitive Andy trying to be just that little bit better than his fellow student. They even managed to squeeze in the G major scale before Graham called time and an opportunity to wrap up the first lesson.

"Well, I hope you two enjoyed that as much as I did. I'll make good pianists of you both yet! I can print out copies of the most useful scales for you to learn as beginners and we can go through them at the next lesson. Maybe in a couple of weeks' time? That work for you, Andy?"

"I'm sure I can find some evening that we can all do," offered Andy.

"But you haven't got a piano to practise on, Andy," worried Janey.

Both students looked towards their teacher for the answer to the conundrum.

"Don't see why you can't come round here, old boy, to tickle the ivories, as long as someone is at home. If that's OK with you, darling?" Graham asked his wife.

Janey paused for effect, and to increase Andy's heart rate. "Yeah, why not? Always easier to learn with someone pushing you on. We can arrange something later, Andy."

And, with all the arrangements agreed to be arranged, the teacher led his students to the front door and bid farewell to his star pupil.

"Thanks again, Graham. Pint on me for Friday. Really looking forward to the next lesson," were Andy's parting words.

And he really was looking forward to the next time he would be able to play the piano.

THE THIRD TIME

Andy was struggling not to look guilty. He certainly felt guilty. As he should, as here he was, committing theft. Theft from the company that he worked for. He had done the same just before Christmas, but this was on a grander scale, and was also to benefit someone outside of the company, albeit unbeknown to them. He had stayed late at work (but not so late as to arouse undue suspicion), and was alone in the compound storage room when he retrieved the twelve-gram batch of WRT743. His reasoning was that no one was likely to flag a missing gram of drug from a batch that was soon to be superseded by a much larger 250-plus grams re-synthesis. The gram he was now weighing out would be good for another twenty doses, of drug which should last him and Janey well past the time when the new batch would have been synthesised and delivered, and probably well beyond the point at which she would tire of him, at least to Andy's reckoning. However, despite the careful reasoning and planning, he felt that he could not relax until the twenty cautiously weighed-out fifty-milligram vials drug (*must be careful to avoid overdosing*) had been driven off-site and stored in the tea caddy in his attic without attracting the attention of either security at Wright and Briggs or his wife. In addition to carrying out this crime, he also had to make peace with Susan for biting her head off in the morning before he'd left for work due to the stress of the knowledge of the upcoming theft, and for the inconvenience caused by him arriving home so late.

It was well after 7pm when Andy unlocked the front door and entered the hallway of 6 Malvern Drive. Not a sound, which rather explained the absence of the people carrier from the driveway. It was only when he decamped to the kitchen that he found out why.

Taken the kids to my mother's as there is no point waiting around for you. Your dinner is in the freezer.

There was no signature attached to the message Andy found on a notepad balanced on the kitchen table, but it was not difficult to guess the identity of the author. *She must really be off on one if she's taken the kids out beyond their bedtime*, he thought. *At least I don't have to find an excuse to go up to the attic to load up the tea caddy.* That was of some consolation to him.

After thus concealing his stolen goods, he returned to the kitchen to pour himself at least a double measure of a particularly strong rum that had been lurking at the back of the drinks cabinet since his last birthday. Nerves needed calming. Guilt needed to be managed. Excuses, apologies and never-agains needed to be conceived and delivered to

Susan before the night was out. "Who would ever want to be a drug pusher?" Andy asked himself, risking a smile. Who indeed?

"So, what's the plan?" asked Andy, who, true to his word, had finally bought coffee for Janey and tea for himself at the recreation centre café.

"Diaries out," answered Janey, at which point both became engrossed in their mobile phones.

"Which reminds me," for a reason he could not recall, "we really must try not to be so explicit in our texts. I know you have a second phone that you use that Graham is not aware of, but is it not impossible that he will get to find it somehow? And although Susan has no idea what my PIN is, it's also not impossible for her to find a way into seeing my texts. I suppose I could use the touch function but she might get suspicious as to why I have changed how I get into the phone. How about having a code?" suggested Andy.

"A bit over the top in my opinion, but happy to give it a try if it makes you feel more comfortable," commented Janey.

"OK. How about this? Going dancing or piano practice is… you know… well… the S-word."

"Really, Andy?" Janey smiled. "Really? A thirty-five-plus-year-old man, married for ten-odd years, three kids, shagging a neighbour, and you still can't say 'the S-word'? You need some therapy, my funny little lover."

Andy could only agree with the sentiment, but therapy was unlikely to change anything. As was becoming normal on these Saturday mornings, he darted a few glances around the crowded café to see if anyone was listening in to their conversation. *Will I always be like this?* he asked himself. He returned to the task in hand. "Don't use your name or address or any other reference to who you are, and I will do likewise. Don't even use people's initials, like 'G' for Graham. In that way, one of us being found out won't mean that the other one is too. Then we can just say that it was a one-night stand with someone random, etc., etc., if we are rumbled. Thinking again, best not to use piano either because it will link me to you. Let's go with dance. What do you think? Do you agree? And please don't write 'XXX' at the end of your texts."

"Whatever rocks your boat, Andy," was Janey's disinterested reply in that rather selfish way that had already started to rankle with him, despite them having spent so little time together. But Andy was only interested in her body and not what was inside the head perched above it. And she reciprocated in kind with his cold sentiment. "Look. Let's get this clear. I'm not in love with you. I don't have any feelings for you, and this tawdry little arrangement is unlikely to last that long anyway. I just want some fun. A chance to go dancing."

"OK. That's settled. And yes, it does make me feel a little less nervous about what we are doing," replied Andy in his defence.

"Doing? We aren't doing anything as far as I can see. So let's get back to the bloody diaries," announced Janey with a rather sarcastic and impatient undertone. "What is it with these amateur teenagers?" She tutted to herself, but even she regretted what she had just rather thoughtlessly blurted out. "I'm sorry, Andy. That all must have sounded rather cold. Of course I have some feelings for you, as otherwise we wouldn't have had the S-word and we wouldn't be planning to have the 'S' word again if that wasn't the case." She smiled at an increasingly confused Andy. "I know I can be a terrible bitch on occasion, but I was just trying to make sure you understand that this was never going to be anything other than a practical arrangement convenient for us both. Hopefully a mutually enjoyable practical arrangement, but a practical arrangement nonetheless. You do understand that, don't you Andy?" She reached her right hand across the table towards him, but without touching, in sympathy with her apology.

Wow! She does have a smidgen of empathy in her soul after all, thought Andy. "No, no. I understand. I fully understand. Not sure why us having a code goes against all that, but let's see how it goes. All I am trying to do is make sure we don't get found out because of a stupid mistake we have made. I wouldn't be having this conversation with you now if I thought there was a likelihood that Susan would somehow find out about us, and I'm sure the same goes for you and Graham. And yes, I fully agree: a practical arrangement is a good description of what we have, and it's no more than that."

Janey continued to soften. "Sure. A practical arrangement. But that doesn't stop us also enjoying each other's company, just as we are doing now. Maybe we can be friends as well as lovers."

I really don't understand women at all, do I? was Andy's rhetorical question to himself. *Always best to just say yes and agree with whatever they say. A much easier life.* He raised his plastic cup of tea towards his lover and new friend. “I’ll drink to that.”

“*Cin-cin*,” replied Janey as their fingers touched by chance between their plastic cups.

Andy put his tea back on the table and moved it first to the left and then to the right. Distracting activity. “Talking about practical arrangements, I don’t suppose you have been more practical than me and thought about contraception, have you?” he whispered almost inaudibly.

“And now you think about the C-word,” teased Janey. “Just put it this way. I have never wanted children and I won’t ever have children, so you don’t have to worry about going out and buying a raincoat. Men!”

The next time the lovers and friends met was their second piano lesson with Graham. Their recreation centre meeting over tea and coffee had broken up with an understanding that they would have a second lesson with Graham before some somewhat more private ‘practice sessions’, so as to strengthen the pretence that they were actually learning to play the piano. That had, of course, been Andy’s suggestion, but Janey had agreed just so that they could agree on at least one thing that morning.

“Lesson number two, I’m afraid, will be much like lesson number one, but with a special treat at the end,” promised Graham.

His students smiled.

“First, I will teach you a few more of the important scales, and then you can have a go yourselves. Here are some printouts of the scales so that you can practise them without me around.” Graham handed them stapled copies.

More smiles.

"And now the special treat!" Graham announced excitedly after over half an hour of his students struggling through the new scales. "A real song for you to learn. Your very first one. Maybe not a classic, chart-topping song, but one I'm sure you will recognise. 'Three Blind Mice'!"

Laughter all around.

Lesson number two drew to a close with a note-perfect rendition of 'Three Blind Mice' by Graham's star pupil, which earned Andy a pat on the back from his teacher.

"In the next lesson we will learn to play the bassline," promised Graham. At least, that was what he thought would be the plan for the next lesson.

An empty house on the 22nd and 23rd.

I am OK most nights next week but 22nd probably works best because I will also have an empty house. See you on the 22nd when I get back from work at about 6 if OK with you?

OK with me. See you on Tuesday evening.

And not a single text rule broken, mused Andy. *A good start.*

"But I thought you had arranged to see your mother tonight?" were Andy's rather agitated first words to his wife as he arrived home from work on the 22nd June.

"Don't panic. We're still going, but Sophie needs to finish off her homework first. Anyway, I thought you were going over the road for your piano lesson tonight?"

asked Susan, busy trying to clear away the remnants of the children's dinners.

"Maybe not, it would seem. Graham's been held up at the surgery, so if we do have one it will have to be later in the evening. Who knows? But a heads-up if I am not here when you get back."

"Whatever. I mean, of course, good luck with your piano lesson, dear," was Susan's sarcastic comment. "Your dinner's in the microwave, and please try not to blow it up this time. You'd think a highly paid scientist would be able to heat up a meal without trashing an oven."

She didn't expect an answer and didn't get one. Andy had more important things on his mind than spitting casseroles.

"My new boyfriend can't even be bothered to turn up on time for our first date. Not a good sign. But there's men for you," teased Janey as she ushered the latecomer through the hallway and into the living room, where two glasses of red wine were waiting for them on the table. Only one of them was full.

Andy did his very best to appreciate her attempt at humour, but his nerves had been shredded by a mixture of performance anxiety and fear of being caught in the act. Not good bedfellows.

"Your usual seat?" enquired Janey, pointing to his 'usual' seat. "I never did get round to asking, but I presume you were able to track down Brian's colleague? Otherwise it will just be the scales and 'Three Blind Mice' this evening. Should I ask? How healthy is one's stash?"

"Pretty healthy," blurted out Andy. "As I said, I still

have some vials left over from what Brian gave me, but I took the precaution of tracking his friend down and have managed to make the stock look a bit more healthy. Enough to take us through the next few months at least, I would say. As long as we stick to the same dose, of course."

"How wonderful! Excellent news. So how much do I owe you?"

"No charge other than your good company," smarmed Andy. "But it wasn't easy. I talked to one of Brian's friends who came along to his funeral. You might have seen him. Ginger beard," he lied.

"I think I might have," answered Janey, which Andy knew was also a lie as the only mourner who'd come close to having a ginger beard had been Susan's Aunt Elsie.

"Anyway, he typed his number into my mobile and said to phone him if I ever wanted to talk about Brian. We both knew what he was getting at," revealed Andy as he took his first taste of a light Shiraz. "It took a lot of nerve for me to contact him, I can tell you, but we arranged to meet in the park next to the cemetery, and that's where I managed to get us another ten vials." He took two from his jacket pocket and placed them on the coffee table between them.

"What, the same sort of vials that Brian gave you? How odd," commented Janey, picking them up for a closer inspection of their contents before returning them to his half of the table. She struggled to cross her legs within the confines of a black pencil skirt.

"I guess they must have come from the same supplier." *That much was not untrue*, thought Andy. "The little bugger tried to up the price, saying there's a low supply and high demand for this drug."

"Well, he would say that, wouldn't he?" observed Janey. "And are you any the wiser as to exactly what the drug is?"

Andy had anticipated this very question. "Some sort of psychedelic, apparently, but he didn't say which one."

Janey put down her glass abruptly. "I knew it," she gasped. "I knew it. Very much like the sort of stuff we used to try out in the group. Amazing. You need to hang on to his phone number, as the stuff he is pushing is the best I have come across. Couldn't you take a bit into work and do some tests to find out what it is?"

Andy smiled knowingly. "Probably a bit more than my job's worth to try and pull that one off as interesting as it might be to find out what it is."

"A shame. But never mind. Whatever it is, let's get on with it!" demanded Janey, standing up. "A lemonade for Mr Jones?" Not waiting for an answer, she walked urgently out of the living room and into the kitchen, returning with two large tumblers which presumably contained lemonade.

Andy unscrewed the two vials containing the white powder he had stolen from Wright and Briggs only days before, and added their contents to the tumblers. He swirled both solutions vigorously before placing them down on the low table separating the two eager 'patients'. "Cheers."

"*Cin-cin.* You said you managed to get ten vials, which is great, but how easy would it be to get more of these psychedelics?" asked Janey, wiping her mouth discreetly with her finger.

Andy tried to work out where she was going with this. "As I said, I can't say for sure that we are taking a psychedelic. It's just what I was told. As for getting more, which I don't think we will need to worry about for some time yet, it's not impossible I guess, but not something I would look forward to doing." *Whatever the reason for her question, best to keep all options open for the moment*, he calculated.

Janey emptied her tumbler. "Fine. Just asking."

"OK. What next?" asked Andy nervously.

"What next? Piano practice, of course," laughed Janey as she made her way over to the instrument in question. She sat on the wooden piano bench and patted the space to her left. "Care to join me?"

Andy took up the offer after finishing his lemonade cocktail, and sat close (but not too close) to the object of his desire.

"I thought we could make good use of the time that this little drug of yours needs to get going and maybe do what everyone thinks we are actually here to do. But this time, if it's all the same to you, Andy, perhaps we could use a bedroom when the time arrives?"

"What? The marital bed?" Andy panicked. "When did you say Graham will be back?"

"Calm yourself, dear boy. We have a double bed freshly made up in one of the spare rooms where we can make as much mess as we like, and Graham won't find us in there because we won't be seeing him until closing time at The Robin Hood has long passed. The C major scale it is, then," announced Janey as she flattened out Graham's printed sheets on the music stand. "You first."

But it was Janey who made the first move some twenty minutes later, just as she had when they had been here before. The drug kicked in early this time. The wash of euphoria had arrived for her, and Andy had almost completed one of his better interpretations of 'Three Blind Mice' when he felt her hand sweep up his thigh and between his legs. His desperate intake of breath completely ruined the last bar of the song.

They never did make it to the freshly made-up double bed in the spare room. They never even made it to the foot of the stairs. That was mostly Andy's fault, because it was Andy who lifted his mistress off the piano seat and pushed her up against the wall behind the piano. It was Andy who pulled down Janey's skirt which slid down over her calves and discarded it on the floor. There was no underwear beneath for him to remove. She reciprocated by undoing his belt and pulling down his freshly washed and pressed jeans and underpants – Susan was a stickler for ironing – to just above his knees. She grabbed his waist, pulling him onto and then into her, and let out a whimper of pain as he entered her dryness. This was no long, gradual lovemaking. It was desperate and urgent. He pulled up her left leg to his waist in order to push himself deeper into her. She wrapped her leg around him and hung on to his shoulders while he concentrated on his timing. Pushing and pulling. Pushing and pulling. Her pain melted away as she closed her eyes to focus on the pleasure he was giving her. Short breaths in and out. Her back arching and relaxing. Without notice, he pulled away from her, her eyes now open to take in whatever was going to happen next. He cupped her head gently between his outstretched hands and pulled her on to his kiss, but then almost immediately moved his hands to her waist and turned her around. Janey was now looking into the empty room with her back being cradled by her lover. Andy guided her slowly to the tall back of the same sofa in front of the piano and on which they had first made love months before. This time he bent her over the sofa and entered her from behind with a thrust that took their breath away. It was in this position that he was able to bring them to an urgent and mutual orgasm that left them gasping frantically for air as they coiled themselves around each other on the floor next to the piano at which they were supposed to be sitting. There they remained, motionless and speechless, as the drug flowed through their veins.

And so ended the third time for Andy.

COFFEE, TEA AND CAKE, PART 1

It must be said that I am as far away from being a city girl as it is possible to be. Not for me the bright lights, the hustle and bustle, the crowds and the noise. I do love the museums, the sights and the history of somewhere like London, but give me the quiet and the space of the countryside any day of the week. If it were up to me, my family and I would now be living on top of a mountain with not so much as a post office for miles and miles around. Our little compromise is to live in a village, although you might see me at the top of a mountain one day not so very far into the future. Still working on Twm for that one!

Janey is a very different kettle of fish, but I think you already knew that. She might have fallen a little out of love with the city, but that was with its people and not the place itself. She will always be a city girl at heart, and so it was with a heart beating a little quicker than normal that she boarded the slightly late 9.40am train to King's Cross on a chilly Tuesday morning in late September.

Forty minutes of staring out of a window for Janey to recall all that had led to her being on a train for the first time in nearly two years. She hated trains, although it was really the people on them that she really disliked. So unclean. She placed her bag on the aisle seat to make sure that she was not going to be disturbed.

Stevenage, 10 Minutes —

It was an honest, often humorous and unusually self-effacing email that Janey had sent to her one-time closest work friend Lucy. Which was precisely why it had taken her so long to craft. What did it say? She was a changed woman. A true woman of the Shires, living with a respectable professional husband in a respectable executive house, mixing with respectable local people. She had even become a member of the respectable golf club; a non-playing member, of course. No more of the wild child.

I can't even remember the last time I went out for dinner, never mind to a club. Other people's husbands? So last year, darling, and one just no longer has the energy.

She hoped that Lucy would take the latter as a reminder of the sort of poor-taste risqué humour they had often shared in the office. It was not meant to demean the upset she had brought to her old group of friends; just serve as an acknowledgement that she had not forgotten what had happened and was not seeking forgiveness for the unforgivable. Janey was treading a fine line. But then again, she always did.

Stevenage Train Station —

It really hasn't got any better, has it? mused Janey as she looked out at the tired station. She peered at a middle-aged couple sitting on an uncomfortable-looking bench and struggling to find something to say to each other. *How sad. But how very normal. A penny for your thoughts.*

The train jerked away from the station as Janey contemplated her real motive for writing to Lucy and asking to meet up; namely, getting invited back into the group of well-to-do junkies. Would her being a changed woman be enough of a reason for them to welcome her back? *Probably not. A big, big, long shot*, thought Janey. *But you just wait until they get to try Andy's whizz-bang new psychedelic. I'll have them all eating out of my hand. Even bloody Jason and his witches' coven.* She allowed herself a self-satisfied smile as the first housing estates of North London suburbia came into view.

Andy had told her that he had managed to secure ten vials, two of which they had taken that June evening. Since then, they had 'met' a further five times. *So it would seem that the little darling has managed to get what might be a regular supply from the ginger beard now that Brian has died. He has a supply – or even a supplier – he can share with me, then*, plotted Janey, although it was not a conversation she was looking forward to having with Andy. But when the time arrived, she hoped that he would just go along with her wishes through the force of her personality and the weakness of his. Janey did not want to go nuclear on this and threaten blackmail; to tell Susan of what her junkie husband was getting up to just yards away from the family home.

The juddering carriages alerted all aboard the train to the start of its slow approach to King's Cross Station. It just remained for Janey to ensure that she was the last to leave the carriage and so avoid having to get too close to her fellow travellers.

London —

Lucy had also taken no little time to reply to Janey, after having initially flipped quickly through her options as to what to do with the very surprising email she had received one morning. Ignore it completely, tell Janey to fuck off, or just agree to meet? It had taken almost two weeks to craft her crushingly neutral reply.

Will be nice to meet up again after so long.

She had at first favoured the option to not bother replying after all that the outrageous slut had done, but she just couldn't resist finding out what had happened to the infuriating but always entertaining Janey. Their meeting was to take place not in their old Costa haunt near King's Cross, but in a place that Lucy had suggested, rather off the beaten track, which (Janey had correctly assumed) had been selected in order to avoid Lucy being seen with her by anyone they knew.

Lucy was surprised to see her perennially late former friend already seated in a corner of Gio's Coffee shop when she opened the door. Both smiled as Janey walked over to exchange elaborate air kisses before leading Lucy to the table she had secured.

"You look fabulous, Lucy," she gushed.

"Thank you. Looks like you're still full of shit, then, Janey. I guess some things never change," replied Lucy.

The mutual, genuine laughter proved to be an immediate icebreaker.

"Two Americanos, please," was Lucy's request to the waiter who had been hovering between the two, now seated friends. They had always drunk Americanos. "And how about one of those large cannolis, Janey?" She gestured to the counter they were sitting next to.

Janey nodded and smiled.

"But look at you," Lucy continued when the waiter had departed. "A floral dress, a cardigan and a warm coat, without a power suit in sight. It becomes you. Looks like you are enjoying country life."

"I did find it a bit of a struggle to begin with, if I'm being honest. So very different to life down here," explained Janey. "But I'm getting there, and Graham has been great. I really landed on my feet with him."

"He's the one, then. The one to finally catch our Janey. I'm really made up for you, old friend." Lucy smiled, rubbing the top of Janey's arm vigorously.

Janey couldn't be sure if Lucy was being genuine. She had never been this complimentary before. "Why, thank you. Very kind of you to say so. I do think I'm in a good place. Looking back, I really regret some of the things I did. Friendships ruined because of my selfishness. How stupid of me to mess you around: the best friend I have ever had. Is it too late to apologise to you?"

"I'm not sure it's me you really need to apologise to. It wasn't my husband you shagged," retorted Lucy rather brusquely.

"Which, I guess, is the main reason I'm here today, speaking to you," was Janey's rather formal start to her pitch. "To try to start again. To apologise to you all for my shocking, inexcusable, indefensible behaviour. You, Jason, Amy – especially Amy – and the gang. Even if you never want to see me ever again, won't you please at least let me apologise to you all face to face? It would mean so much to me. A chance to clear my conscience; to expunge the person I used to be," implored Janey.

Lucy hesitated. "I'm not sure. I can't see Amy agreeing, for one."

"Of course, I understand. But doesn't everyone deserve a second chance? I'm not asking for anything other than a chance to meet you all and try to make up just a little bit for all I have done. That's all I am asking for. Can't you at least talk to them about this? Please, Lucy."

Lucy stared at her Americano in the hope of receiving divine inspiration. "I'll try Janey, but I'll be very surprised if anyone agrees. It all really sounds like a way for you to relieve your guilt rather than something that will make any difference to the likes of Amy, but, as I said, I'll give it a try."

"Thank you, Lucy. Thank you so much. Please try your best and let them know how sincere I am about this. They are good people, and an apology is the very least they are owed," pleaded Janey.

"We'll see," said Lucy. "We'll see." She picked up the bigger of the two cannolis and expertly bit off one end without dropping so much as a crumb of pastry.

Janey smiled. Job done. "And what about you, Lucy? Is that an engagement ring I see?"

Stevenage, 12 Minutes —

The meeting had gone as well as Janey could have hoped. Lucy had seemed approachable, if not exactly the Lucy of old, which was not surprising given how they had parted. She trusted Lucy to make good her promise and contact the group. It was very unlikely that they would all agree to meet Janey, but she was confident that she could weave her spell over whoever turned up and at least start the process of reintegrating herself back into the friendship group. She just needed that opportunity; a foot in the door. *How nice it would be to be able to enjoy those amazing gatherings again*, she thought as the train slowed in preparation for arriving at Stevenage. *Step two is to get a healthy stash of Andy's drug with which to really wow them. Easy-peasy.* She smiled to herself. *Maybe.*

However, the overwhelming feeling in the pit of her stomach as the train left Stevenage was nausea at having to demean herself in front of someone who had rejected her and walked away from her friendship. Her natural instinct was screaming at her to tell Lucy to just fuck off, but that was a measure of just how much she wanted to be a member of that circle of middle-class junkies once more.

"More fool me," muttered Janey through the cold train window.

Meanwhile, back in sleepy Ulstown, two residents were discussing the ups and downs of married life.

"Don't you ever worry about Ian's behaviour from time to time? Not that there's anything obvious to worry about as far as I can see. I'm just talking hypothetically," was Susan's foray into being able to talk about her own worries.

Meera finished swallowing the first bite of her meringue. "I stopped worrying about my husband's behaviour long ago. These days I just get annoyed sometimes, and very annoyed at other times. What's on your mind, Sue?"

They had arrived late at the coffee shop, and their table by the door was exposed to the full blast of a windy October afternoon every time a shopper wanted to escape the privations of the charity shop stacked High Street. Susan tutted and pulled her coat tighter around her as a family of five struggled to get their possessions through the door kindly held open for far too long by "Hi, my name is Jo."

Here goes, thought Susan. "You'll probably laugh or even be a little bit annoyed by what I'm going to say, but I know Andy, and the only thing that has changed in all the time I have known him has been his shoes." She did not want to get into a heavy conversation, but she was, nevertheless, more than a little concerned about her husband, and would welcome the opinion of someone she could trust to keep the matter to herself.

"Annoyed? Never. Laugh? Probably." Meera smiled. "Believe me, I would be very surprised if you could surprise me."

Susan warmed her hands on her coffee. "I guess it all started sometime around spring. Where are we now? October. So over the past six months or so. Not a sudden change in behaviour – not even that obvious to begin with. But it is now," she prevaricated. "Bottom line: I suppose he just seems so much happier, so much more outgoing. Yes. Happier. Definitely."

Meera laughed. "See, I told you I would laugh, didn't I? So where's the downside? When are you going to tell me about all the juicy bad news?"

"I suppose it does all sound a bit strange and I really should be pleased, shouldn't I, but Andy is not the type to just wake up one day and decide to be happy. Something has changed. But what?" asked Susan, taking an obviously unwashed spoon to her tiny slice of dry carrot cake. She put the spoon down and started to eat the cake with her fingers.

"The usual suspects? Changes at work. Maybe work is going well, or some stresses have just gone or at least got better. And, of course, there's the elephant in the room to consider: whether he's having an affair." Meera moved quickly to take the sting out of the latter usual suspect, as she feared the worry it might cause someone already prone to worrying. "I'm assuming here, of course, for argument's sake, that Andy has not suddenly 'seen the light' and taken to hanging around churches?"

Susan smiled. "Andy is not one of those few scientists who find a way to buy into immaculate conceptions. Work? You might be right. Apparently he is heading up trying to sell his project to another company. He certainly seems happier to talk about what's going on at work these days. But happy enough to spring surprise Spanish holidays on us? He always used to shout me down for wanting to go abroad with the kids; now, right out of the blue, it's 'Costa del Sol, here we come'. Which was great, don't get me wrong; we had a fabulous time, as you know."

Meera did her best to hide a grimace at the memory of all the Jones family holiday photos she'd had to look through the week after they had returned. No Spanish holidays for the Stevens family. Not even under canvas.

"Then there's the family meals out most weekends. He used to hate taking the kids to pubs or restaurants, and I mean *really* hate it. Not any more, it would seem. And look at all the money he has been happy to spend on the house. Decorators in. He always used to insist on doing all the DIY himself. That new living-room suite we have ordered. That wasn't cheap, as you know."

Meera did indeed know.

"And I won't tell you about the bloody tent we bought which we still haven't taken out of the box. Now he's a camping fanatic all of a sudden after that holiday we all took together. None of this is the Andy I know. An affair?"

"I think we can rule that one out with Andy, can't we? Not that he isn't an attractive man, of course," was Meera's rather rushed reply. "He's just not the type. He's the archetypal family man, and I think everyone would agree with that."

Susan swirled her mug of coffee and finished off that which was drinkable. "Every man is capable of an affair, as is every woman given the opportunity. But Andy? Right now? If he is having an affair, then it's not as if he's spending much time with her – assuming it is a her, of course. I mean, he's either at work or with me and the kids. The only hobbies he has are the poor excuse for exercise the boys have on Friday nights, and piano lessons with the Robinses." She thought it best not to mention to Meena how sex with Andy had perked up in recent months. She'd never even really talked to her husband about sex, so she was not going to open up to a friend. But there was no denying that Andy's appetite and energy in bed had returned after years of disinterest from them both.

Meera was relieved that Susan had herself ruled out the possibility of Andy having an affair, even if she was not as reassured as Susan that he was not. "Men are pigs. Bastards. And if they are offered a new bit of arse without any strings attached, they will take it with both hands," muttered Meena across the table. "Andy may not be spending all of his Sunday afternoons singing hymns but that doesn't mean that he hasn't had some sort of near midlife epiphany. Like an awakening; a sort of deep reflection on his life," she offered up as a final explanation for the change in Andy's behaviour.

"I do know what an epiphany is, dear," was Susan's gently sarcastic reply. "But you could be right. Who knows?"

"Who knows indeed, my good friend? Two coffees, a meringue and a disgusting-looking carrot cake down, and we are still none the wiser. Another coffee?"

"What a good idea," agreed Susan.

"You're late," commented Susan as Andy laid his laptop bag on the kitchen table. It was not meant as an accusation, but more an observation.

"Tough day but a good one. Difficult to avoid late days when we are talking to the US, especially West Coast companies," he replied. "Kids OK?"

"Sophie's not in a good mood for some reason or

another that she won't tell me about, but she's OK. That's our Sophie for you. Did you have a reasonable lunch at work? Bacon sandwich for you tonight?" asked Susan a little apologetically.

"Sounds nice," lied Andy as he took up his usual position at the kitchen table. "Any homework to help out with?"

Susan pulled out the breadboard from the dishwasher. "All done and dusted, you will be pleased to know."

"Good news from work for a change. Well, sort of. I was told today by Allison that I will not be considered for redundancy next month as I am too important to the ongoing business development activities around trying to sell the project. Not completely brilliant news as they have just pushed the review date back six months, but better than nothing," was Andy's account of his day. He put the kettle on.

"That is very good news," enthused Susan. "A Christmas without the sword of Damocles hanging over our heads. Unlike some of your poor colleagues, I guess."

"Indeed," agreed Andy. "Poor buggers, but I still think they are out to get me, and they will show me the door as soon as the project is sold or deemed unsellable. Just you see. Six months' grace to find another job. I'll start looking after Christmas."

"I can't believe they will let you go after all that you've done for them over the years, but I suppose it's sensible to find a backup strategy." Susan was smelling the open packet of bacon, past its sell-by date, when her husband's attention was diverted by Rachel running down the stairs. *It won't kill him*, she hoped.

"How many times? Don't run down the stairs. Walk," shouted the man of the house. "Loyalty doesn't count for much these days, even though they expect yours without question," he moaned as he rose from the table to make his tea. "Coffee?"

"No thanks, dear," replied Susan. She pondered. "Maybe here's my chance?" she whispered to herself. "On the theme of good news, Ian thinks you're much happier in yourself these days, at least according to Meera." She served up the sandwich and presented the bottle of tomato sauce. "Sounds like it's because work is going well. You do seem happier."

"Ian said that?" asked Andy, preparing to take the first bite of his sandwich. He paused to swallow. He had forgotten to add the sauce. "I must say that I'm surprised that Ian said that. Our Ian is hardly the most emotionally intelligent of hombres."

"Well, that's what Meera said, but don't go talking to him about it. She told me in confidence," advised Susan, anxious to conceal her little lie. "But never mind who said what – I do think that you are a bit easier to live with these days. Not so snappy with the kids, for sure."

Andy was not sure whether to consider this an insult or a compliment. Consistent with the theme of him being more contented, he went with the latter. "I suppose the job is less stressful these days and I am enjoying this new business development stuff. Get to meet lots of people. Is this bacon all right? Tastes a bit funny."

Susan nodded her head dismissively.

"Anyway. But I think Brian's death had a big impact on me; maybe bigger than I thought at the time. Dying that young, with all that living gone in a heartbeat. If anyone wanted a reason to squeeze the life out of every day they're given, then there it was. I'm sure I wasn't the only one to think that at the service. A tragedy." Andy had surprised even himself. *What a brilliant cover to hide why I'm really happy*, he thought.

"I didn't think you thought that much of him. You didn't seem to have much time for him when he was alive," Susan accused. "And my mother would vouch for that."

"And with good reason, I would say. But no one deserves what happened to him; a young man with all that time to really live," added Andy. "Imagine the children dying before us."

This last sentence tipped the balance for Susan. It all made sense now: his change in mood and behaviour. How could she ever think that he was having an affair?

At that very same moment, a high-resolution image of Janey's arse from the day of Brian's funeral wandered into Andy's brain.

And there, in a nutshell, is men for you. Pigs to a man. But not my Twm, of course, as he would never dream of doing such a thing. Not if he knows what's good for him!

AND LIFE GOES ON

Janey was sitting on the dressing table's matching chair in the spare bedroom, facing a bed containing her still-naked lover, who was watching her carefully pull on her stockings. Always stockings with Janey. Never tights. And Andy just loved that.

"As I said, Graham will be back not long after eight tonight, so you had better get a move on, young man," ordered Janey.

Andy's experience over the past few wonderful months, of enjoying trying to learn the piano followed by an energetic 'dance' or two, had taught him to be more relaxed about the whereabouts of the friend he was cuckolding. But the warming and relaxing effects of WRT743 slowly leaving his circulation certainly helped calm him. "I know. But it's just so hard to get out of this bed and walk away from you once again. If only I could stay the night," he murmured.

"Funny you should say that." Janey smiled. She was now fully stockinged, dressed and made-up in anticipation of welcoming home her hard-working husband. Theatrically, she whipped off the duvet of the king-sized bed to further encourage her lover to leave the love nest so that she could strip the bed and wash out any incriminating evidence.

"Do you really need to change the bedclothes in the spare room so often, darling?" Graham had asked on more than one occasion. "It's not as if we have guests here every weekend."

"You're absolutely right, dear. But I just hate stale bedrooms. Can't resist freshening them up even if no one has slept in them," Janey had lied. *Note to Janey's brain*, she'd thought. *Make sure you only wash the sheets when Graham is out.*

"OK, I get the hint," admitted Andy, who had at least made the effort to sit up on the side of the bed. "But what did you mean when you said, 'Funny you should say that'?"

"I'm assuming you didn't know that my birthday is coming up in a few weeks' time. The 10th November, to be precise. So, I was thinking, why don't we do something a little bit different than the usual piano lesson to celebrate the occasion?" suggested Janey, who was now facing away from Andy and brushing her hair with the aid of the dressing-table mirror.

Andy slowed momentarily in buttoning up his favourite dark green shirt. *Is this relationship changing? Is she actually starting to like being with me rather than just using me to get access to 743?* he dared to think. "I know now. I won't ask the number. What did you have in mind? Aren't you celebrating your birthday with Graham?" he asked.

"I'm sure we'll be going out to some nice restaurant or

other, so no need for you to worry about that. What did I have in mind for *us*? How about going to a nice hotel for the night? An afternoon spent dancing. A lovely evening meal. Maybe a slow waltz before falling asleep, and then a rumba in the morning before saying goodbye. That work for you?" asked Janey, her eyes teasing.

Andy's thoughts were a jumble of excitement at the prospect of spending a night and the following morning with a beautiful woman, and the excuses and guilt at cheating his family. "Sounds very appealing indeed, but what will we use for an excuse?"

"*Excuses.* No need for us to have the same excuse. I've not really thought this through, but I could tell Graham that I'm stopping overnight in London with an old friend. Nothing to alarm him there, I would have thought. And couldn't you just say you're at some business meeting or, better still, some sort of residential conference?" pondered Janey.

"Not a bad idea," replied Andy, who had roused himself to get dressed fully, aside from the shoes he couldn't find. "Have to give it some thought," was the line they'd both known he was going to use. "But where and when?"

Janey pointed. "They're under the bed where you left them. Let me sort out the hotel. Somewhere not too far away, but far enough away to make it unlikely that anyone there will know us. Me and Graham have separate credit-card accounts so it's not a problem for me to book and pay. We can settle up after. But there is one thing I will need to warn you about: it won't be cheap!"

"I think I might have guessed that." Andy smiled as they descended the stairs, Janey first.

"Best lesson yet, I thought," she whispered in his ear as she opened the front door for her fellow student.

"We've had worse," commented Andy with a subtle wave as he crossed the street to a still-empty 6 Malvern Drive.

First step agreed. Now all I need to do is come up with a convincing script to tease a few doses out of my little lover to take down to the London gang. Perhaps just before he falls asleep after a long night of dancing, mused Janey as she waved goodbye and shut the front door of number 4 Malvern Drive.

The anaesthetist was correct in that Andy had felt a small prick in his arm, and he was now advising his patient to count backwards from ten. As a fully paid-up and very active member of the unofficial Royal Society of Hypochondriacs, Andy was sufficiently terrified to do precisely as he was told without further comment. One of his keen worries peculiar to such occasions was that he would end up counting down into negative numbers. However, he'd only managed to get to four when it was lights-out time.

The next thing he was conscious of was seeing the surgeon hover over his abdomen. A scalpel was requested.

They haven't started? But I'm still not under! panicked Andy. "Stop! Stop! I'm still awake," cried the patient.

No one in the room changed what they were doing.

Andy tried to raise his arms and lever himself up off the table, but nothing worked. He couldn't even clench his right fist, although he could almost feel the signals being sent from his brain down to his hand. *They must at least be able to see that my fucking eyes are open.* "Help! Stop now," were the last words he thought he had cried out before the first incision was made, yet the sensation he felt was more one of someone drawing a line on his chest rather than actual pain. *At least the anaesthetic is having some positive effect.* The scene was becoming more and more like one of those gory recollections, so beloved by hypochondriacs, from patients who are convinced that they remained conscious through a major operation. Andy had never been persuaded by such accounts, but he was now willing to reconsider his earlier scepticism. He was pretty sure that he could feel the surgeon peeling back the skin covering his abdomen and clamping it tightly back. But – mercifully for the horrified patient – it wasn't painful, just unnerving. Very unnerving. Andy could hear the surgeon breathing heavily, and the rattle of surgical instruments to the right of operating table. Strangely, the bright lights above were starting to dim. And then go off. Darkness.

"Shit!" shouted Andy to a roomful of people who weren't listening. "A fucking power cut!"

Again, no comment from the surgical team to either confirm or deny the patient's observation.

Now in complete darkness, Andy felt his bed moving slowly down the room and then plunging, feet first, off the edge of the cliff the room had become. He could feel himself falling dramatically the only noise being the passing rush of air past his bed. Surrounding him on all sides throughout his free falling descent were what seemed like the windows of hospital wards, each with gowned patients watching him fall further and further. He fell past floor after floor of hospital wards as if he had been thrown off the top floor of the atrium of a grand hotel. Some of the patients were standing, and some stared at him from hospital beds pushed up against the windows. Some had mutilated faces; others looked as if they were dying. All were transfixed, staring at Andy falling past them. Ward after ward as he plunged. Just as he wondered why there were no women in these wards, the women appeared. They were all naked, all old, and all pointing and laughing at him, apart from two who suddenly came into view, standing together and holding hands. They were Susan and Janey. Both were crying.

Andy woke up violently, his body immediately snapping into a ninety-degree position. He could feel the bile rise from his stomach into his throat. He rushed into the en-suite bathroom and vomited into the toilet. Gasping for air, he was aware that Susan was standing behind him within the door frame.

"Are you all right? I mean, do you feel a little better now?" asked a clearly concerned Susan.

"I'm fine," replied a clearly not fine Andy, who had climbed up off his hands and knees, flushed the toilet, and was now swilling his mouth under the tap.

"You look really pale. No chance of you going to work looking like that. Why don't you just go back to bed, and I will bring up some dry toast and tea after you have had some more sleep? You look terrible," added Susan for extra effect. "Perhaps you've come down with a bug, or maybe you had a bad reaction to that salmon you had last night, but I remember that you didn't exactly look a hundred per cent when you came back from your piano lesson. Definitely a bit spaced out."

"Who knows?" answered Andy, keen to get away from the subject of how he'd looked after coming back from Janey's. He flushed the toilet for a second time, walked like an old man back into the bedroom, and (following an expletive) climbed into bed.

Susan resumed her position next to him.

"But you're right. I'll have a little lie-in to recover and see how I feel in a few hours. No rush."

"Very sensible. I'll get up to sort out the kids, but that won't be for a good hour or so," said Susan, glancing at the bedside clock. She turned towards her husband and rested her arm on his chest. "Time for a quick one to follow up after the long, slow one we had last night? Only joking, dear. But last night was very nice. Very nice indeed."

Andy tried to remember last night. *Back from Janey's quite early. A sneaky tumbler of rum as a quiet celebration of a very enjoyable piano lesson. I must hide that bottle better, although I suppose there's not much left. I don't even really like rum that much. Susan and the kids back just after nine. Yes. And then bed and sex. Surprising that Susan has not linked my piano lessons with us having sex. Definitely will not do that next time, just in case she's getting suspicious.*

But Andy's bigger concern was the way he felt the morning after taking WRT743. Typically, the week after was never a problem and he actually felt very relaxed for the first few days. It was just the morning after (and sometimes the rest of that first day) that was the problem, although this was the first time he had actually been physically sick. Usually it was just a bad headache and brain fog.

Janey too had said that she got headaches the morning after, but she'd brushed them off in a rather typical Janey way. "I always get headaches, and you should expect some sort of payback after such naughty enjoyment."

All very unscientific, thought Andy, *although it is reasonable to conclude that headaches are a side effect of taking WRT743.* But on this particular morning the thought was bothering him that there was something more sinister going on with this drug other than just the odd headache.

He rose from bed to rummage around the medicine cabinet in the en-suite bathroom. He took the Full Monty option, maxing out once again on doses of both ibuprofen and paracetamol. He did not want to consider going any further than what he could easily buy from pharmacies, although there was little doubt that his headaches were gradually getting worse with every dose of WRT743 he took. Adding to these concerns was some preliminary data he had received at work indicating that WRT743 caused mild vacuolar degeneration in rat brains. Quite a rare finding but, as well as being marginal, it was not dose-related and so the consensus of the project team was to carry on with the development of the drug and, in parallel, look into this potentially concerning finding in more depth. The definitive toxicology read-out would take time. Months.

How nice it would be if every morning was like this. Andy smiled to himself as he dunked a piece of shortbread in his strong tea. He was sitting alone at the kitchen table, enjoying the autumnal morning sun streaming through the window. The children were at their various schools, and Susan was busy buying 'essentials' they didn't need on her way back from dropping them off. Andy's crushing headache was starting to become a memory, and the tranquillity of the morning had taken care of his brain fog. *This must be what every morning is like for Janey*, he thought as he reached for a second piece of shortbread. *But I bet she doesn't eat until well after midday. I wonder if she gets these strange dreams after taking 743? I must ask her.*

He finished his shortbread and his tea and started to get ready for work. He also decided to focus his thoughts on what to do about the recent toxicology data. It was very preliminary and should not be considered significant, but those were insufficient reasons to deter Andy from worrying.

Harlow, 24 Miles —

Plan A was quickly arrived at. Andy's health was top priority, so he would book an appointment, this time with his usual GP at the Ulstown surgery, and discuss bringing forward the MRI scan he had discussed with Graham earlier in the year. It seemed sensible not to see Graham about this, just in case Janey had shared her side effects with him and he noticed the parallels. An MRI would show up any unlikely vacuoles in Andy's brain.

Plan B was going to be a bit trickier. In fact, a lot trickier. Regardless of whether 743 was creating vacuoles in brains – "Very, very unlikely," whispered Andy to himself as further reassurance – it clearly had some unpleasant side effects, and so was not worth taking unless one was a patient for whom successful treatment of an illness, such as severe depression, was a good trade-off for getting headaches. But was sex with that beautiful, unobtainable woman a good trade-off?

"Only one thing for it," announced Andy to the empty car. "We need to compare 743 against a placebo." As in all good placebo-controlled trials, the patient would not know if they were taking the placebo or the drug. The title of the very small clinical trial was to be *Will Janey Reach Orgasm with Andy When on a Placebo?*

How the bloody hell will she react when I tell her afterwards? was the worry he could not quite put out of his mind. *But a night in a luxurious hotel might not be the worst place in the world to start the trial.*

HOTEL

And that night was turning into everything Andy could have wished for. That was, aside from the mildly inauspicious start caused by him not being able to leave work until later than he had planned and consequently had received a gentle rebuke from Janey. One does not keep Mrs Janey Robins waiting. Having to park the car in a side road outside the hotel also hadn't helped, but the hotel car park had been full when he'd arrived. But all that was soon forgotten over a lavish dinner for which both had made the effort to dress for the occasion: he in a tie and jacket, and she in the black dress she had worn at the funeral.

"Now you can stare at my arse with impunity," teased Janey as she walked in front of him down the hotel corridor. And he did.

The dinner was heavy, with wine to match. The conversation was relentless, each with much to tell of their life and their loves, their dreams and their hopes. There was laughter, but also a little sadness and some regrets.

The lovers might have spent many hours learning to play the piano and dancing, but they had never really had the time to properly talk about anything other than arranging the next lesson. Or was it that they'd chosen not to talk? A case of deliberately not wishing to know too much about a person they were never supposed to be with? If so, then tonight was undeniably different. Andy dared to dream that Janey was attracted to him, and not only because of the chemicals.

Both were on a natural high after dinner and drinks when Andy failed to get his key card to work on the door to the Deluxe King Suite at the grandly named Royal Cavendish Spa Hotel. Janey rescued the situation by managing to get into the room with her card, and then she locked Andy out.

"What are the magic words?" she whispered from behind the locked door.

"Oh, I don't know. All very childish. Don't be so annoying, Janey." Andy looked up and down the corridor to make sure that no one was witnessing his embarrassment.

"Wrong. Two more goes and then you are sleeping in your car tonight."

Silence, other than the noise of the cogs whirring in Andy's brain. "Would Madam like to sample some hard drugs?"

"Is the right answer. Or close enough," announced Janey as she opened the door with a flourish.

Andy walked in and went to kiss his lover in the doorway.

"Hold on, big boy. First things first," was Janey's response as she backed into the room. "Hard drugs first and then the kinky stuff. If you're lucky, so don't push it," she teased. She went to the lavishly stocked and outrageously priced minibar and brought out a chilled plastic bottle of Coke. "Will this do instead of lemonade?" she asked as she walked over to the table to pick up two glass tumblers. She filled both of the small glasses to near the brim.

"Don't see why not," answered Andy as he made his way over to his suitcase and opened up the zipped side pocket and retrieved two vials. *The usual Janey, then. Drugs first, second and third*, he thought. *How could I ever think that she had some genuine feelings for something other than chemicals? But never mind. There are worse things to do on a freezing November night.* "And I nearly forgot," he called out, rather too loudly. "Your birthday present." He proceeded to take out a small Bluetooth music speaker (with extra base), which he placed on the table next to where Janey was standing. *I hope to God that Susan has not noticed that it has gone missing*, he worried.

"You've bought me a music player for my birthday? How thoughtful, but you really shouldn't have."

"No, no," replied Andy, wondering if he couldn't have handled this better. He picked up his mobile phone and held it up for Janey to see. He scrolled through his playlists and pointed to *Birthday Songs*. "I put together some songs I thought you might like for your birthday, and, if you like, we can play them as background music for whatever we choose to get up to tonight." He smiled in the hope of getting approval from the impossible-to-impress Janey.

"How sweet," was her genuine reply, and she felt compelled to lean forward and kiss him on the forehead.

"You really do know your way into a girl's knickers, don't you?" laughed Janey.

If only you knew how long it took me to put that playlist together. Andy smiled to himself. *We might have known each other for months, but I still have absolutely no fucking idea what music she likes. At least she seems to like the idea in principle.* "The least I could do. It's your birthday and I really should be paying the whole bill for tonight," he offered, wincing at the thought that she might accept his generous offer.

She didn't. There were more important things on her mind. "Why don't you start the music and sprinkle some of that pixie dust of yours onto the Coke? There's a good boy." And with that, she pushed her hand through her hair provocatively in preparation for enjoying the benefits of some hard drugs.

They stared at each other as the pixie-dusted drinks were finished.

"*Cin-cin.*"

"Cheers."

Janey looked again at the label on the Coke bottle. "Diet Coke? I'm sure I can taste sugar."

"That's what you get with five-star hotels," quipped Andy. "Sweet-tasting diet drinks. Time to slip into something more comfortable?" he asked, trying to steer the conversation away from what he knew had been added to the drinks. Sugar. And only sugar.

He led the way in undressing, diving under the soft duvet of the king-sized bed and tossing his unfolded clothes on top of his suitcase rather than folding them and placing them in the shared wardrobe. He was ready and waiting for whatever might happen next. Janey then delighted in playing the seductress; an imaginary temptress from an erotic black-and-white French film. But it suited them both. She was in control, and started by undressing so very slowly while he lay in bed naked, watching her. Each item of clothing was delicately folded and laboriously deposited in the wardrobe, except for her black stockings, which were still on when she pulled back the duvet and lay down next to her lover, who had just remembered to start playing the birthday music selection.

"Celine Dion? Really?" Janey frowned as the first song started.

"Let's try the next song," said Andy apologetically as he reached over to his bedside cabinet for the player. "It was very difficult to imagine what you like, you know. Took me hours."

Janey stroked the back of his shoulder. "I know. Leave it on. Music when in bed. It doesn't get any better."

But it did. A locked door. No worry about Graham returning early. No Susan and the kids to rush home to. No bedclothes to wash. They had all the time in the world. There was no urgency in their lovemaking that night. No frantic coupling. No desperate gasping for breath. Not so much as a shared bead of perspiration. Just a long and relaxed night of intertwining bodies and blissful sleep.

Andy was the first to wake in the closing hours of a November night. The playlist was on its third cycle and Elton John once again stepped up to his piano.

Tiny Dancer.

What perfect words, thought Andy to himself as he stared at the tiny dancer lying asleep next to him. *If only she could hear those perfect words now at this perfect time.* Her face had an unblemished, porcelain-smooth complexion and the innocence of youth. At that moment she was no older than twenty-five, and she was Andy's girl. The perfect girl. The perfect woman. The perfect moment. He looked at her and dreamed of a life that might have been.

In that very brief moment when life could not possibly get any better, Andy paused to recall the life that he had lived up to this moment in time. Did his dream of the life that might have been mean that he had made all the wrong choices? Picked the wrong wife? Followed the wrong career? Never been the person he could have been? But he had no regrets about marrying his university sweetheart. He knew he had got lucky with her. He didn't deserve her and she deserved better, just like her mother had always insisted. He had never made a better decision than asking her to marry him; a perfect wife who then became a perfect mother. He would never, ever leave her, his family or their home, even if Janey took it upon herself to offer him the life that might have been. This practical arrangement was just for sex and for the confidence he gained from being able to entice a beautiful woman into his bed, regardless of how that had happened. *All very shallow and selfish*, Andy often thought to himself in his many introspective moments, but he also managed to convince himself that this new confidence made him a better man. A happier man, and one more content with his life than he had ever been. This fragile reasoning was delicately balanced against a clawing and inescapable guilt.

After the end of Elton's song, he reached over to switch off the speaker, but in doing so unintentionally roused Janey.

"Sorry," apologised Andy. "You looked so peaceful just lying there, dozing. Does it get any better? A lovely dinner, some fizz and a bottle of red, and the S-word to finish off the night." 'The S-word' was now a well-established shared phrase with which Janey often teased him with.

"'Finish off the night'?" asked Janey, slowly raising her head off her deflated pillow. "Not even midnight yet. No rest for you just yet, young man. It is my birthday, don't forget." She quipped as she made her way to the en-suite bathroom, throwing a hotel dressing gown around her naked shoulders.

Andy smiled to himself as she closed the bathroom door. *I think we can confirm from this particular experiment that Andy doesn't need drugs to deliver to specification! But do I risk telling her that the Diet Coke was not quite Diet Coke and the sweetness she had picked up on was because I added fifty milligrams of white sugar?*

A wash, a quick touch-up of her make-up, a dab of perfume here and there, and Janey was ready for action again. She slid open the bathroom door and walked around the bed, making sure that Andy had time to appreciate what he could see under the open dressing gown.

"That was all very nice, Mr Jones," she confirmed as she took off the dressing gown and slipped back under the duvet next to him, "but there's definitely something different about tonight. Are you sure you put the full dose into the Coke? Don't get me wrong, the S-word was great, but I'm really not getting that warm and relaxed feeling afterwards tonight. You know, that sort of psychedelic glow we've talked about before." She faced Andy with a puzzled look in her eyes. "Could it be that the ginger man has stiffed you? I would certainly be taking it back if I had bought that at Boots. Not doing what it says on the label. How about a top up right now?"

Probably best to come clean and just come out with it now, considered Andy. *If not now, then when?* "Well, it was the side effects. You know, the headaches, the brain fog, the dreams, and I was actually sick after the last time," he began.

Janey looked even more confused.

"What I'm trying to say..." prevaricated Andy. "What I'm trying to say is that I was worried enough about the side effects – and you've had headaches as well, don't forget – to see what would happen if we just took a placebo."

"What you're trying to say..." mimicked Janey in an attempt to impersonate Andy. "What you're trying to say is that you pretended to give me the drug when actually you fucking didn't." She was now sitting up in bed, staring at him.

Andy also sat up. Maybe it would have been better not to come clean about this right now. worried Andy to himself. Janey was moving into very angry mode. "Well, obviously I couldn't tell you that it was a placebo, otherwise the experiment wouldn't have worked," he argued, opening his hands in an apologetic gesture.

"So I'm a fucking experiment now," she countered as she left the bed and walked naked over to the minibar to see if there was anything in there that would dampen her anger.

God, that woman just is *sex*, Andy thought, watching her bend over to reach for a small bottle of negroni cocktail.

She poured it out into her empty tumbler without asking him if he wanted anything from the minibar.

"You enjoyed the sex, didn't you? At least, that seemed to be the case from where I was looking, so doesn't that prove that you don't need the drug to reach orgasm? To enjoy sex?" was Andy's QED.

Janey decided to curtail any further titillation by pulling on the dressing gown and tying it securely at the front. She moved towards the window and opened the curtains enough to be able to look out onto the brightly lit hotel car park two floors below. "You just don't get it. You just don't fucking get it, do you, Andy?" she insisted, whilst shaking her head in exaggerated exasperation. "The sex is just a small part of the experience." Now facing him, she squeezed together her finger and thumb to show just how small. "The euphoria. The feeling of confidence. Everything in the world being just fine, thank you very much. The muscles being relaxed better than after any fucking session in a spa. Happiness and contentment that last for days afterwards. That's what I'm looking for. Do you get it now? Will you ever get it?"

Andy had no idea where all this was going. "Of course I do, and it's not that I don't also get those feelings, but perhaps me having sex with you is more enjoyable than you having sex with me."

"And please don't give me all that 'poor little me' shit,

Andy," spat out Janey. "The bottom line is that you lied to me. Lied to me and lied to me on my fucking birthday celebration." That was her attempt to occupy the moral high ground.

"Mea culpa, Janey. But don't forget, we don't know anything about this drug. We've no idea what it is or how it works. I was just trying to be careful – for both of us," lied Andy.

"Indeed," replied Janey. "And that is all a bit strange, isn't it? I mean, you still not knowing anything about a drug you have managed to magic up out of nowhere." countered Janey who had now sat down at the table. Cocktail number one had almost been finished. "You said that you only had ten vials, of the drug but here we are, some twelve or fourteen vials later, and you've not said anything about running out. Got yourself a nice little supply there? A nice big stash?" There was an edge to her voice; perhaps even some vitriol aimed at her lover. "Anyone you would care to introduce to me? I wonder if I need the middleman anymore?"

Andy paused in an attempt to craft a convincing lie to end this ugly spat which was ruining the night. He could not tell her the truth. Janey must never know the real source of the drug, as that would just open another can of worms and another angle with which she could blackmail him if she wished to. "OK. Hands up. I can get more out of the contact I told you about, but I don't want to risk involving you in all this. No need for you to know the details. If you – if *we* – want more of the drug then I can get it. You just don't need to know anything more about it. Why take the risk?"

In a heartbeat, Janey's demeanour changed. "So you can supply on demand, then?"

"I don't know about supply on demand, but there doesn't seem to be a problem with getting what we need. At least for the moment," replied Andy, guessing where this conversation was leading. She had backed him skilfully into a corner, and he knew it.

"So, if I asked you for some vials to use for just me on my own in my own time then it wouldn't be a problem for you and your supplier to humour me? Not talking lorryloads here, just a little 'something for the weekend' sort of thing. And of course, I would pay for it," said a now much calmer Janey. She even smiled.

"In theory, I suppose. In theory," was the best he could come up with.

"OK, OK. Sounds promising and worthy of further discussion, my good boy, but still, you have rather fucked up tonight, haven't you my little love? You ruined my birthday," teased Janey.

"Maybe not." smiled Andy. "One might have considered a contingency plan."

"And what, pray, might that be?"

"A couple of vials of the real McCoy, just in case the experiment didn't work."

"What an excellent scientist you are. Here's my glass." Janey raised her empty tumbler in eager anticipation.

"But they're in the car. In the glovebox, and I will have to get dressed and go out and get them."

"So you will," agreed Janey. "But why didn't you just put them in your case?"

Andy didn't want to disclose that the real reason to not

pack them in his suitcase was because he'd wanted to avoid taking the easy option of giving out WRT743 at the start of the night. "What if there had been a fire, or someone had broken into the room when we were out, or—"

"We were raided by the vice squad?" interrupted Janey. "Not very likely, is it? And why do you insist on using those attractive but very suspicious-looking vials which cry out, 'Drugs inside – please try me'? Why don't you hide them in an empty salt or sugar container?"

"What a very good idea. I'll do that with the rest of the vials when I get home." Andy realised what he had said only when he arrived at the end of the sentence.

"More at home? Definitely some to spare for poor old little Janey, then. Very much looking forward to it. Don't let me stop you getting dressed." She smiled as she opened the minibar in search of her next drink.

"But it's getting on for one in the morning," argued Andy, looking at the clock above the table. "Why don't we just get some sleep and take them in the morning after a nice breakfast in bed?"

"What a good idea," Janey replied, which surprised him.

"No need for me to get dressed, then?" he said, relieved.

"The good idea was actually that we take some now, *and* again after breakfast," countered Janey.

"Is that wise?"

"Wise? It's bloody brilliant." She poured out a second bottle of negroni. "As I said, please don't let me stop you getting dressed. I'll rustle up some Diet Coke, and this time it will really be Diet Coke, won't it, Andy, rather than the sugared version I'm guessing you gave me last time?"

She was still smiling as Andy quietly closed the hotel-room door behind him on his way down to his car and some sugar-free hard drugs. Her main take-home message from the night so far was that Andy could not be trusted. *Pretty much like all pushers, I guess*, she concluded rather ungraciously. The sooner she could use some samples from him to reintegrate herself back into her old group of misfits, the sooner she would not have to rely upon just one source of recreational drugs. *But*, she pondered, *perhaps I should give some credit to the man. Very naughty of him to lie about the drug, but that was some great sex and I definitely did orgasm, and all without the aid of chemicals. Pleasantly surprising, really.*

Andy was similarly thoughtful as he took the stairs, rather than the lift, to the ground floor. Not a good time to get stuck in a lift, without socks or underpants under his long overcoat, trousers and shirt. He waved meekly to an expressionless concierge as he passed reception, mouthing, "Forgotten something," to a member of staff who could not have been less interested in what one of the night's many adulterer guests had to say. *Just as well that I brought four vials along with me, but I'm certainly not going to take one in the morning as well.* He considered whether he should take some headache tablets before the WRT743. Then the gathering chill of a very early November morning reminded him once more that he was not wearing any underpants.

STOLEN CAR

Kev looked up and down the dimly lit side road. It was just before midnight so it would be surprising if anyone had a good reason to walk down a road where there were no buildings unless they were up to no good, and getting up to some no good was exactly what Kev was contemplating. *How fucking stupid can you be, parking an executive car in a side road with no houses?* He rubbed his hands in gleeful anticipation and reached into his rucksack for the electronic bag of tricks that had served him so well up to now. He kissed the beeping box as the driver's door opened first time. "You little beauty," he whispered to his electronic best friend. This wasn't the first car he had broken into in the street leading to the Royal Cavendish Spa Hotel. He could usually be sure of rich pickings outside the five-star hotel with its small and outrageously expensive car park. Rarely did he not get a good return on the cost of his train fare to get there. Much to his delight but no little surprise, the car started first time.

"Got a great one here for you, buddy," advertised Kev by text on his mobile phone. He had parked his newly acquired car in a lay-by a few miles before the A10, wanting to drive back in daylight so as not to arouse any suspicion that he was driving a stolen car. Then straight to D&W Autos to drop off the car, and thus he could avoid having to take the car home.

"A great fucking what?" was the reply from the W of D&W Autos. "Do you know what fucking time it is?" At least W had made the effort to phone. He was indeed interested.

"Yeah, sorry, mate, but you're never in bed before two, are you, and I know this is just what you were looking for. You get first dibs. A very smart 70-plate VW Passat two-litre TDI auto with loads of cracking options," continued Kev, fiddling with the sports drive setting. "Very smart black leather, and even a sunroof. Looks like a pearlescent white to me but I'll have to check. Epic car and great to drive."

"And how the fuck is that what I want?" was the comeback.

"No need to get all arsey with me, mate: and we both know that you're just fucking with me to get a good price, so you can just fuck off right now and I can take it to Mags if you're not interested. In fact, you know what? Fuck it. I'll do that," countered Kev.

"All right, all fucking right. Calm yourself. Bring it down to the garage tomorrow morning, but after the punters have dropped off their cars. After ten. But I'm not buying shite."

Kev smiled. "No problemo, 'cause I'm not selling shite," were his last words before ending the call.

Resigned to sleeping in the car overnight, Kev looked to see if there were any goodies in the boot. A large umbrella, a pair of walking boots and a car blanket were not going to make him rich overnight. But he did take the blanket as a way of keeping warm in the car against the frost that was beginning to form on the grass verges. Back inside the car, he glanced at the back seats. Nothing, other than an outsized road atlas of Britain. *Why the fuck would you waste money on that when you've a top-of-the-range satnav? Must be an old geezer.* He thought some more about the owner. Probably someone with a family, given the type of car he was sitting in. Definitely a man, based upon the lingering smell of aftershave. *On the pull? Lucky fucker. Some suited executive wanker who thinks he's better than the likes of me. Serves him right to get his car pinched.* But there's something more to this man, considered Kev. *Not top dog at work or I'd be sitting in a Range Rover, so my man is probably some bellend middle-manager type, up to his bollocks in stress. Poor bastard. Pissed on all day at work, and then goes home to sniff his brats' nappies and get served up shit for dinner by his wife, who looks nothing like the woman he married and is getting shagged every morning by the Amazon man. Having his car nicked is the least of his worries. I'm doing him a favour, really.* He afforded himself a smile for not being like the driver. *Wanker.*

Contemplation completed, he then leaned over to the glovebox, which was easily unlocked. *You'd think the ass-fucking Germans would be able to work out how to lock a car, wouldn't you?* Inside were the expected car manual and locking wheel nut. Not so expected was a cellophane bag containing some vials. *'Ello, 'ello, 'ello! And what little beauties do we have here? No wonder the wanker bothered to lock the glove box.* His pupils dilated in anticipation of his pupils soon to be dilated. He opened the seal and shook out the four vials onto the passenger seat. *Who's a lucky boy? And just look how pure and white. Must be some quality, tip-top gear.* He unscrewed the black cap of one vial and sprinkled a sample onto his middle finger before tasting it. Not a taste he recognised, and he knew all the tastes. A little metallic, and a bit sharp. "What the fuck. What's the worst that could happen?" commented Kev as he emptied the contents of the vial into his mouth and washed the powder down his throat with his first swig from a bottle of vodka he had brought with him as company for the long night ahead.

The next hour was spent watching hard porn on his phone while listening to his music played through the car's top-of-the-range entertainment system. He felt relaxed, but no more than that. *What sort of shite gear has Percival the Posh Pusher left me?* he pondered before washing down vials two and three with even more vodka. The fourth vial was put in his rucksack for another day. *Don't want to go mad.* He smiled to himself.

Essex Police had been called to the scene by an early-morning jogger who'd heard music from a car parked up in a lay-by and found a man lying awkwardly across the front seats. The jogger had not managed to rouse the driver by banging on the window, and could not get into the car as it was locked from the inside.

The policewoman and her partner who were first on the scene thanked the jogger and broke into the car by smashing a side window, to find the driver unconscious but still breathing. An ambulance took him to the Princess Alexandra Hospital in Harlow, and the officers attending arranged for the car to be picked up and taken back to Harlow Police Station.

The driver was identified as Kevin Elvis Aaron Aspinall of Epping, based on a driving licence that was found in a rucksack on the passenger seat. The registered owner of the car was Wright and Briggs Pharmaceuticals of Harlow.

part four

THE RECKONING

NEXT STEPS

"Andy!" barked a surprised Susan as she peered around the kitchen door to see who had let themselves in. "I thought you weren't getting back till this evening. Wasn't that right?"

"That was right," answered Andy as he wheeled his suitcase to attention in the hallway. "But not any more. Someone stole the car."

"What? The Passat?" breathed Susan in disbelief.

"Taken from right outside the conference hotel."

"What are you going to do now? How will you get to work? Will you get in trouble for this?" She was flustered, confused by a clutter of her own questions.

"I don't know, to be honest. Never had a car stolen before. I was going to phone HR when I got home, so I had better get on with it, I suppose. At the end of the day, it's just a car that Wrights lease through some agency or other and the insurance will be sorted out by them somehow." Andy rummaged in his inside jacket pocket in search of his mobile.

"Aren't you supposed to inform the police?" asked Susan.

"I'm not the owner of the car, so I guess HR will do that. I really don't know. I'll talk it through with them and find out what to do." Andy was also starting to become a little flustered again, in sympathy with his wife.

"You're not going into work today, then. But what about tomorrow and the rest of the week, and how did you just get home?" asked Susan, realising that she hadn't yet asked the most obvious question.

Andy had had plenty of time to think about that during the mostly silent drive home with Janey, who had dropped him off just outside the estate. "One of the guys from work was leaving the conference early anyway and he offered me a lift back as he's quite local. He dropped me off at the front of the estate," he lied.

"Lucky," sighed Susan. "Cup of tea?"

"Lovely. I'll ring up work from the lounge. Kids all right?" asked Andy, who was now beginning to recover his composure.

Susan didn't answer her husband's throwaway question, but instead busied herself with filling the kettle. She delivered Andy's tea on a tray she had just bought as a reward for not buying a rather expensive new dinner set she had obsessed over for several months.

"All sorted, it would seem." Andy beamed and put down his mobile on the armrest of the sofa. "HR already knew about the car being stolen because the police had been in touch. They'd found it not that far from the hotel – abandoned, I presume. Anyway, the police then phoned the lease company, who picked up the car and they will arrange the repairs and get it back to me. Sounds like it's been damaged. In the meantime, the lease company will deliver a temporary replacement car to the house tomorrow. All very efficient, I thought – if they stick to their promises, of course."

"Repairs?" questioned Susan. "What repairs? Was it in a crash? Did they catch the thief?" She had almost come to the end of her questioning.

"I don't know. I don't think so. HR said there's just a broken side window. I didn't ask, but I guess it's just how the thief broke in. No idea if they caught anyone. I'll find out soon enough, I suppose. Anyway, it's not like it's actually my car or there was anything of any value to steal from inside, so I'm not too concerned," commented Andy, who was enjoying dunking shortbread into his tea.

"Are you OK? Must have been a shock. You're not going to get into trouble for missing the conference, are you?" repeated Susan.

"It'll be fine," answered Andy, who had decided to focus his worries on what would happen to the four vials he had left in the glovebox. Would the garage handling the repairs look in there? If they did, hopefully they would just leave everything as it was given that the glovebox had been locked. Andy had reassured himself, at least for the time being.

Harlow, 13 Miles —

"Good morning, Andrew Jones speaking," shouted Andy into the hands-free phone receiver of his Ford Focus courtesy car. *So much for getting my Passat back within a week. What the hell are they doing with it?* he snarled to himself.

"Good morning. My name is Louise Jeavons and I'm speaking to you from the Harlow BUPA Clinic regarding your MRI scheduled for the 16th December. I appreciate it's very short notice, but we can squeeze you in late this afternoon due to a cancellation. Would you be able to come in today?"

This was exactly the sort of situation to send Andy into a tailspin and make him panic. And it did. "Um, I'm not sure. Can I ring you back?" pleaded Andy.

"Well, I really need to know now, but I guess we could wait thirty minutes for you to decide, given that we haven't given you much notice. Please ring me back on this number. Thank you."

Andy said goodbye to someone who had already hung up on him. Louise had people to call and patients to meet.

Despite being a card-carrying hypochondriac, he had put to the back of his mind the consultation he'd had with the neurologist nearly a month ago, as his mind was already flooded with thoughts of hotel adventures, stolen cars and work. No doubt another reason why it was not at the top of his agenda was that it was very much hush-hush. He had not told Susan about his appointment or the neurologist's recommendation that he have a brain scan to determine the cause of his chronic headaches and brain fog. *No point in getting her all worried.* He'd also thought it best not to share with the consultant that he was taking some very unconventional medications from time to time. Despite reluctantly agreeing to sign off on the scan, the consultant considered it unlikely that they would find anything untoward, unlike Andy, who thought they would. And that might happen sooner rather than later if he agreed to the new appointment time.

He parked up at work with ten minutes to make the call. He was still shaking. "Hello, is that Louise Jeavons? Andy Jones speaking."

"Ah, Mr Jones. Can I book you in for 4.45pm today, then?"

Andy could hear someone talking in the background, distracting Louise. "Hello? Hello? That should be fine. Can you hear me?"

"Yes, sorry. All a bit busy around here. OK. Let's confirm 4.45pm, but it would help if you could get here by about 4.30. Thank you, Mr Jones. We will see you later today. Goodbye."

Immediately Andy wished that he had kept the December appointment. But he knew he would regret any decision he ended up making. Nearly a whole day of worry in front of him. "Brilliant," he muttered as he once again entered Wright and Briggs towers.

Why is this thing so bloody cold? wondered Andy as a constant stream of chilled air passed his sides. It felt like being strapped into a coffin, with extra ballast so as to prevent even the slightest movement. The bulky headphones and face mask provided the coup de grâce.

He heard the piped voice of the radiologist, who was speaking from some distance away, in a separate room from the monolith that had swallowed the patient. "Would you like some music through your headphones? Radio 2 OK? The scan should take around forty-five minutes."

Andy didn't know whether to laugh or cry. It had come

to this. He looked like a Radio 2 person, and now he had to listen to it for the best part of an hour. "Fine with me."

And then the noise started. Noise that was allegedly caused by the machine, but seemed to Andy to have been taken directly from the CIA's torture playbook. Loud, random and intermittent noise that broke through the whine of Radio 2's DJ. Not that there was anything that could terrify Andy more than what he thought the results of the scan would reveal.

"Very well done, Andy. One more scan sequence and we will be done. Just four minutes to go," was the final announcement from the radiologist.

Will I get a sticker for being a good boy? wondered Andy, though his biggest concern was elsewhere. *If they don't get me out of here right this minute, I promise I will piss myself, and won't that be a funny story for the radiologist to tell her friends?*

He didn't. But it was very, very close.

"Thanks for all your help," gushed Andy after he had returned from the bathroom. He looked very carefully into the radiologist's face to see if he could detect any signs of concern following the scan. Nothing. "When should I expect the results?" was the question the radiologist had already fielded six times that day.

"Your consultant should get back to you in about two or three weeks. Do you have any other questions, Andy?" She was rarely bothered by any other questions, and this patient was no different.

A relieved Andy said his goodbyes and waved to a somewhat surprised receptionist on his way out to the car park and towards his embarrassing Ford Focus, which had been hemmed in by two large, German people carriers. *The face of private healthcare in Britain*, he mused, looking at all the shiny new cars surrounding him. He took time to settle into the driver's seat and commence some reflection before actually starting the car. He had made the right call. But he wouldn't tell Susan about this. Not unless the result forced his hand, of course.

He hated the winter, and the drive home in the dark reminded him that winter was well under way, but it was during that drive back through heavy traffic that he came up with a way to at least have something to look forward to this season. A Christmas holiday. A Christmas holiday by the sea, with fantastic views and big beaches for the children to run around on. *Maybe somewhere in the West Country. A long old drive, but worth it*, he thought as his mind turned towards steepling cliffs and wild waves. *The credit card is going to take another hammering, but time and memories are more important than money. And just imagine Susan and the kids' faces when I tell them!*

Perhaps Brian's death had had some small effect on Andy after all. He also couldn't rule out the possibility that the long-term effects of WRT743 were lifting his mood, as was known to be the case with psychedelics. But surely nothing could compare with the joy that being with Janey could bring.

THE NEXT TIME

How about another piano practice? Don't forget to bring along those four whisky samples you told me about last time. Very much looking forward to it. I can do Wednesday or Thursday next week.

Wednesday after work is best for me.

"I must say that I am a little bit concerned about letting you have this," Andy said as he handed over a vial to Janey on that Wednesday evening. She was still lying in bed in the Robinses' spare room, luxuriating in the after-effects of her latest experience with WRT743. He was sitting on a bedside chair, starting to get dressed. That evening he had abstained once again, and it was obvious from looking at Janey what effect the drug was having even some two hours after taking it. "It's like I'm becoming a pusher."

"Don't be such a silly person," argued a clearly intoxicated Janey. Andy suspected that she had also been drinking before he had arrived, or was it merely a sober person looking at one who wasn't? "And anyway, I thought you had four vials in your car. Where's the missing one? Two will last me longer than one, and then I won't need to bother you any time soon." She had presumed that Andy had partaken before they went to bed, though the reality was that he had found a way to empty most of his drug cocktail into the toilet after excusing himself on their walk to the bedroom.

Andy reminded himself that the Passat had not been returned for a reason he really should have chased up. It had been two weeks since that night at the hotel. "Still haven't got the car back, so the vials I brought tonight are from what I've got in the house."

"You have even more?! I wonder where my little lover keeps his never-ending stash?" teased Janey, pulling back the duvet in anticipation of dressing. "Under the sink? No. No red face there. Back of the sofa? No red face still. In the—"

"Give it a rest, won't you, Janey? All you need to know is that it is there for when we need it."

Janey quickly gave up on the chase that was supposed to have happened at the hotel before events had intervened. She sent herself a memo to remind herself to resume her crusade on another, more sober day, before walking naked past an almost fully dressed Andy as she made her way to the bathroom. She made sure to draw a finger across his chest as she passed by.

That woman will be flirting right up until she is six feet under, thought Andy as he watched her arse disappear out of sight.

With the minimum of further discussion, they both got ready to return to normal life.

"Nearly forgot," began Andy as they descended the stairs. "And I suppose I really should tell you since you are also getting headaches. I had an MRI scan to see if there is anything going on up here." He mentioned this matter-of-factly, as he usually tried to do with potentially life-threatening medical matters. "Should get the results back in two or three weeks, but please don't tell Susan about this. No need for her to worry unless there really is something wrong."

"Are you really *that* worried about these possible side-effects?" asked Janey as she opened the front door.

"A little bit, if I'm being truthful." Which he wasn't. He was far more than a bit worried. "But it's just as likely I'd be having these headaches and the rest even if I wasn't taking this drug. Who knows?"

"Oh, poor you," cried Janey, kissing her finger and pressing it onto his forehead. "I'm sure you'll be OK, but do tell me when you get the results."

You can be sure of that, Janey, thought Andy to himself as he walked in darkness across the road and into 6 Malvern Drive. *If only I could be as relaxed as that woman.*

MEANWHILE, BACK AT THE STATION

I don't suppose my job is much unlike most other people's: about ninety per cent boredom and ten per cent excitement. That elusive and unpredictable ten per cent – where you think that you're really making progress, making a difference – offsets all the crap you usually have to put up with every day.

It was almost time for tea, one rather quiet Thursday morning in mid November, when something in that ten per cent turned up. Didn't sound like anything remotely interesting when DC Simmonds tried to get into my eyeline. The man can be irritating from time to time, not least because he's so annoyingly young and thin, but at least he doesn't hide anything from me, which can't be said for some of his male pals. Anyway, I turned to see what he wanted…

A note just in from the agent: 'Give me a break and drop all the italics and first-person crap, why don't you?!'

So…

DC Simmonds had the eyes and the excited demeanour of someone with something terribly important to say.

"OK. Out with it," demanded DS Elias, putting down her pen and adopting her well-honed weary expression. "Another fight at the chip shop? Our reg caught with his trousers round his ankles in the park again?"

"No, ma'am. A car theft."

Elias swivelled on her chair to show her back to her colleague. "Can you see anything on my back? Does it say anything like, 'Please come and talk to me about car thefts'?"

"No, ma'am."

"So, pray, why do you stand before me, Simmonds?"

"I think you will find this one very interesting, ma'am. The King was found unconscious in a car he'd pinched, and—"

"Sorry. Must stop you there, DC Simmonds," interrupted Elias. "But who exactly is 'the King'?"

"Well, Kev Aspinall. Kevin Elvis Aaron Aspinall. I thought everyone round this shop called him 'the King.'"

"It would seem not, wouldn't it?" responded Elias. "What's the little scrote been up to now? Selling some more of his shocking-quality speed to the masses?"

"Not exactly, ma'am. As I said, he was found unconscious in a stolen Passat." Simmonds opened his notebook. "Whisked off to the Alexandria, where he didn't come round until late the following day. Bloods were taken and the hospital lab found a high concentration of a substance they hadn't come across before. Forensics then found that this substance matched up with a white powder they found in some glass vials in Aspinall's rucksack." He smiled.

"Yes, I suppose some people might find that quite interesting. Have you had a chance to have a little chat with our poor patient?" asked Elias.

"We need to get him round to the station when he's discharged from hospital, but he said when we spoke to him briefly in his hospital bed that he found the substance in the car's glove compartment. Not his, he said, but of course he would say that, wouldn't he?" Simmonds turned the page of his notebook. "And I quote: 'A shit drug that nearly bastard killed me; you tossers should leave me the fuck alone and bang up the criminal wanker who owns the fucking car.'"

"Indeed," replied Elias.

"But he might actually be telling the truth, ma'am. Forensics found someone else's fingerprints on the vials as well as Aspinall's, and those other prints were found all over the car." Simmonds paused for dramatic effect. "Reasonable to assume that they belong to the car's owner, I would say."

"Who, of course, we need to bring in at your earliest convenience," advised the DS. "Do we have a name yet?"

"The car is registered to a lease company and is currently being used by someone at Wright and Briggs Pharmaceuticals just up the road. We have contacted them but not yet got through to someone who can help. Typical big company. But we're on the case." Simmonds moved on to the next page. "But the best is still to come, ma'am. I know you think forensics are a bunch of uncommunicative sociopaths, but they've really delivered on this one."

Elias did her best to look suitably impressed, although she chose to remain suspicious regarding forensics' competence.

"They were able to work out the chemical structure of the substance found in the vials by sending a sample off to some contract analytical lab. It looks like Aspinall probably took most of what was in three of the vials but left one untouched, although we can't be certain about that. We will need to talk to him again. Forensics had never come across this compound before. Completely unknown in the chemical literature, or so they said to me. But here's the clever bit. Some bright spark then searched the patent literature and found a reference to exactly the same chemical structure in a patent that was filed in 2021. The assignee of the patent was none other than Wright and Briggs Pharmaceuticals of Harlow!"

Elias straightened in her chair. "Very nice work, DC Simmonds. And well done. Very interesting. Very interesting indeed. Forensics do seem to have delivered for a change. Right! A plan."

"Yes, ma'am. A plan." *What a brilliant idea*, Simmonds thought sarcastically. *Now why didn't I think of that? I guess that's why I'm not a DS.*

"Arrange to interview your King; get a signed statement presumably backing up what he has already told you, and hopefully without his usual colourful language; then nick him for car theft. Can I leave that with you?"

"Yes, ma'am."

"Let me have Wright and Briggs' contact details and I will get on their backs. Perhaps I can kick a response out of them. At least get the name of the employee who's using the car, and thus our number-one hombre as to who's got hold of this drug. Perhaps your Elvis man was actually telling the truth for a change. You can come along with me when we go to see them at Wright and Briggs. They have got some serious questions to answer, including how the fuck their security allows presumably toxic chemical substances to be taken off-site."

"Yes, ma'am."

"Good stuff, Dave. Very interesting indeed. I'll need to push all this past Jurassic Park upstairs, but I can't see them having any problem with us running with this one rather than giving it to someone else. Now. Off you toddle."

"Off I toddle, my arse," mumbled Simmonds as he toddled off back to his desk, leaving his boss to rub her hands in gleeful anticipation of spending her time on something interesting.

THE CAR

Andy felt he now knew what a panic attack felt like. He had just waved goodbye to the delivery driver who had dropped off his sparkling-clean Passat in the visitors' car park at Wright and Briggs. Even the sand left over from the family's summer holiday that Andy had just not been able to get out of the carpets had miraculously disappeared. But it was not the excitement of finally getting his clean car back that was uppermost in his mind. It was what he would find in the glovebox. His heart rate was already raised before he even opened the compartment.

Nothing. That is, nothing other than a car manual and a locking wheel nut.

He tried not to appear frantic as he quickly searched the rest of the car for the four vials. Boot. Side pockets. Floor. Nothing other than some paperwork from the valet company wishing him a pleasant day, which they had left in a side pocket. *Where the fuck are they?* It didn't make sense for the lease company to have them, unless one of their staff had stolen them. *Possible, but hopefully very unlikely*, considered Andy. Likewise for the valet company. Most probable was that whoever had stolen the car had taken them. That was something that Andy considered to be of low potential risk to him. Once the thief took the drugs, they would be gone and never seen again. *But what if they can trace the car back to me and come knocking on my door for more?* "Fuck!" shouted Andy within the confines of the Passat.

He sat back in the passenger seat to catch his breath and his senses. He knew he was thinking about the worst-case scenario – he always did – and the most likely outcome was that he would hear no more about it. But then the real, *very* worst-case scenario came to mind. *What if it's the police who have the vials?! But surely they would have informed me that they'd withheld something from my car? Wouldn't they? And why would they carry out a search of my car just because it was stolen? Is that the sort of thing they do? Fuck knows.* His heart rate started to pick up again. It was time to consider mitigating any downside to all of this. *Maybe I need to get rid of what's left in the attic in case the thief and his mates – or even the police – pay me a call. I can always get new supplies from work if nothing happens. I need to get Janey to get rid of her vial. Fuck! What am I going to tell her? I can work all that out later, but she must get rid of that drug pronto.*

He reached for his phone in his breast pocket.

You should throw away that sample of whisky I gave you ASAP. I was sick after drinking one of them. We need to talk.

It didn't take long for Janey to reply. It rarely did as of late.

See you at the usual place tomorrow morning? We can talk about it then.

Yes.

At least that bit's sorted, thought Andy as he locked up his car and made his way to reception. *But fuck knows how I'm going to explain this to Janey. She will go ballistic with whatever I say. Should I tell her the truth or spin her another lie?* He was no nearer to working out what he was going to reveal to Janey, but at least his heartbeat had finally returned to something near normal. He convinced himself that this was just another case of him overreacting to a set of circumstances that were very unlikely to amount to anything serious.

Ulstown, 17 Miles —

Could you please contact Harlow Police Station on this number at your earliest convenience?

Andy vowed there and then to never again look at texts while driving. He quickly realised that he hadn't suffered a panic attack earlier in the day when he couldn't find the vials. *This* was what a panic attack felt like. Fortunately – very fortunately – for him, the next service station was only two miles away, and in its car park he was able to slowly calm himself to the point of being mildly terrified.

They've got the vials. The police have got the fucking vials. I was right. And how the fuck did they get my mobile number? Must have been those wankers in HR who gave it to them. Shit, shit. But so what? It's not a crime to have powders in your own car. Why would they immediately assume that every substance they find is a drug? Calm down, Andy boy. Calm down. Nothing to see here.

"Hello. This is Andrew Jones replying to a text about contacting you."

PC Knight could detect the worry in the caller's voice. "Ah, Mr Jones. Let me have a look… Yes, here it is. Could you please come down to Harlow Police Station to meet with one of our officers?"

"Could you please tell me what for? Why do you need to speak to me?" fretted Andy.

"Erm… Just routine as far as I can see," answered PC Knight rustling some papers on her desk, for no obvious reason other than to reassure the caller that she knew what she was talking about. "Apparently, you had your car stolen. Is that right?"

"Yes, that's correct."

"Well, I suspect it's related to that. Just routine, I'm sure," added Knight, trying to reassure him, although she had no more information than did he to justify her soothing words and tone.

A marginally less terrified Andy switched to the calendar on his phone. "I could make the morning of Monday 28th," he lied. He had a meeting with Grace Chaval at work booked in for that morning, but the latter could wait. It could definitely wait.

"Let me have a look… Yes. That should work. How about 10.45am on the 28th?"

"Yes. Fine with me," replied Andy, as he would whichever time she'd proposed.

"OK. We will see you next week. Please report to

reception. Thank you for getting back to us so quickly. Have a nice weekend."

Andy knew that was going to be impossible.

DIFFICULT CONVERSATIONS

I

Andy would have expected Janey, and certainly the Janey of old, to launch into an expletive-filled tirade accusing him at least of lying to her, and probably of many other crimes. Therefore, he was more than mildly surprised to see her pause, take a drink of her coffee and look him directly in the eye. It was time to tell her the truth. *Well, at least some of it.*

"By rights I should storm out of this café and out of the recreation centre right now after the sorry truths you have finally told me. You have lied to me. Taken me for an idiot. You've put my health at risk. But I'm not going to shout, although you fucking deserve to be shouted at," menaced Janey, leaning over the table to look closely into Andy's face. "No, I'm not going to shout. I'm going to be sensible and reasonable. And why?" She paused. "Obviously there are risks in taking this drug, but you're nothing if not a very careful man," she said, with a little warmth. "Maybe even too careful sometimes. Yes, far too careful. So, if you have done your sums – and you will have – and you've been prepared to take the risk of trying this drug, then it's safe to assume that you are not being reckless. And you know what? We're still alive. But most relevant to all this, to this risk, are all the times in the past when I have mixed drugs without any idea of what many of them were, and, yes, even taken concoctions I fully knew had not been tested in proper clinical trials. So you see, it would be rather hypocritical for me to come down too hard on you, at least for that. But the lying? Pretending that Brian – and, after that, his friend – gave you the drug, when all along you were giving me some experimental substance you had taken from work? Unforgivable. You lied. Why?"

Andy was struggling to accept Janey trying to take the moral high ground given her history of deceit, but he was now standing in a glasshouse of his own making. "Why?" He carried out his usual surveillance of those sitting at the surrounding tables. "Imagine the police coming to your house and finding the drug. Your and Graham's house. I'm taking a risk telling you all this, but I think it's better that you know the truth as I don't think you would get rid of your vial if I just asked you nicely and without any justification. True?"

Janey frowned in confirmation that she agreed. "Maybe."

"Get rid of that vial," demanded Andy, as far as Andy was capable of demanding anything. "And now!"

"I will, as soon as I get home. Promise," lied Janey. She wanted to keep her options open with Lucy. And who would ever look inside a tiny, almost empty salt cellar kept at the very back of a kitchen cupboard? A little salt had even been added to mask the taste. She tried to ignore the thought of Graham mistakenly sprinkling the drug onto his fresh pasta and rocket.

"Let me and only me take the risk of the police finding the drug in our houses," finished Andy.

This is just crap. What's all this about police raids all of a sudden? Why should the police be turning up at homes for no good reason? thought Janey, as she stirred her coffee for no good reason. *Andy has been spooked by something that will never happen. Why now? But stealing from work? That does surprise me, and maybe that's what is really behind all this. His fear of getting sacked for stealing company property.* She stopped stirring. "But hold on. Hold on a minute." She paused to work out how best to articulate what precisely she was asking Andy to hold on for. "Why are you telling me all this now? Your car's been stolen; you've got it back. How does that change anything? What's it got to do with your ridiculous panicking about the police raiding Malvern Drive? Is it that your car being stolen has suddenly made you realise that you are stealing from work? A lifetime non-thief, thieving?" She was trying out her theory. But it was Janey who was the one to suddenly realise something. "Oh! The vials were not there. Not in the car. Someone's taken them."

Andy nodded resignedly.

"Well, that will be the car thief, won't it?" concluded Janey, picking up her coffee. "Probably just another junkie stealing to get a score, and here he finds a few in the car. I'm sure he had a good time. So what's the problem here? Why all this bullshit about getting rid of your wonderful drug from my house when there is no risk of anyone even looking for it, never mind finding it?"

"You might well be right, Janey. That's exactly what I thought, and it's probably what happened: a junkie got lucky. But there's a complication. More a potential complication." Andy could not downplay it any more without himself appearing suspicious. "It's the police. They called me in for an interview. On Monday."

"Fuck! The police? It's just a stolen car. Why do they want to talk to you about a stolen fucking car?" countered Janey, in a tone of voice that was picked up by an overly made-up mother busy ignoring a conversation about breaststroke at her table. Janey noticed her interest and fixed her with a glare that would stay with the poor woman for the rest of the day. Breaststroke suddenly didn't seem so boring after all. "Let's take this outside," demanded Janey, who had already stood up and picked up her bag ready to leave.

"But what about the drinks?" asked a still-seated Andy.

Janey leant over the table and suggested, sotto voce, "Fuck the drinks." She threw her coat over her shoulders and stormed out of the café, barging past two members of Junior Archers Group Two.

Andy followed her and apologised on her behalf. "So sorry. We're in a terrible rush."

They met again outside Janey's car. "Get in," she advised strongly.

Andy slumped down into the passenger seat, closed the door firmly and tried to regain his composure. "I'm almost certainly overreacting. They told me over the phone that it's just routine. But, as I said, we should get rid of any traces of the drug at our homes. Just in case."

Janey decided to be selfish. "OK. For argument's sake, let's say that the police *are* the ones who have the vials, and not the thief. It's actually not a drug, based on what you have just told me, so the worst that could possibly happen is that they charge you with something like company theft. I'm assuming you didn't have written permission to take the vials out of work. And even if they charge you with stealing, what's all this got to do with me? There's no link to me. No evidence that I have been using this stolen drug, and certainly that it was stolen by me."

Andy couldn't blame her for taking this selfish line given his own misdemeanours, but he thought that she could have dressed up the sentiment a little better. She was being rather brutal. "Janey. Look. You're almost certainly right, and of course I would never dream of dragging you into all of this," he replied, trying to reassume the moral high ground. "Surely you must know that? My only link to you that they would be able to find is our texts."

"But they're all in code. How the fuck would the police be able to work out what we're talking about?"

"This is not a new millennium version of the Enigma code. They would at least ask questions about all of the strange texts between us, I would have thought. Again, that's why I'm telling you this. Forewarned is forearmed and all that. We need to come up with a consistent story. The drug bit should be very easy: I will just say that I never gave any to you, and you will deny any knowledge if asked. But all those texts? They will surely ask about our relationship, our affair, which is obviously not a criminal offence, but it's not something we would want anyone to find out about. If they convince themselves that we are having an affair, then they might doubt that we are telling the truth about anything else and so dig deeper. They should keep that sort of information confidential, but would you trust them?"

Janey put aside the minor inconvenience of the possibility of her lover being charged with theft and instead chose to focus on the prospect of their affair being discovered. "That would kill Graham. He could probably tolerate me having an affair. I wouldn't be surprised if he actually thinks I *am* having one. Not with you, of course. He would be comfortable bumbling on with our lives as long as no one else finds out. But what would devastate him would be everyone down at the surgery – his colleagues, even the patients – gossiping about him behind his back if this all comes out into the open. He doesn't deserve that."

"Maybe you shouldn't have fucking started this in the first place, then," muttered Andy under his breath. "Look," he continued, "I'm very sure I'm hyperventilating about all this, and the police just want me to fill in a few forms. If they do have the vials, I'll tell them that I took them out of work to try myself as an experiment. Very naughty, but not something they'll lock me away for. I'll then have to make my apologies to Wright and Briggs." It was the latter possibility that was of most concern to Andy. Would they come down hard on him, or just give him some sort of rap across the knuckles? He could well believe either scenario being acted out. "I just want to make sure that we're both fully prepared if they come round asking some difficult questions. You have never taken any drugs off me. Agreed?"

"Yes," snapped back Janey.

"The texts are mostly about piano lessons, and it is in your nature to be a bit flirty, but that's all they amount to.

Some healthy banter. There have been no sexual relations. No affair. Agreed?"

"Agreed. And you agree not to involve me in any of this if at all possible?" added Janey, rather ungallantly.

"Agreed," answered Andy.

"So. Is that it? No more dancing for us? No more drugs? The end?" probed Janey.

"I really hope that is not the case. Let's see what the police have to say on Monday. If it's nothing, which is bound to be the case, we can be up and running again with the piano practice or dancing or whatever you want to call it, as soon as I can half-inch a few vials from work." Andy put his hand over her forearm. "This is not something I want to give up any time soon."

"Nor me." Janey smiled for the first time that morning. "You know, I rather think you have got it all very wrong this morning as surely the police would have appeared at your house already rather than waiting until next week to see you if they thought they were on the tail of a drug baron. I'm sure it's just a meeting to discuss your car being stolen. Bottom line is that you really didn't need to tell me any of this and we could quite easily have carried on just as we have done for the past six months or so. Mr Jones has miscalculated, methinks."

"I really do hope so. And you are almost certainly right, Janey. But I just didn't want to take the risk of not being able to agree a common way forward in the event of shit hitting the fan." Andy paused for reflection. "We view risk differently. We're just very different people, really."

"I think that is something neither of us will have any trouble in agreeing with." Janey smiled.

"Best to keep our heads down until the police have stopped sniffing around," suggested Andy. "Let's keep on with Graham's piano lessons going, though, even if we won't be able to practise by ourselves for a while. Good to keep up the excuse."

"That'll be nice," whispered Janey. "I would miss seeing you, my little lover boy."

That almost sounds genuine, was the surprising thought that came to Andy's mind.

Just as he was about to respond to her warmth, she grabbed his wrist and turned it so that he could see the face of his watch. "Maybe time you should be somewhere else?"

"Shit! The kids." And with that, Andy careered across the car park and back into the recreation centre faster than any member of the veteran athletics team who were warming up outside the recreation centre could have managed.

It was not until he arrived back at 6 Malvern Drive that Andy could mull over the morning's drama. He had said all that he wanted to say, even if the revelations had left him open to potential blackmail by Janey. *But surely she wouldn't do that? Not after all we have been through?* He was reasonably sure that he'd got the key messages across, but it had been difficult – *Very bloody difficult!* – not least because it had all been so contrived. Janey was absolutely correct. He hadn't needed to tell her the true source of the drug. The morning's pitch had been mostly about keeping her from telling the police the original lie he'd used on his lover. That the drugs were from Brian, and then from his friend. With Brian having been a known pusher, the police would have probed deeper and maybe even suspected Andy of dealing other drugs and making use of Brian's network. At that point, Susan's family would likely be drawn into the investigation; a scenario to be avoided at all costs. *Box ticked.*

But Andy was also keen to unburden himself of what he considered the most heinous of his recent crimes: giving someone an untested substance without telling them of the risks that they were taking. That was as unforgivable as it was dangerous. But now Janey knew what the risks were, and if she decided to resume taking WRT743 at some point in the future, she would do so with full awareness of the potential threat to her health. Her choice. *Box ticked.*

Although Andy was still carrying around the heavy weight of the police interview to come on Monday, he had at least unburdened himself of some of it by removing all traces of WRT743 from 6 Malvern Drive. A trip to the attic when Susan was out with the children had been followed by a thorough bleaching of the kitchen sink in which he had washed out the vials. *What a shocking waste,* thought Andy. Susan was both surprised and pleased to see a glistening sink when she returned. "Long overdue for a clean," explained her thoughtful husband. He also felt comforted by Janey's promise to rid Number 4 Malvern Drive of any traces of WRT743. *Box ticked.*

Or so Andy thought.

II

If Andy had slept at all that Sunday night and Monday morning, then he was not aware of having done so. He certainly had not benefited from it. The headache he took to the bathroom that morning was worth at least the usual cocktail of ibuprofen and paracetamol he swallowed before getting ready for another working Monday. Everything he did that morning was just as happened on countless Mondays, until right up to the point at which he usually turned left at the traffic lights before leaving Ulstown. Today he turned right and headed for the park. He had the choice of almost all of the parking bays. Sent a text to Allison at work.

Problems at school to sort! Should be back at work around lunchtime. Could you please cancel our meeting arranged for this morning? We can reschedule when I get in. Apologies and thanks.

"That's work sorted out. Time for a walk," announced Andy to the rear-view mirror.

He had spent almost all of his waking hours on the preceding Sunday going through the most likely questions he thought the police would ask and the answers he would provide. Now the chance to go through them all again in the chill air of a November morning. Andy often wondered just how anal he could manage to be. It was far too cold to walk the length of the park and so, with still over an hour to go before his appointment, he sought shelter in his car. Time to drive in circles around town a few times to count down the time. All this to avoid telling Susan what he was actually doing this Monday morning.

"My name is Andrew Jones and I'm here for my appointment at 10.45. Apologies if I'm a little early."

"Ah, Mr Jones. That's fine. No problem," replied PC Knight, looking at the computer in front of her. "Please take a seat over there and someone will be with you shortly."

Andy did as he was told.

"Dave? Your 10.45 is here. You're in Interview Room 2." Knight terminated the phone call.

11.05am —

"Mr Jones? Mr Andrew Jones?"

Andy got up from his chair.

"Great. Sorry for keeping you waiting. Really busy this morning. I'm DC Simmonds. Please follow me to the interview room. This way. Thanks." Simmonds opened the door to allow Andy into a room 'decorated' with office furniture which had surely seen better times.

DS Elias dropped the papers she was holding onto the uneven table and stood to greet her third interviewee of the day. "Ah! It *is* you. You are not the only Andrew Jones I have come across. Quite a few of you about. Should have paid more attention to your address. My maiden name was Jones, as I might have told you when we met earlier in the year. Can't remember if I did tell you, to be honest. Anyway, please take a seat and excuse my ramblings.

"So, good morning, Mr Jones, and thanks for coming along this morning." She could almost hear Andy's jangling nerves. "First of all, let me put your mind to rest, as I would imagine you are a little worried as to why we've asked you here today. We would just like to clear up a few outstanding issues regarding the theft of your car. Is that OK, Andrew? May I call you Andrew?"

"Of course. But please call me Andy."

"Andy it is," confirmed Elias. "I will leave it to DC Simmonds to formally conduct the meeting, although I am very likely to chip in here and there. I have form, don't I, DC Simmonds?"

"Yes, ma'am," replied her report. "Just a few points of procedure before we start the recording, Andy."

"What? You're going to record the interview?" asked an increasingly panicky Andy.

"Just standard procedure, Andy, and as much for your protection as for ours." Simmonds, adjusted the laptop in front of him to optimise his view. "Let's get this fired up. Can you see the camera in the corner of the room?"

Andy nodded.

"That will record both the sound and the visuals of this interview. As we said, just standard procedure and nothing for you to get alarmed over."

This doesn't sound much like routine process to me, worried Andy. *But surely there's nothing in all of this?*

Simmonds proceeded to go through all the formalities that Elias was always so keen to avoid, which included Andy agreeing to have his fingerprints taken. "Just to match up with some prints we found in the car which we are assuming are yours. We want to make sure we can rule out a third party being there. All just routine," reiterated Simmonds once again.

The interview started by establishing that Andy was responsible for and in charge of the car that had been stolen from outside the Royal Cavendish Spa Hotel on that early November morning.

"Andy. Was there anything in the car that night that

you would consider unusual? Something you would not typically keep in there?" asked Simmonds.

No messing. Straight to the point, thought Andy nervously. *They found the vials. But how the fuck do they know it's a drug? Only someone at Wright and Briggs would be able to say that it might be a drug one day.* Might *be. No point in spinning a lie that can be easily pulled apart.* "There were four vials in the glove compartment," he admitted.

"What is in the vials?"

"Samples of a compound from a project I am working on at Wright and Briggs Pharmaceuticals."

"What compound? Is it a drug?" probed Simmonds.

"It wasn't a drug. It's one of many thousands of compounds we have made in the course of the project, but it is not a drug."

Simmonds glanced sideways at his boss to see if she wanted to intervene. She didn't. "So... er... what is or was the purpose of the project? Wasn't it to make a drug?"

"All our projects are started on the basis of trying to find a drug, although very few are successful and actually end up with a drug that goes into humans," answered Andy, who was starting to think that focusing on the science might not be such a bad option. *Introduce some confusion.* "The project I am working on is in its very early stages, and if we are fortunate enough to end up with a marketed drug from it, then that compound is very unlikely to be on the market – and thus be considered a drug – for at least another five years, and that's being very optimistic indeed."

Elias could see that her colleague was starting to struggle. Time for an intervention. "All very clear, Andy, and thanks for the detailed explanation. The vials do not contain a drug. But I'm still struggling to understand why you were taking them home – I'm assuming you were taking them home – if it's not a drug. Some sort of homework for the project? What would you have done with the drug – sorry, the compound – had you managed to take it back home?"

Andy had anticipated this question and, although he could sense that he was being manoeuvred into a corner, he had prepared an answer. "I wanted to see if the test compound worked as an antidepressant. I was going to try it on myself." He was grateful that they had not asked him why he had been staying at a hotel, as that *would* have led to him telling a lie. Still, he assumed that at some point he would be asked from where the car had been stolen.

"Obviously I'm no pharmaceutical scientist, Andy, but wouldn't that be something rather frowned upon in the industry? Taking drugs – sorry, compounds – off the premises and trying them out at home?" Elias frowned to reinforce her point.

"Yes," answered Andy. "And I sincerely regret ever doing so. It is not something I have ever done before, and, believe me, I will never do it again, but it was the result of very unusual circumstances. But more important is that, in the end, I never took anything out of the vials. You have it all. I never took the compound out of the glove compartment and into the house."

"Well, that's not exactly—" began Simmonds, before being cut off in mid-sentence by Elias.

"Thank you, DC Simmonds. Of course, there's no reason for us to doubt what you are saying, Andy, but we obviously don't know for sure that these are the only samples you took from work. You mentioned unusual circumstances. Could you please elaborate?"

Routine questions and routine process, my arse, pondered Andy. *These bastards think they have something on me and are going for it. Thank fuck I had that conversation with Janey.* "The unusual circumstances? I was not in a good place. Work is very stressful with the threat of redundancy hanging over me. Brian had been killed, as you know, and that had affected my family, especially my wife, very badly. I was depressed. Constant headaches and brain fog. So I thought I would try out the drug – I mean compound – we were working on to see if it worked in humans."

"But why didn't you just go to your GP and get some prescription antidepressants?" asked Simmonds, which earned him a sideways glance from Elias.

"You're right; maybe a bit stupid of me, really. In fact, in retrospect, definitely stupid of me not to take the obvious option. But there is still a stigma around admitting you are depressed, and, from all the reading I have done, I'm not the only one who remains to be convinced that the current drugs on the market for treating depression don't really work as well as them having some addiction concerns to boot." Andy paused to see if there were any comments. There weren't. "Also, I wanted to convince myself that we were working on a project which had a good chance of being successful." He bit his lip. Too much information. Keep it simple. Keep to the argument that he was depressed and needed relief.

"Well? Did it work? Were you less depressed after taking it?" asked Elias.

Andy paused, contemplating the very naive trap that had been set for him. “Like I said, I did not take the compound.”

“But you would have at some point in the future?”

“That was my intention. But would I have taken it had the car not been stolen? I really don’t know, but my best guess is that I would have chickened out. I’m a very risk-averse person.”

“But not risk averse enough, it would seem, to prevent you stealing from the company you work for?” posed Elias.

“I wouldn’t say stealing.”

“So you had permission to take these samples off-site?”

Andy paused. “Not as such, but, as I said, it wasn’t as if I stole them.”

“What would you call it, then? Items removed from work without permission?” asked Elias, leaning back in her chair.

“I’m the project leader. I don’t really need permission,” lied Andy, fully realising the precariousness of the stance he was taking.

“Again, no reason for us to doubt what you are saying, but it will be something we will need to confirm with your employers. Just routine and I’m sure there will be no issues,” replied Elias, who had glanced up at the clock above the door and realised how short her lunch break might now be. “Fine. And thanks again for coming in to talk to us this morning, Andy. Before we finish, could you confirm that you have not given this compound or any other compound from Wright and Briggs Pharmaceuticals to anyone else either inside or outside of the company?”

"Yes," replied Andy. "I have never given any compound made at Wright and Briggs to anyone else."

"On the basis of your reply, our working assumption will be that the four vials we found and the powder contained within were the only materials you took from Wright and Briggs Pharmaceuticals. However, we will likely be looking to confirm this directly with the company."

Andy noticeably stiffened on hearing Elias's last sentence; a gesture that was picked up by both officers. "I understand," was the best response he could manage, for his mind had already turned to the very difficult questions he would likely face at work in the not-too-distant future.

"Before I formally end this interview, is there anything further you wish to say?" asked Simmonds, looking directly at Andy.

"Er… no, that's fine. There's nothing more I want to say. But what happens next?"

"Next?" said Elias. "As I said, we will get in touch with your employer to confirm what you have said – and, to be frank, to determine whether they wish to pursue charges if a property theft has taken place, but I hope it won't come to that. Nearly forgot – perhaps you would be kind enough to leave your mobile phone with us so that we can check any correspondence you have had with Wright and Briggs? I see you have it in your shirt pocket. We should be able to get it back to you within a couple of days, but please get in touch with DC Simmonds if it takes longer."

Simmonds pushed his card across the table and received Andy's phone in return.

"I'm guessing we will be able to access all the data we need through your phone, but we might ask you to hand over your computer if not." Elias smiled. "I think we're all done here."

That prompted Simmonds to initiate the formalities of ending the interview.

As they were leaving the interview room, Elias turned to Andy. "It must have been a terrible few months for your family after Brian's death and not helped by all the coverage in the local press, but hopefully you will have had some comfort from knowing who we believe are his killers are behind bars and will soon be on trial. We think we have a very strong case against them."

"Yes. Thanks for keeping us informed about that," replied Andy.

"This interview might have seemed rather heavy to you, Andy, but you must understand that we have to be diligent in following up these things," remarked Elias as she edged towards the coffee machine.

"I understand," said a barely understanding Andy as he looked towards getting out of the building as quickly as possible.

"What is it now, DC Simmonds?" asked a clearly exasperated DS Elias. "I would like to get home before midnight. Dinner to cook and maybe even eat. House to clean. Life to live. You know, all those trivial things one has to do."

"Sorry, ma'am, but I thought you would be interested in this summary of the texts I found on Andrew Jones's phone," said Simmonds, with undertones of him being pretty busy as well. "Took me quite a long time," was added to emphasise the latter point.

"OK, thanks," replied Elias, glancing at the printout she was handed without actually reading it. "Anything interesting? Any suspicious texts with his ex-brother-in-law, Brian Tyler, or anyone else in that mucky little circle? Wouldn't it be interesting if we found out that Jones was supplying Tyler."

"Nothing along those lines, ma'am. At least not from what I have seen so far. But there are a lot of text exchanges, dating back to the spring, with a number linked to a Janey Robins of 4 Malvern Drive. One of Jones's neighbours, I guess."

"Interesting," muttered Elias.

Simmonds pointed to a few of the texts as examples. "As you can see, some sort of weird code which might suggest that they are trying to hide something."

"Could be. Could be. Having been down that Malvern Drive place myself to meet Jones and speak to him about Tyler's murder, I wouldn't say that it is the most obvious place to deal drugs. Maybe they're just mixed-doubles badminton partners? Who knows? But it's something we really should look into a bit deeper in case we are missing a trick or two." Elias shuffled the printouts into a neat pile and attached a staple to the top left-hand corner. "Let me have a look at these and decide whether or not we should have a chat with our Ms Robins."

Simmonds stood back from the desk.

"Don't know about you, young man, but I for one am going home. Goodnight."

III

Harlow, 15 Miles —

"One fucking thing after another," muttered Andy venomously to his car windscreen.

He was travelling to see his consultant neurologist on his way to work, following a phone call from the hospital the day before asking him to attend a meeting he had not been expecting so soon. *Surely they would just send a letter rightly accusing me of being a hypochondriac if everything was tickety-boo? They wouldn't want to see me. But they do. A letter is apparently not sufficient to convey these results. Something's fucking wrong*, fretted Andy as the driver of a two-section lorry swayed marginally into his lane. *Get off your fucking phone!* he shouted within the confines of his brain. *Car stolen. Janey chewing my arse. Police trying to lock me up, and now the news that my brain is not what it should be. Well, if my brain really is screwed then I don't think I will be struggling into work later today.*

"You bastard," shouted Andy through his closed sunroof to a God he had ignored and abused for longer than he could remember. "You bastard."

"Please take a seat," offered Professor Svensson as Andy entered the consulting room: a brightly lit and sparsely decorated office featuring a side room with a bed, presumably for more intimate examinations. Andy hoped there would be no need for any of that.

The professor, a reassuringly distinguished-looking and well-dressed gentleman with the very slightest hint of a Scandinavian accent, pressed a few keys and completed a full circle with his computer mouse in search of an errant cursor. "Ah! Got it. Here we are. Right. Thank you for coming along this morning at such short notice, but I thought it would be better for us to discuss this face to face as it would be difficult to discuss over the phone. A perplexing case, for sure." He frowned at his screen.

Andy's heart was pounding so hard and fast that he was sure that the professor would notice. He wanted to say something, anything, but thought it better to wait until the professor had earned at least some of his huge consultation fee.

"To cut to the chase, I suppose – isn't that the saying one uses? Anyway, we found what appear to be minor lesions in three distinct areas of your brain, which might be indicative of you having multiple sclerosis, but I emphasise here the word 'might'. They are marginal, very small lesions and may just be artefacts, but it is something that the radiologist has flagged up." The professor paused to see if Andy had anything to say, which he didn't. "Now, the behavioural tests you did when I first saw you did not show anything untoward, and I would expect to have come across a few red flags if you were presenting with MS, such as fatigue, or balance, muscle or visual abnormalities." The professor scrolled up one page on his computer. "You tested negative for all of those."

"What about headaches and brain fog?" asked Andy in a quivering voice. "Are they symptoms of MS?"

"Headaches, yes, but headaches are so common in the general population that I wouldn't consider them useful in diagnosing MS by themselves."

"So," replied Andy tentatively, "do you think I have MS, based on all you have seen?"

"From all I have seen? No. I wouldn't conclude that you have MS based on the picture we are seeing at the moment. However, I also wouldn't rule out you developing it at some time in the future based on what we have seen in the scan."

"How likely do you think that is to happen?" whispered Andy in the forlorn hope that his question would not be answered in the way he feared it would.

"At this point, with how you have presented, not very likely at all. But we should be prepared and vigilant," answered the professor, fully aware of how nervous and fearful his patient was. "Moving forward, I would suggest the following." He scrolled down two pages to the notes he had written just before Andy had arrived. "A repeat MRI scan sometime in the New Year to determine if what we have found is real. If it is – and I repeat *if* – we will need to consider follow-up scans to see if it develops further, as well as some blood tests and rerunning the behavioural tests. But as I said, lots of ifs and maybes. For the moment, let's just focus on booking you in for another MRI in, say, five to six months." More typing from the Professor. "I'm just sending an email to my PA to get that arranged. Of course, Mr Jones, please do come back to me should you notice any marked changes in your balance, fatigue levels or vision. Does all that sound reasonable, Mr Jones?" Professor Svensson looked up from his screen to face Andy and smiled.

"Of course, and thank you for your detailed explanation. I know a little bit about MS from my work, but are there any marketed drugs that cause MS?" Andy realised he was going out on a limb with this question.

"You know, I'm not sure a patient has ever asked me that question before," answered a genuinely surprised professor. "Prescription drugs that cause MS? Maybe in rare cases with some of the new, very potent anti-inflammatory drugs and I recall some publications linking non-specific drug abuse to MS, but I wouldn't say prescription drugs are even a minor cause of MS." Yet again, he looked at his computer screen. "And according to my notes, you are not currently on any medications anyway."

Andy tried to move the conversation away from this topic having got some sort of answer and a modicum of reassurance. "Just asking out of general scientific curiosity, really," he lied. "Should I have MS, what would the prognosis be for someone of my age?"

"Once again, Mr Jones, that remains a very big 'if'. But people who are diagnosed with MS these days have a good choice of drugs, not only to treat the symptoms but also to modify the course of the disease. There are some even more compelling options coming through trials; remyelinating therapies which might reverse disease progression. Exciting times."

"All sounds very interesting," replied Andy, making a mental note to do some research of his own, as is a hypochondriac's duty.

"Any other questions, Mr Jones?"

Andy could not think of any, although he knew that many burning questions would come to mind as soon as he left the hospital. "None that I can think of at the moment."

They rose from their seats simultaneously.

"Thank you for your time today, Professor."

"And please don't worry too much," advised the professor, offering his hand. "We are a long way away from ringing any alarm bells."

Both men smiled as Andy let himself out of the consulting room and out through a maze of near-identical corridors to the car park and the sanctuary of the driver's seat of his (still very clean) Passat. An alarmingly old woman was carefully wheeled past the front of his car as he strapped himself in. They caught each other's gaze, and Andy a watery smile from her which he thought was one of either pity or resignation.

Old women. They know everything. Much closer to any God that might just be out there than the rest of us. They have a direct line. She knows what's wrong with me. She knows. Andy smiled back.

On the very short drive remaining to get to Wright and Briggs, he made a vow to himself. *Whatever happens to me in the days and weeks to come, I personally will make sure that WRT743 gets tested in every toxicity assay I can find. I don't want my legacy to be a drug that harms before it heals.*

IV

The CEO of Wright and Briggs Pharmaceuticals looked around the oval boardroom table to see if there were any follow-up comments. Andy was not the only one present who thought that Dr Judith Meredith had aged noticeably over the past year. Nor was anyone surprised, given the huge changes ongoing at the company.

"Thank you, Allison, for those words. Very helpful and much appreciated. Unless you want to add anything,

Andy, I think we have arrived at the point where I can sum up the key decisions we have arrived at in this meeting."

Andy shook his head.

Judith picked up the notebook in which she had been writing and turned back two pages. "First of all, Andy, and maybe most important of all, I personally very much regret that there has been a need for us to have this meeting this afternoon; that recent events have led us to make the decisions we must now enact. I would like to go on record to thank you for the invaluable contributions you have made to the company ever since you have arrived here. That sentiment has also been substantiated by the contributions we have heard today from your direct supervisor, Allison, and from Claude, representing the personnel department. But I'm afraid there is no escaping the fact that you have admitted to taking company property – highly confidential and proprietary company property – off-site without seeking written permission. As we heard in detail both from Claude and from our company lawyer, Steffan, such an action amounts to gross misconduct and thus an option of immediate dismissal for us to consider." She paused to take a small sip from her water bottle. It was obvious to all that the CEO felt very uncomfortable. "Andy, you have also heard today a brief summary of the meeting we had with DS Elias and DC Simmonds in which the possibility of you being formally charged with theft was discussed. However, because of your previous exemplary record at Wright and Briggs and the mitigating personal circumstances you raised at this meeting, we will not be approaching the authorities with a view to you being charged with theft." Judith once again reached for her water, and opened up an A4 card wallet from which she took out an envelope. "Our compromise proposal is to offer you redundancy with terms broadly consistent with those currently being offered to some of your colleagues." She pushed the sealed envelope across the table to Andy. "Your particular terms differ in that there are clauses to ensure confidentiality, such that neither you nor Wright and Briggs Pharmaceuticals will disclose to any third party the circumstances of this compromise agreement. No one in this company other than the people in this room will know of the theft of company property that has taken place. I'm sure that will be your preference. As is company policy for all our leavers, we will provide you with a standard reference."

Andy took possession of the envelope and placed it in his own folder. "Thank you, Judith."

"We do hope you will accept what we think is a very generous offer, which stipulates that you will work through your notice period up until Christmas, with the 23rd December being your last day with us. I'm sure that your colleagues would like to give you a good send-off, and we will honour your invitation to the company Christmas party. Our intention is for your leaving to be seen by the staff as just one of several redundancies the company has made, and no more remarkable than the others. We will allow you a week's grace to review the terms we have offered. Do you have any questions, Andy?"

Andy toyed with the idea of signing the agreement now, given what the CEO had outlined, but he resisted the temptation. "No, that all sounds very clear to me. I will take this with me to read, and I will get back to you with my answer as soon as I can." He looked around the room at the people who were soon to be his ex-colleagues. He had known Judith and Claude since his first day at Wright and Briggs. "However, I would like to say to you all – but especially you, Judith and Allison – just how sorry I am for the stupid error of judgement that has led us to this point and this meeting. I have let you all down, and without any real justification other than my own personal issues which I have talked to you about today in some depth, but this should by no means be seen as an excuse for my untypical behaviour. Just a reason. I hope, in time, you will forgive me for what I have done and instead remember the positives: our successes, and the personal interactions I personally will remember very fondly. I only wish I could turn back the clock and avoid making such a terrible decision. But I can't, and I will have to live with the consequences of my rash stupidity for the rest of my career." He could sense that they had genuine empathy for his predicament and did not wish to wreck his career, though that was easily within their power. "Not sure I have anything else to say other than thank you for your understanding and your willingness to find a way to help me despite my being so undeserving of that help. I hope in the years to come you won't think too badly of me for this one stupid decision I have made. I'm certain I will come to look back on my time with Wright and Briggs as some of the most enjoyable years of my life."

He wondered if his well-rehearsed closing remarks were too saccharine, but maybe not, based on the genuine smiles and handshakes that followed. He was to be made redundant and left with an uncertain future. But it could have been worse. Far, far worse. This horrific mess had also left him with a very different view of Allison, who had spent over an hour with him prior to the main meeting. It was from her that he'd found out that Wright and Briggs, much to the annoyance of DS Elias, did not know how much WRT743 had been taken by anyone, whether on- or off-site. This was because the internal process for monitoring stocks of non-drug, research-stage compounds only required scientists to flag if stock levels were too low. No record was ever kept of who had taken what and when. Therefore, no paper trail existed to document Andy taking any WRT743, and so the police were unable to determine whether or not the four vials they had found in his car amounted to all that he had taken. Thus they were, not surprisingly, very critical of Wright and Brigg's internal processes, which they felt fell far short of good practice. This much was obviously true. Maybe it wasn't so surprising, then, that the company had chosen to offer Andy a compromise agreement and not press charges. They were as reluctant as he was for this sorry story to enter the public domain. The bottom line? The police had no evidence that Andy had taken off-site more than the two hundred milligrams of WRT743 he had admitted to taking, despite their strong suspicion that he had. Allison hadn't been obliged to reveal any of that to Andy, but he was very grateful that she had, as he was now aware that the police would have to find another way of proving that he had removed more than he had admitted to. The only way they could do that would be to talk to Janey. Andy was not out of the woods yet, but surely he could rely upon her to keep to their agreed story. Couldn't he?

V

"That didn't take you long," observed Susan as she entered the kitchen to load the dishwasher. She glanced up at the clock just above the window. "I make it less than half an hour since you got back from work."

"Would forty-five minutes be more acceptable?" asked Andy over his freshly poured large single malt. "I didn't know we were keeping a record of such things."

Susan closed the dishwasher and looked across the kitchen at her husband, who was now sitting at the table. He looked pale and tired. He looked old. "We aren't. Can I say something to you without you biting my head off?"

"Be my guest," invited Andy, in a manner that suggested that he might just bite her head off.

"And there you go again. Using that tone of voice. I don't think you even realise you are doing it, do you?" accused Susan, who was now standing at the opposite side of the table. "You have not been easy to live with these past few weeks, but whatever is bothering you, you won't get rid of it by drinking or by taking it out on us. It was poor Sophie's turn to get it this morning. You really should say sorry to her before we go to my mother's."

Andy stared into his glass. It already needed refilling. "You're right. Work is a real handful at the moment although I know that's no excuse for me to take it out on you all. Guilty as charged," he admitted as the second large whisky was poured.

"That's a start. But the drink. Are you going to carry on like you have been doing lately? Cracking open the bottle as soon as you get home and then cradling a glass for the rest of the night? This is not the Andy I know.

You've had hard times at work before. What's different this time?"

There was no way that Andy was going to talk to Susan about the meeting he had endured just hours before. Of course, he would have to tell her sooner rather than later about Judith's offer, but not tonight, and certainly not before he had worked out a convincing script he could use to obscure the real reason for him being made redundant. "I know, I know. But it helps. Helps me put out of my mind the shit I have to put up with at work. Takes the stress away, at least a bit."

"But you can't carry on like this, Andy. Have you taken a look in the mirror lately? You look terrible."

"Well, thanks for that. You really know how to cheer someone up, don't you?"

"Just trying to hold up a mirror for you, Andy. Only you can change things. I can't stop you drinking, but I am here if you want to talk about it."

Andy hated the thought of 'talking about it'. He always did. "Nothing to talk about. Work's a pain in the arse. I'm enjoying a few drinks to take the edge off things, and I will stop as soon as things get back to normal. You know I can stop drinking whenever I want to. You know I'm not an alcoholic."

"The words of every new aspiring alcoholic. But you know what? I've said my piece. I've offered to help. I'm here whenever you want to talk about all this. But if that doesn't stop you drinking and lighten your mood, then perhaps the children will be reason enough for you to bring back the old Andy. The real Andy. He wouldn't ignore them as you have lately. Up to you, Andy," advised Susan, taking her coat off the back of a chair and walking into the hall. "Come on, you lot," she called up the stairs. "We're late. Nanny will be waiting."

Of course it was up to Andy, but he was in no mood to feel anything but angry and sorry for himself as Susan closed the front door behind her and headed off to her mother's house in the company of the children. He ignored the pasta dinner that she had prepared for him, and instead retired to the lounge carrying the whisky bottle and a tumbler. This was going to be a long night. The TV was switched on and left on whatever channel had last been watched. Andy had no particular interest in watching anything. He just wanted company to help him drink the night away. If only Janey was with him right now. He imagined them naked, in that living room, doing all the things that had so recently been such a big part of his life. That would be no more with access to their nirvana now removed. The job to which he had devoted so much time and effort, often at the cost of missing various rites of passage for all of his children, would be no more. Keeping up the ridiculous mortgage payments on a house they could only just afford with his well-paid job at Wright and Briggs – the house in which he was currently drinking himself senseless – that would soon be no more. Maybe the solution to all of this – a way for him to avoid causing his family any further hardship, disappointment and sadness – would be for *him* to be no more.

Andy struggled to get out of his chair, but was aided by holding on to an adjacent sideboard. He made his way to the bottom of the stairs before making a slow and steady ascent to the landing and then moving through to the en-suite bathroom. He opened the cabinet above the sink. The usual stock. He wondered briefly if he would be the first man to commit suicide via an overdose of female contraceptive pills, but decided that he should remain to the end the conventional and traditional man he had always been. His frequent headaches meant that they had far more than a safe stock of ibuprofen and paracetamol. These were taken out of the cabinet, along with some co-codamol he had only recently bought. *That should be enough.* But before he closed the door, he noticed some bottles of children's liquid painkiller and sedative antihistamine. *That'll do nicely. Something to help wash all the pills down.*

Back in the living room, he arranged all the medications on the low table in front of his armchair, in a neat semicircle around the bottle of whisky and his glass. He needed a refill. *Maybe a few drinks first.* An oft-repeated saying is that suicide is a coward's way out; an easy solution. They seemed like very brave cowards to Andy that evening as he faced down his killers. Another drink. And another one. *What should be the last TV programme I should see in this life? An action film? Sport? Music? Comedy? But of course, comedy! What better way to see out my ridiculous life? A comedy it will be.* But he had inadvertently dropped the TV remote on the other side of the room, and the armchair was becoming ever more comfortable. The consensus of his meandering thoughts was to first have another drink and watch to the end a life-affirming documentary about a family struggling to live in a sink estate, and then take the pills.

"Wake up! Wake up! Andy, can you hear me?" shouted Susan. "Sophie, can you please take the others upstairs to your bedrooms? I'll be up soon. Daddy has a bad cold."

Daddy spluttered to some low level of consciousness. "What's happening? What are you doing?" Slowly, his eyes opened. "I feel sick."

And with that, Susan helped him to the downstairs bathroom, where he vomited profusely into the toilet bowl. "That's better. Get it all out," she advised. "I'm going to call an ambulance. How many pills did you take and when?"

"What pills?"

"The fucking pills on the table in the living room."

"But I haven't taken any pills."

"Are you sure? Look at me, Andy. Look at me. Have you taken any pills?"

"No."

"So why are all those pills on the table?"

Andy paused to try to collect his thoughts; to remember what he had done that night. "I was just thinking of taking them, but I never took any. I just drank whisky." He turned around and threw up once more into the toilet.

Slowly, Susan's blood pressure started to fall and the pounding of her heart to recede. But she wanted more reassurance, and so she went back into the living room and brought the medicines to show Andy as he hunched over the toilet bowl. "Look, Andy. These. Did you take any of these?" she asked as she presented each bottle, one by one, to her bleary-eyed husband. "Did you take any of these?"

"No. I told you, no." Andy was beginning to get irritated with her insistence upon repeatedly asking the same question. "I promise you. I never took as much as one pill."

The word 'promise' seemed to work. It so often did with Susan. "So, you're just pissed, then?"

"Bingo."

"Me and you. We need to talk."

Susan joined Andy in the living room. He was sitting in the armchair, looking a little further from death than he had appeared less than an hour earlier, but not much. She placed two large glasses of chilled water on the table between them. She had cleared up the alcohol and drugs lying around the living room, returning them to their proper homes. She'd even managed to switch off the TV. The children had been reassured that everything was fine with Daddy and had settled down to sleep, although Sophie had done her best to stay awake and listen to her parents' conversation, if not for long.

"So. What happened tonight?" was Susan's opening question, and a very good one.

"Isn't that rather obvious?" answered Andy, who had reverted to self-pity mode. *And rather obvious*, he thought, *that I couldn't even manage to kill myself? Pathetic.*

"But why? That's far from obvious. At least to me."

Fair point, thought Andy. *Very fair point.* Susan deserved better. The family deserved better. "Why? Because I've let you all down and life would be so much better for you if I was no longer around, making your lives a misery."

Susan gulped heavily but she held back a tear. "Whatever makes you think that? I thought we were a close family. A strong family. Strong families help each other out when things get bad. That's what strong families do. That's exactly what you did for me when Brian died, and now it looks like it's my turn. My turn to help you. But I can only do that if you tell me what is really troubling you so terribly." She wondered if she actually knew Andy at all; her husband and the father of their children.

Andy had some thinking to do. Decisions to make. Susan didn't need to know all the gory details. It would destroy her if she ever found out about Janey. Nor was there any need for her to be told about what had been happening with the police, as it might all amount to nothing, so why let her worry? But he needed some justification as to why he had considered taking his own life, even if it was not the full story. "Two things, I suppose. They offered me redundancy this morning. Not that it's really an offer, though. They've made me redundant."

Susan was not sure whether to be angry, sorry, or just relieved that it was not the worst fear she had been harbouring. "You're best shot of that place and the people there anyway," was her first thought. "At least the management. You knew it was coming but it must still have come as a shock, even if they are a bunch of bastards. But I thought your project was going well? Are they offering you a good deal like they have with the others?"

"The project's dead. We had some very bad toxicity data through last week. Redundancy terms? Four weeks' pay for each year worked, which will mostly be tax-free. We won't be poor for a good while yet."

"We'll never be poor. Never," announced Susan defiantly. "You'll be snapped up quick enough, and even if that didn't happen, I could go out to work. But first of all, I'll help you from home and start contacting some employment agencies. We'll sit down at the weekend and write out a plan. I will be your new PA."

"We're not so very different after all, are we, dear?" Andy smiled.

"Did anyone ever say we were?"

"But wherever I end up, it's unlikely that I will find a job that pays the mortgage on this house," he pointed out.

"I wouldn't be so sure about that. But even if we have to move house, it's not exactly the end of the world, is it? How many real friends will we miss around here? How many friends have the kids made? Exactly. In fact, I would look forward to moving out of this place. Maybe somewhere cheaper up north, with a decent garden for the kids and some open spaces to play. A new life for us all."

"Let's drink to that," added Andy, raising his glass of water.

And they did.

"But you said two things, didn't you?" remembered Susan. "Two things that were troubling you."

Andy then took her through a very convoluted story involving headaches, GPs, neurologists and brain scans. All meat and drink to a seasoned hypochondriac like him. The tale was mostly truthful, although it lacked any possible link to taking WRT743, with or without Janey's company.

"Why didn't you tell me about all this? Keeping it to yourself for months..."

"I didn't want to worry you or the kids," was his

truthful reply. "And I'm a bit unsure about telling you now, since it will most likely be nothing."

"But it was enough to contribute to you considering taking your own life, so it clearly was something." Susan paused. "You must promise me something, Andy. No more secrets."

"I promise. There are no more secrets."

If only she knew.

When all the others were asleep, Andy lay awake in bed, waiting for the recommended dose of painkillers to chip away at his fully deserved hangover. He was replaying the memories of the evening before that would stay with him forever, including the drug-free night of passionate lovemaking that had ended with him and Susan falling asleep in each other's arms. She was no Janey. She didn't need to be. She was Susan. His wife. Whatever had made him think that anything could be worth risking what he had with her? With his young family? Foolish, stupid, idiotic, selfish and ungrateful. All of those, and several other adjectives that had not yet come to mind. He was still in the game. Still had a wife and family to stand by and support him. But would the strong family that Susan had talked about survive the fallout of the police interviewing Janey, which they would surely do once they had seen all their text messages? Their one last hope of charging Andy with at least something.

MY LITTLE BROTHER

There are few days that go by without me giving it at least a passing thought, and it has been nearly two years since the day I found out that I have a brother. A much younger brother. My baby brother. I have not yet gathered the courage to tell anyone in the family; not even Twm. But I guess I will have to at some point, not least because this secret is burning up inside me and needs to be let out. A career in the police force is not good training for keeping secrets! Maybe I will share my big secret when I retire (which is now within touching distance), as at least then there will be no fallout from a legal standpoint.

It all started innocently enough when I asked PC James – but everyone calls her Jas, as do I – to do a bit of digging around in Andy's extended family. There was something really nagging at me after that second meeting with him. His eyes, his nose and even his mouth so reminded me of my father. Yes, the one who kicked me out of the family home when I fell pregnant. That *father. He even spoke the same way. Or it could just be my memory playing tricks. After all, it's over forty years since I last spoke to that man, and I have done my very best to forget him ever since. Yes, Andy and I are both Joneses, as are millions of others, but I'm sure I picked up at least a twinge of a Yorkshire accent in him, and I know that's where my parents chose to run away from me. Ridiculous to even imagine that we might actually be related, but I just couldn't resist being nosy. I am a detective, after all.*

If you ever want these sorts of searches to be done around here, then Jas is your girl. Very meticulous in everything she does, and you can rely upon her to be diligent even with the dullest of tasks, and this assignment very much fell into that category.

I was at least intrigued to find out that Andy's deceased parents were Emrys and Gladys Jones, and that they'd lived in a small village just outside Harrogate in Yorkshire. Now, Jones is obviously a very common Welsh surname so it would, perhaps, not be so very strange if Andy and I had parents with the same first names.

"Thanks for the report, Jas, but do you mind looking a bit deeper? Could you look into where his parents were born and their dates of birth? You'll have to trust me on this one."

"Not a problem. I am on it," was her reply.

But that's exactly when it did *become a problem. Jas was waiting for me, hovering around my desk, when I arrived at work the very next morning.*

"Who left that bloody tinsel on my desk?" was the first thing I said to her when I sat down.

"No idea," admitted Jas.

"Well, please get it destroyed, there's a good constable."

She ignored me. "I've been chasing up your request to

find out more about Andy Jones's family. Do you think we could discuss it in one of the empty interview rooms?"

I thought she looked worried. "Do we have to?" I moaned.

"I think it would be best."

So off to Interview Room 1 we went, and sat at opposite ends of easily the worst table in the whole station.

"Over to you, Jas."

"First of all, I might have got this all terribly wrong. I don't think I have, but it's probably best if you or someone else double-checks it all."

"OK. Understood. I'm listening."

"Not an easy search as Jones is one of the worst family names to chase up, but at least the combination of the names Emrys and Gladys helped. I chased them back through a few census records from Harrogate, where they are listed as living with their son Andrew, who seems to be an only child. All as expected. So I chased back a bit further, as you asked me to, until I got to the 1981 and 1971 censuses." Jas pushed two pieces of A4 paper across the table for me to read. "As you can see, during that period they lived in 17 Grove Terrace, Pontycymer, and had a daughter called Mary Angharad, who I think is you. Andrew Jones might be your brother."

That certainly was me. Right address, name, parents and time. I couldn't remember their exact dates of birth but the numbers Jas had looked close enough. I remembered that cramped little house I couldn't wait until I was old enough to leave. "But he can't be my brother. Impossible," I laughed.

"That's for you to decide, ma'am. I'm just showing you what I found. Can't rule out that he was adopted, of course."

"But even if my parents did adopt him – and they are definitely my parents – he would still be related to me, wouldn't he? Sort of?"

"Like I said, ma'am, I'm just showing you what I found."

As you can well imagine, my mind was spinning. It had blown. Do I really have a brother? Someone I knew nothing about for the past forty-plus years? He has children. I'm an aunt! My children have cousins. *It was all too bizarre for my mind to take in, and I think Jas picked up on that.*

"Look, I will leave all this with you, and you can do with it as you wish," she said as she made for the door and away from this madwoman.

I thanked her, but as she was about to leave the interview room, I called her back and asked her to close the door and sit back down. I then asked her to not breathe a word of what she had found in her searches; nor tell anyone what we had discussed that morning. And as far as I know, she never did, bless her. I, of course, should never have put one of my reports in such a position, but even had the truth come out, I could easily have claimed that I'd become aware of my relationship to Andy only after the case had been closed. I'm pretty sure I could have avoided any awkward insinuations.

Now for the guilty-as-charged bit, I'm afraid. That same day, just before lunch, DC Simmonds came to see me to ask me what we were going to do about Janey Robins.

"Criminal that Wright and Briggs can't even monitor their stock, but I still think we've got a way forward on this one, ma'am," was his opening statement. "Looking through their texts again, I reckon those two are definitely using that drug, and maybe having an affair to boot. Interesting to see

what you think. And we've still got to fully look into any links Jones might have with Tyler."

He then picked out for me a few texts which, I agreed, looked very much like some naive code for exchanging and using drugs. The substance in question was, no doubt, WRT743, but it was nothing we could prove as they would surely deny everything and, at best, Simmonds' interpretation of the code would be seen as ambiguous and tenuous. Still, he was quite right to suggest that we should at least bring Janey in for questioning. She was our last hope of getting a conviction in this case. Andy Jones passing on stolen 'drugs' to Janey Robins with the intention of her taking them. A long shot, but we should be diligent in following it up. And that would have been my recommendation, right up until my conversation with Jas.

"Good stuff, Dave. And I agree: we should probably get Janey Robins in for a little chat, but leave this with me and I will go through all the texts myself. Some nice bedside reading all about drug-taking and affairs. Who needs Scandi noirs?"

I recall that he looked a little disappointed that we weren't moving faster on this. Simmonds will make a good detective, mark my words. I promised him I would get back to him soon.

But, boy, did I have some thinking to do! So it was off to the local park for a brisk walk around Route B. My favourite. Along the river and around the lake, which that day was frozen solid. What should I do? What could *I do? By the time I had started on the return leg of my walk, I had come to a decision. Well, sort of. Don't tell anyone. Not even Twm. At least not yet. What to do about the case involving Andy.*

Difficult! I can keep a secret and, as I said, no one yet knows that I have a brother aside from Jas; not even my brother himself. What sort of parents keep such things secret? A discussion for another day, perhaps, but you already know my opinion of my and Andy's parents. It was very near the end of that freezing-cold walk around the park, thank God, when I finally sorted out what to do about it all. Nothing. Well, nothing in the sense that I decided not to bring in Janey Robins for questioning, and so not to progress with a case against Andy for passing on to her what could be construed as a potential drug of abuse.

How did young Simmonds take all of this? Not well, but he soon calmed down when the next case came along. Much more interesting. And he, as well as I, could see all manner of difficulties in trying to convince the CPS that we would get a successful prosecution in this case. WRT743 was not a classified drug of abuse. We had no way of proving that Andy had taken more than two hundred milligrams of it from Wright and Briggs, although we were pretty sure that he had. Even if, for some bizarre reason, Janey had admitted to taking substances off him, it would likely have been her word against his. Theoretically, we could have searched her house, and that was something Simmonds pushed for but I reckon that we would have struggled to justify such heavy-handed tactics and obtain a search warrant. If we had, not even Simmonds would have emptied out Janey's salt cellar and been able to justify forensics analysing what looked and tasted like salt! Imagine the fallout in that genteel little close if Plod paid a visit to the Robinses' house. Which brings me to the below.

The real reasons why I swept this case under the carpet were, of course, personal. Personal only to me. What useful purpose would it serve anyone to chase down my little brother and see his family and home put at risk, as surely would have happened had we brought Janey in and charged around her house, and had the affair been discovered by the families? All for the long shot that would have been the chance of getting a conviction? He's my brother and he deserves another chance. And that's exactly what I gave him.

Italics! Oops. So sorry.

COFFEE, TEA AND CAKE, PART 2

Andy was scattering salt on the very icy path outside his front door when he heard a ping from his phone. Padded coat unzipped. Cardigan unbuttoned. Phone taken out of his shirt pocket.

Would you be able to meet me one lunchtime this week at the Costa on the Broad Walk in Harlow? Just an informal chat about finishing up with the stolen car issues, and an update on the court case. Thanks. DS Elias.

It was only when Andy had read the text for the fifth time that the words took hold fully. Did this mean that they were no longer going to chase up what he had been doing with WRT743? That they were not going to question Janey? His view of life was that if things seemed too good to be true then they invariably turned out not to be true. He was not going to treat this potential good news any differently, although he struggled to dampen his optimism. *Assume the worst, hope for the best,* was the phrase that came to mind as he typed his reply.

See you at about 1pm on the 20th. Regards, Andy.

Only one day to wait. Could this be the beginning of the end of his nightmare?

Although Andy knew Harlow well, he had never before been to the coffee shop to which Elias had invited him, and so he was unfamiliar with the layout of the large, brightly lit room that he walked into. He could see Elias in the far corner, struggling to remove tinsel from the back of her chair. She quickly noticed him and waved him over to her table.

"Take a seat, Andy. What would you like to drink?"

"No, I'll get these."

"The police invited you here, so the police will pay."

"That's very kind of you. A black tea, please."

"I was going to treat myself to a cake as I haven't had lunch yet," lied Elias. "Any for yourself? Or perhaps a biscuit? Shortbread?"

"Thanks very much, but no thanks. I've not long had lunch," lied Andy.

Not a long queue for Elias to navigate, but long enough to provide her with an opportunity to look over at Andy, who was focused on wasting time with his phone. *Definitely my father. Clear as day. Maybe even a bit of him in Alex, perhaps? The mouth?* she thought. *Just has to be a blood relative with that nose.*

"One black tea," she announced as she pulled out her chair to sit back down. "Brutally hot as usual, so be careful." Gingerly, she placed the tea in front of Andy. "Right. First, thanks for finding time to leave your work to see me. As I said, just an informal meeting, hence this place rather than the station."

"No secret recording devices anywhere in the vicinity?" joked Andy, burning his hand on the ceramic cup.

"I couldn't possibly comment," said Elias, trying to match his attempt at humour. "So, the trial," she announced, swiping her phone. "Scheduled to start on the 23rd January. It is, of course, your prerogative to attend, but it is not something I would recommend based on some of the more upsetting evidence we have relating to how Brian died. But, as I said, completely up to you and your wife. We can send details of the trial, which will be in Chelmsford Crown Court, closer to the time if you choose to attend."

"Thanks," replied Andy. "I can't see us going, not least for the reasons you have just given, but I'll talk it through with Susan and, I suppose, her mother as well. We'll let you know in good time."

"Now. The theft of your car – or, more to the point, what we found in your car," began Elias.

Here comes the crunch point, thought Andy, tensing his whole body in expectation. *A few words that will affect the rest of my life.*

"As you might have already heard, Wright and Briggs do not want us to charge you with theft, which will no doubt come as a great relief to you," said Elias.

"Very much so," answered Andy. "A huge relief. They

have been very good to me." He was not going to volunteer that he had been made redundant.

"And that is, of course, their choice. No doubt they are very mindful of adverse publicity. So, no further action will be taken by us regarding the theft," concluded Elias.

"All of which I know. But what about the texts? What about Janey?" muttered Andy under his breath.

"Now I want to say something completely off the record," whispered Elias. "Something just between the two of us, and something that must always just remain between the two of us. By no means should you even tell your wife about what I am going to say. Understood? Can I trust you?"

"Of course," answered an increasingly worried Andy.

"This may sound strange, but I am trying to do you a favour. Provide you with some advice you would do well to listen very carefully to. Give you a second chance, I guess."

"Sounds very ominous," interjected Andy rather lamely.

Elias chose to ignore the remark. "We have spent a good deal of time sifting through the many texts between you and Janey Robins of 4 Malvern Drive. It is clear from those texts that there is, at the very least, a close ongoing relationship between the two of you. The nature of this relationship is not of interest to us. That is a private matter between consenting adults, and there is no need for you to elaborate upon it. However, we remain strongly of the opinion that you were supplying Janey Robins with WRT743 with the intention for it to be used as a drug of abuse, regardless of whether it can be legally defined as a drug."

She paused to see if Andy would respond to this accusation. He didn't.

"So why aren't we pursuing you with the intent of

charging you with supplying drugs?"

Andy's heart missed several beats. Had he really got away with it all?

"Lack of evidence," Elias continued. "Obviously. Any defence lawyer worth their salt would have little problem getting this case kicked out of court. WRT743 is not a known drug. Due to Wright and Briggs' poor protocols, we have no evidence that you stole more than two hundred milligrams of it. Mrs Robins would very likely deny ever having received anything from you, and we have no evidence to prove otherwise. So, a case not worth pursuing from our point of view."

Andy nodded to show that he understood. He knew better than to smile at this juncture.

"However." Elias exhaled. "However. I think we should all be grown-up about this. Andy, please don't insult me by claiming that you were not supplying Mrs Robins with WRT743. As for why, and what you got out of taking such a risk, I don't need to know. But we both know that you have committed a serious crime."

She looked intently at Andy, who just continued nodding at his accuser. *No sense in denying or admitting to any crimes as her mind is made up anyway. And she just happens to be correct*, he thought.

"So why am I telling you all this?" asked Elias rhetorically. *Because you are my fucking brother!* she screamed inside her head. "Because I think you, Andy, are one of life's good guys. You have made a terrible mistake which could so easily have led to you being handed a long jail term. Your lovely young family being blown apart. Your career and future prospects being damaged irreparably.

Why did you ever take such a risk? Like I said earlier, that is for you to mull over. But I do so hope that you will never consider taking such a risk again. You are better than that. Your family deserves better. You've been given a second chance. Please don't go and fuck it up, Andy."

Andy finally replied. "I understand. And please believe me when I say how much I appreciate what you have told me in confidence today. I don't deserve a second chance, but I am so very fortunate to have been handed one. And no, DS Elias, I won't go and fuck it up."

"You know what, Andy? I think I believe you."

Both parties left the coffee house a good deal happier with the world than when they'd arrived less than an hour before. Andy found it strange that Elias had asked him to forward his address to her should he ever move house. *Why would she want that information?* he thought on the short drive back to Wright and Briggs. *Is she going to hound me to see if I carry on supplying dodgy compounds? Surely she can get hold of that sort of information by other means? But it's been a very strange day all round, so who knows?*

"And just why are you so bloody happy tonight?" was Susan's light-hearted accusation over dinner that night.

"I just can't win, can I? I just can't win," was Andy's humorous reply. "Guilty as charged, M' Lord. Lock me up and throw away the key. Oh, and by the way, when I said that there would be no more secrets, I was lying."

"What do you mean? What secret?"

"It wouldn't be a secret if I went and told you. You'll just have to wait until Christmas."

"I hate you, Andrew Jones! I really do."

part five

A NEW LIFE

CHRISTMAS BY THE SEA

Few would deny that it was a bleak day. But it was also a beautiful day, with patches of blue scudding across the sky, letting out the sun from time to time. A fierce north-westerly wind blew across the beach, and huge waves crashed onto the rocks framing the cold sand. A true winter's day on the North Devon coast. The foolhardy were celebrating Boxing Day by tiptoeing into the arctic-like sea. But that was not something that Andy contemplated as he huddled into his brand-new woollen winter coat at the top of the beach.

"That really suits you," Susan had enthused when he'd put her present around his shoulders early on Christmas morning. "Now you have no excuse to hang around indoors all Christmas!"

A Christmas holiday in Devon had been Andy's surprise present to the whole family. The secret about which he'd dropped hints to Susan. *Saves me going out shopping*, he'd thought as he completed the online booking. The unbudgeted-for extra expense was easily a good exchange for the joy on their faces when he'd told them of the holiday just a week before. *The best Christmas present I have ever bought.* Still, he felt a bit mean not buying something for the children to open hours before dawn on Christmas Day – not that they didn't have more than enough presents to open, courtesy of their mother.

In the years to come, Andy would consider the Christmas that fell at the end of that tumultuous, life-changing and even life-threatening year to be the start of the next part of his life. A chance to start again, to reset his priorities, to smell the roses. But all that was far from his mind on that winter's day as he sat on a beach, watching his son do what all men and boys do given the opportunity: dig holes. Andy hoped that Josh would not go looking to dig holes the like of which his father had managed to dig and then fall into. *What advice should I give the young man who will soon be Mr Joshua Jones?* he pondered, smiling encouragingly at his young son. *Don't do as your father did? Be a better man than your father was? Be a better husband, and a better father to your children? Enjoy life more than your father did? Not bad advice, perhaps.* He turned his gaze to the waves and the horizon beyond. *Be the best you can be? True, but more than a bit corny. Be kind and thoughtful? Definitely. Be happy? Yes. Be happy. The only advice anyone needs. But easy words to say. Perhaps in time I will know enough about being happy to teach all my children how to be so. I do hope so.*

"Hurry up with that hole, young man," he advised Josh. "The girls will soon be back from the Boxing Day sales, and we will have lots to carry back to the car." He struggled to lean forward from his camping chair to see if

Susan and their daughters had appeared from around the headland. Not yet. Time for some more relaxation. Some more doing nothing other than watching the tide come in.

The lead-up to the Christmas holiday had been a strange time for Andy. Anxiety about the true reason for him leaving Wright and Briggs becoming common knowledge. It hadn't. Anxiety about becoming unemployed. Not as much as he had feared, as he had already had positive responses to the few job applications he had submitted. He had his wronged wife to thank for that, as she had pushed him to apply for jobs for which he didn't think he was qualified to be considered. But these understandable and not unexpected anxieties were easily eclipsed by the surprising but genuine good wishes he received from his work colleagues for the future that lay in front of him. Cards, presents, speeches and even a party to see him off all of which left him with warm memories of his time at the company despite all the ups and downs. He was both sorry and glad to leave the place that had offered him his first job.

And then there was the Robinses' Christmas party! The evening before, Andy was able to tell Janey all about the conversation he'd had with DS Elias, as Graham had been dispatched to get some 'essential' snacks and drinks after teaching his pupils a very basic version of 'All I Want for Christmas is You'. The tension drained from her face when he told her that the police were not going to chase up the texts. She hugged him and kissed his forehead.

"Thank you, Andy," she whispered. "Thank you."

It was then that he remembered just what a beguiling and enchanting woman she could be.

All in attendance said that the party was the event of the year in Malvern Drive, and one that would be remembered for many years to come. Janey was the perfect hostess and surprised even her husband by going out of her way to make sure that none of the guests wanted for anything. *If I didn't know better*, Andy had thought towards the end of the evening, *I would say that our Janey is changing.* He hadn't really had a chance to be alone with her, but he had got a smile and his arse felt when they'd passed one another in the hallway. Now there seemed to be an unspoken, mutual realisation that their relationship had changed. It had had to. Their 'practical arrangement' was now just a memory. They were nothing more than just good friends with a shared secret and a few memories of some very special moments.

"And finally," announced Andy to no one in particular, "they're back."

Joshua dropped his spade and abandoned an impressive hole to rush off to see if there was anything for him in the many bags the girls were carrying, which of course there was. "Look what Mummy has bought me!" He beamed as he held up another toy car to join his collection.

"Don't I get a hug?" asked Susan. And she did.

It was towards the end of the long walk back to the car, surrounded by his young family, that Andy turned round once more to look at the sea. *Time to smell the roses.*

THE LAST TIME

The night before, they had enjoyed what Andy considered to be an outrageously expensive dinner with drinks to match. With the wine flowing, the endless conversation had laughter and even the occasional wiped eye as Andy recalled his aborted suicide attempt.

"But why didn't you tell me, Andy? Why didn't you tell anyone? I'm so sorry that I contributed so much to you feeling that you wanted to end it all. How much you must have been suffering…"

Suffering and suicide were soon to be far from Andy's mind, on the last night he was ever going to spend with his lover.

It was like old times. Lying asleep next to him was the most beautiful woman he had ever met. He recalled that this was when she was at her most attractive: as morning was breaking. He studied her lips, her angled nose, and the wisp of hair that had fallen over her face. She woke as he gently brushed it aside.

"Andy." She smiled.

"And a good morning to you," he replied.

She turned to glance at the bedside clock. "But it's not even eight in the morning!"

"Says the woman who probably didn't even know that such a time exists."

Janey feigned annoyance. "You know, I'm really glad that this will be our last time together."

"How different it was to our first time," posed Andy. "No drugs. No alcohol. Well, maybe a teeny little bit of alcohol."

"No regrets?" she asked.

"Why do you *always* manage to ask the toughest questions?" he teased. "More regrets than you could ever imagine, but they don't add up to nearly as much as I would have regretted never meeting you."

Janey could never hope to match the warmth and sincerity of what he had just said, and so instead she just stroked the side of his face and smiled. "Has anyone told you, Andy Jones, that you are a terrible, soppy old romantic?"

"No." Slowly, he edged his way out of the bed and over to the hotel bedroom window. He pulled back the long curtains just enough to be able to look out upon open fields and an early spring dawn. "This is such a lovely part of the country. Not a bad hotel either. I will miss the warm days down here in the south."

"I'm not great at geography but I do recall that Yorkshire is not in the Arctic Circle," replied Janey from the sanctuary of the now, thoroughly tousled bed.

Andy turned to her. "And how would you know? You've never been north of Birmingham. But I am looking forward to going back home."

"Any movement on the house front?" asked Janey, struggling to sit up.

"We've had a few people around but no bites yet. I think Susan is asking too much and we will have to bring the price down a bit, but we'll see. Not that we are in a rush, as we won't move until the kids have finished for the summer. Not sure they are that pleased with the move and the new schools but hopefully they will come round in time. That's where my new job is, so it's not like we have much choice, really."

"A coincidence that the new job is taking you back home," teased Janey. "Susan happy?"

"She'd prefer to stay somewhere in the south of the country, but I genuinely couldn't find anything local, and she likes the Harrogate area anyway. My penance is to have signed a Faustian pact which will end up with the mother-in-law coming up to live with us. I've put that to the back of my mind for the time being!"

"So, when are you off?"

"Next week, before the May bank holiday, to look for a suitably dingy one-bedroom flat," replied Andy, pulling back the duvet to re-join his lover. "First day in the new job will be the Tuesday although Susan thinks my main job will be house-hunting." He reached over to the bedside table for his phone. "Anyway, enough about new jobs and new houses. Ready for a bit of Celine Dion?"

"Can't wait! Just like the old days."

And then they made love for the very last time.

Andy loaded Janey's huge suitcase into the boot of her car and carefully laid her jacket and coat on top of it. With the boot secured, he opened the driver's door. Janey paused and turned to face him.

"So this is it, then," stated Andy with a hint of a watery eye. "No more dancing. Time to put away our dancing shoes for the last time."

"Oh, I don't think so," replied Janey. "There are many more years of dancing left in us both, trust me. But with different partners." Was there at least a suggestion of emotion in her voice? "The next part of our lives. The second part – no, maybe it's the third. The part of our lives that will be spent with our families. Long, fulfilling, healthy, chemical-free lives."

"We'll never see one another again?" asked Andy, failing to suppress a visible gulp. He was struggling to push down his emotions to the very bottom of his stomach.

"I do so hope not. The Robinses will always try to stay in touch with the Joneses, and of course there will be the big Malvern Drive goodbye party to look forward to when the time comes," she assured him as she wiped away the beginnings of a tear. "You and I might not take to the dance floor together again, but didn't we have such a wonderful, wonderful time?"

"Even if we never did get to learn the piano." Andy smiled as he too found something in his eye that needed rubbing.

"I'll never forget you, Andrew Jones. I'll never forget us or the memories which will last however many new lives we get to live. And the next time you are ever daft enough to even consider ending yours, just remember these words." She grasped his right hand and looked intently into his eyes. "I have been so very fortunate in my life to have been able to meet the kindest, most generous, most thoughtful and most sensual person that anyone could ever wish to meet. You have made me think deeply about the person I am and, more importantly, the person I could and should be. I'll never be able to put right all the stupid, selfish things I've done in my life, but at least I can try to avoid hurting anyone else from now on. Who would ever have thought that I'd be saying such things a year after first meeting you? Not me, for sure. The world is a better place for you being in it, Andrew Jones. And so am I. Make sure you don't leave it any time soon."

"No longer on the agenda, Janey. I promise."

"Oh, and one last thing. It's no longer Janey. My real name is Jane." With that, she leaned forward to kiss her lover one last time, brush his arm gently, and climb into the driver's seat.

Andy closed the car door and watched a part of his life that would stay with him forever drive out of the car park and under the towering oaks of the hotel driveway, and slowly disappear from view. On that fine spring morning he was sure that the grass looked much greener than he could remember it ever looking. He could swear that the sky had never looked so blue, nor the birdsong sounded so sweet, nor the spring flowers ever smell so fragrant.

"Goodbye, Jane."